Edge of Darkness

Troy Kennedy Martin was born in 1932 in Scotland and educated at Finchley Grammar School and Trinity College, Dublin. After doing his national service with the Gordon Highlanders, he worked as a teacher until he wrote his first television play *Incident at Echo Six* (1958). Subsequent work for the BBC included the creation of *Z Cars* (1962) and *Diary of a Young Man* (1964). *The Italian Job* (1969) and *Kelly's Heroes* (1970) are original screenplays and more recent work includes *Reilly – Ace of Spies* (1983) and an adaptation of Angus Wilson's novel *The Old Men at the Zoo* (1983). Since 1985 he has been writing film scripts for Hollywood. He is currently finishing a new series for the BBC.

EDGE OF
DARKNESS

Troy Kennedy Martin

faber and faber
LONDON · BOSTON

First published in 1990
by Faber and Faber Ltd
3 Queen Square London WCIN 3AU

Photoset by Wilmaset Birkenhead Wirral
Printed in England by Clays Ltd, St Ives plc

Appendix Two, 'Nuclear Power' © Walter C. Patterson, 1990
Troy Kennedy Martin is hereby identified as author of this
work in accordance with Section 77 of the Copyright, Designs
and Patents Act 1988.

A CIP record for this book is available from the British Library

ISBN 0–571–14194–3

2 4 6 8 10 9 7 5 3

CONTENTS

Edge of Darkness has a Gothic feel to it. Dark, with a gloomy view of nature, and strong on melodrama, it may seem something of a departure from the usual run of television mini-series, but in fact it derived much of its strength from a British literary tradition which goes back many years. While the modern novel has developed on mainly personal lines, the television mini-series has inherited many of the characteristics of the nineteenth-century public novel, particularly its strong narrative and characters; *Edge of Darkness* was consciously written to reflect this.

Its unfashionable gloominess – 'paranoid' was the unkind description given by one critic – came about because it was written in paranoid times.

Edge of Darkness is the product of the years 1982 to 1985. These were the days before *détente*, when born-again Christians and cold-war warriors seemed to be running the United States. It was the time when the White House changed its nuclear strategy from the thirty-year-old notion of mutually assured destruction (MAD) to the idea that a nuclear war was winnable. It was a time when 30,000 nuclear weapons were thought too old and too few and the whole armoury had to be modernized. And on top of that, 25 billion dollars was to be spent on space weapons. In March 1983 President Reagan made his 'star wars' speech allocating this money to the Strategic Defence Initiative: a defence umbrella which would safeguard America.

Edward Teller, the power behind the Lawrence Livermore Laboratory in San Francisco, and General Graham, with his 'high frontier' concept of space warfare in Washington, were the two strongest advocates of 'star wars'. What surprised me at the time was how closely President Reagan's views mirrored those of the beam-weapons fanatics who had been advocating the use of lasers for many years. They were supported by the maverick US millionaire Lyndon La Rouche, a one-time candidate for the US Presidency and a fervent anti-Communist. I was familiar with La Rouche's magazine *Executive Intelligence Review* and its related magazine *Fusion*, where beam weapons were seen as the ultimate defence weapon. With his SDI speech President Reagan brought these crazies centre stage. It was from this source that I began to draw the character of Jerry Grogan, the space-race entrepreneur.

At the centre of the star wars strategy during this the first phase was the X-ray laser, produced by the Lawrence Livermore Laboratory and a favourite with the beam-weapon warriors. Dozens of these lasers were to be placed in geosynchronous orbit around the planet to shoot down Soviet missiles. What was overlooked at the time was that these lasers were to be energized ('pumped') by nuclear explosions and were in fact Teller's third-generation nuclear weapons in another guise.

Later President Reagan was to place these lasers outside the SDI remit. They were too dirty to be part of the umbrella. But from these lasers came the basis of the sub-plot in which Jerry Grogan goes looking for plutonium in England to ensure the development of his own weapons system.

The situation in England during these years was just as bleak. The bitterly fought Inquiry into Sizewell B and the continued problems at Sellafield contributed to the feeling of a country moving remorselessly towards a nuclear state, with all that meant for the loss of civil liberties. There was no hint of the privatization of the CEGB as yet, but with a battle with the miners looming, it was obvious that nuclear power was becoming a more attractive option, and a permanent way of crushing them. It was only a matter of time before Mrs Thatcher's entrepreneurs would get their hands on the nuclear-waste business. This created another plank in the story, the creation of IIF and its devious managing director, Bennett.

Meanwhile, the cold-war rhetoric was getting hotter. There were Cruise missiles at Greenham and elsewhere. Mrs Thatcher began to outdo the White House when it came to talk about the 'Evil Empire' and the need to replace ('modernize') one nuclear system with another, and the Falklands War had produced a jingoism that hadn't been seen since 1914. Furthermore there was a growing concern about the environment.

It was against this background that *Edge of Darkness* was written, so it could be said that it was driven by a political pessimism. And yet there were positive responses to all these events. Organizations such as CND, Greenpeace and Friends of the Earth became household names. The Greenham women fighting their campaign against Cruise survived years of mud-slinging and legal harassment and many hard winters to draw attention to their cause. More books were published on the nuclear issue than on any other subject with the exception of women's studies. There was a growth of networks – the beginning of an alternative lifestyle and way of thinking similar to what had developed in the sixties but with less bullshit.

Nevertheless, there was something lacking: people were against various things but what were they *for*? As the decade progressed they gradually realized that they stood for something very important: the planet. The idea became concrete with the now famous photograph of the earth taken from one of the Apollo spacecraft, and the hypothesis that seemed to legitimize it, although its creator would be reluctant to acknowledge it, was Gaia.

The 'Gaia hypothesis' was formulated by the British earth scientist Doctor James Lovelock and his American colleague Lyn Margulies. Lovelock believed that the planet and its surrounding atmosphere was a single living system – a self-regulating mechanism built to maintain the optimum conditions for life. This was why the salinity of the oceans rarely changed, and the amount of oxygen in the atmosphere and its temperature did not vary beyond carefully defined margins. All these systems were regulated by a complex series of feedback mechanisms, involving some of the millions of systems that make up the biosphere.

Lovelock's hypothesis, besides being a stunning piece of imaginative thinking, was a metaphor that satisfied many people's intuitive need to re-evaluate their relationship with nature. Like Rousseau before him, Lovelock forced us to rethink our relationship with the planet. Most importantly, he placed the earth at the centre of events, and put the human race on the periphery, where it might even be expendable in certain circumstances.

Thus the idea of Gaia gave the groups struggling to find a focus for their legitimate unease something to fight *for*, rather than against.

But the metaphor is capable of more than one interpretation. Indeed it spans the spectrum from 'a positive vision of the wholeness and interdependency of the earth, a wholeness that it is a delight to be a part of' to quote a recent article in the *New Scientist*, to a blind faith. In *Edge of Darkness* Emma believes that Gaia is acting through her and through her colleagues, who have seen how the proliferation of plutonium endangers Gaia's existence. At this point Gaia ceases to be a metaphor and becomes a religious belief. And it is towards this kind of moral certainty that Craven journeys. It is uncertain whether Craven, or indeed Emma, would have shared the conviction of some 'deep' ecologists that nature, 'red in tooth and claw', should be allowed to take its course (arguing that Aids, for instance, should be understood as one of Gaia's ways of dealing with overpopulation); I should like to believe that they would have rejected this kind of eco-fascism whilst understanding the spiritual feelings which the idea of Gaia inspires in many people.

So while there was a political pessimism at the heart of the script, there was also a moral optimism inspired by the idea of Gaia – an optimism that informed not only me as I wrote it, but also everybody in the production who came in contact with these ideas.

Running parallel with Craven's journey but on a quite separate track was the notion of Craven as a 'green man', unconscious of his own past, his nature concreted over by generations of urban life – a man who has lost touch with his roots, not in terms of family and place, but of ancestors and folk memory. For the formulation of this part of Craven's character, I drew on ideas from *The Real Camelot* by John Darrah. Darrah sees the Arthurian romances as a series of encoded stories which disguise much earlier tales, revealing the presence in Bronze Age Britain of a druidic civilization. I wanted to fashion Craven's ancestors from this period, to make him the reincarnation of the original 'green man', whose destiny was to confront and destroy in the name of the planet the free-market forces of modern entrepreneurial capitalism, as represented by the chairman of the Fusion Corporation of Kansas, Mr Jerry Grogan.

However, it was inevitable that when a 'green man' is metamorphized into a detective in a TV thriller, those things that he might have represented in Bronze Age Britain tend to become marginalized. Furthermore, both the actor playing Craven and the director baulked at the idea that at the end of the story he would turn into a tree. This aspect of *Edge of Darkness* usually separated the men from the boys at Television Centre. 'I am writing this story about a detective who turns into a tree.' 'Oh, yes,' would be the guarded reply. 'Who's this for, Channel Four?' Eventually I was persuaded out of the notion but not before some of its spirit had rubbed off on Craven's character.

I derived the black flowers that replaced the idea of Craven turning into a tree at the end of the story from Lovelock's description of the dark marsh grass that spread across the planet at some distant time in the past, when the earth was further from the sun than it is at present. This grass attracted sunlight, enabling life to evolve. It was one of his examples of how the planet reacts to maintain the 'optimum conditions for life'. The way I used the black flowers, of course, ran counter to Lovelock's hypothesis, for today the earth is too hot, rather than too cold. So I have to plead dramatic licence in creating these flowers with the intention of melting the ice cap; the fact that we now know this might happen without their aid is perhaps an example of life, or Gaia, imitating art.

Finally, I have to confess that there are even more obscure elements within the drama. These are traceable to a third story which underlies the text. The first story, Craven's, begins with Emma's murder and is fairly straightforward. The second – what American scriptwriters call the 'back story' – traces the events that have happened before her death and produces some of the answers to the question facing Craven: why was she killed? (See Appendix I.) The third story, of which only minute fragments exist, concerns the rivalry between the characters Jedburgh and Grogan in what appears to be a reincarnation of previous quarrels played out many hundreds of years ago. Both Grogan and Jedburgh I easily imagined inhabiting the world of the medieval knights. Not the world of chivalry, but that which reflects the arrogant independence of the knightly orders established in the infant European states.

I had long been interested in stories of the Templars, however apocryphal: how they guarded some special wisdom in the Temple of the Dome on the Rock, and how they brought it back to Europe when they retreated from Jerusalem, and how in some way it became part of the alternative culture of the Elizabethan age and, eventually, of the Enlightenment. I was always struck by the likenesses between the world of the Templars and the rise of today's military castes, led by men who seemed in some way to stand outside time. It seemed to me that the knowledge that has brought us nuclear fusion and that will one day take men off the planet had its roots in the knowledge which the Templars are said to have guarded in the Temple.

The idea that there existed in the Middle Ages a secret way of seeing things that countervailed the rigid scholasticism of the day was attractive, as was the idea that it survived to become the prevailing ideology of our own times, with its own – nuclear – priesthood. So I made Jerry Grogan a descendant of one of the Templars: a man who dreams of building 'a new Jerusalem in the Milky Way', as Jedburgh sardonically puts it.

If Grogan is a Templar, then Darius Jedburgh must be a knight of the Marches, a Teutonic defender of the borders of Eastern Europe, a warrior from that strife-torn basin that for a thousand years has produced the world's most bitter battles and its hardest soldiers. It was here that the great military machines of the modern world were forged.

Thus this aspect of the 'back story' read something like this: descendants of the Templars, disestablished and unaware of their past, act in concert to bring the human race to the point of departure from the planet. By the human race they mean, of course, a small band of privileged soldier–scholars whose mission will be to conquer the galaxy by fire and by sword.

The funds for their galactic ambitions come from the mutual fear the two great empires, Russia and America, have for each other. This fear allows them access on both sides to unaccountable resources with which to pursue their goal.

In the meantime, scattered descendants of the Teutonic Knights recognize the danger in the Templars' ambitions and try to stop them. In their view the Templars are diverting humanity from its prime duty, which is the defence and protection of the planet. But a sea of 'sanctimonious shit' (Jedburgh's words) protects the Templars, as a result of which the efforts of the Teutonic Knights are deflected and ultimately defused. Craven himself is deemed to be a part of this struggle – Jedburgh jibes that he has been 'freeze-dried from some earlier epoch' in the scene at the hunting lodge.

These elements are so obscure that they are not meant to be picked up by the viewer, but may be of interest to the reader. Rather like yeast in the making of bread, they were an essential element in developing the characters.

In 1985, the year that *Edge of Darkness* was produced, the world's atmospheric scientists met at Villach to warn of the dangers of the greenhouse effect. A decade which had begun with a preoccupation with the cold war was all set for change. Today we have the beginning of a new world in Europe and the missiles are going from Greenham. There are a new set of priorities: the greenhouse effect, the ozone layer, pollution, acid rain. In the light of the greenhouse effect, even the nuclear option has to be re-evaluated.

Edge of Darkness was very much a reflection of its time, although it had, I hope, some qualities which have transcended it, notably its appreciation of the ideas of Gaia, and its attempt to expand the television detective story using humour and depth of feeling, which are so often denied by the industry's corporate process.

Because of the amount of rewriting that went on during production, what is being published here is the original script of Episode One, and the final version of Episodes Two–Six, which have only minimal descriptive passages. The first episode, therefore, gives a slightly better understanding of what a script looks like before the director and cast get their hands on it.

In broadcasting, scripts are not perceived as the sacred items they are in the theatre. They have to be robust enough to withstand constant probing and hammering by those involved in producing them. Therefore the writer must take great care to provide detailed research which can be used to defend the scripts. The appendices here give some idea of the work involved, and go some way towards illuminating the text.

Troy Kennedy Martin, London, November 1989

Edge of Darkness was first shown on BBC Television in November 1985. The cast and crew included:

RONALD CRAVEN	Bob Peck
DARIUS JEDBURGH	Joe Don Baker
EMMA CRAVEN	Joanne Whalley
JAMES GODBOLT	Jack Watson
PENDLETON	Charles Kay
HARCOURT	Ian McNeice
JERRY GROGAN	Kenneth Nelson
ROBERT BENNETT	Hugh Fraser
CLEMENTINE	Zoë Wanamaker
ASSISTANT CHIEF CONSTABLE ROSS	John Woodvine
TERRY SHIELDS	Tim McInnerny
Producer	Michael Wearing
Director	Martin Campbell
Make-up	Daphne Croker
Costume	Denver Hall
Sound	Dickie Bird
Photography	Andrew Dunn
Film Editors	Ardan Fisher
	Dan Rae
Designer	Graeme Thomson
Music	Eric Clapton
	Michael Kamen

Edge of Darkness won six BAFTA Awards in 1986. They were presented for Best Drama Series, Best Actor (Bob Peck), Best Music (Eric Clapton with Michael Kamen) Best Photography (Andrew Dunn), Best Editor (Andrew Fisher and others), and Best Sound (Dickie Bird and others). The BAFTA committee does not present an annual award for best script.

Compassionate Leave

1:1   A rail junction. Night
*It is raining. A freight train carrying thermal oxides makes its way
slowly through the freight yard of a northern city, its wheels clattering
over the points as it slowly crosses them. It carries the logo of the storage
company, IIF. It bends round the side of a hill, and its brakes begin to
hiss as the driver brings the train almost to a halt. At walking speed, it
snakes into a special siding, past a big warning notice and the sign for
radioactivity.*
*The freight train comes to a halt by a board which says 'International
Irradiated Fuels'. Again we notice the logo. A member of the UKEA
Police Authority stands by the notice with a machine-gun, watching as
the train comes to a halt. Almost immediately a big low-loader switches
on its lights, revs its motor and begins to trundle across the freight yard
towards the siding. It, too, carries the logo.*

1:2   Outside the British Legion Hall, Craigmills. Night
FIRST DRIVER: (*Voice over*) Just look at him . . .
   (*Four cars are parked on the broken concrete apron, just off a
   grade three road. It is raining hard. Water pours down a farm
   track to meet the road just opposite the hall; then it swims down
   towards the valley hidden below in the mist. Despite the rain, a*
   DRIVER *stands swabbing the bonnet of the biggest car, a
   Granada. He is being watched through the fogged-up windows of
   a second car by two men. They look like police drivers.*)
   (*Voice over*) There has to be some reason for that kind of
   behaviour.

**1:3   Inside the second car, British Legion Hall, Craigmills.
Night**
The two DRIVERS *watch the man throw a bucket of water over the car.*
SECOND DRIVER: He's scared stiff of his boss. That's the reason . . .

I

1:4 Inside the British Legion Hall, Craigmills. Night

GODBOLT *stands on the platform, facing the almost deserted hall. The wall behind him is draped with the union flag and the colours of the local Territorial Regiment. Above him is a large trade union banner. It almost brushes* GODBOLT'*s head. He is a huge, confident man of fifty and he stares down at* RONALD CRAVEN, *who sits alone in a stack of bentwood chairs in the centre of the floor. The rain drums down on the corrugated roof. They stare at each other in silence, stubbornly.*

To one side is a trestle table on which are assembled piles of twine-tied voting papers. Standing behind it, and studying the papers in an offhand way is the Assistant Chief Constable, ROSS. *He is more intent on the confrontation between* GODBOLT *and* CRAVEN *than the ballot papers, but he does not want to show this.*

GODBOLT: In God's name, man, I'm not asking you for much. All I'm asking you to do is delay the inquiry till we get back from Blackpool. (*He comes down the stairs.*) It's only two weeks. (*He crosses to the island of chairs.*) I've been into your office, Ronnie, I've seen your workload, you've got cases piled on your desk. Frauds, rapes, robberies – (*He pauses.*) I thought you would have welcomed an opportunity to get some of that cleared up.

CRAVEN: (*Speaking quietly, but firmly*) I want to get *this* cleared up.

GODBOLT: So do I, Ronnie. It were me who said you should be called in! Remember?
(*The rain drips down through a small hole in the roof and wets some of the ballot papers on the long table.*)
But to say you're going to come to Blackpool with ten men and start poking around, asking questions in the middle of the Trade Union Conference – about a voting irregularity in my union –
(ROSS *pushes the papers out of the rain.*)

CRAVEN: It was fraud, Jim.

GODBOLT: We're talking about three hundred bloody votes. And what were my majority? Two *thousand* three hundred!
(*He looks across at* ROSS, *who shrugs. It's not up to him. It's up to* CRAVEN. GODBOLT *turns back to* CRAVEN.)
And we're on the brink of a national strike and you want to divert the attention of the conference to an alleged election fix. 'Miners' Union in Vote Fraud': the media would have a field day.
(CRAVEN *raises his head and looks at* ROSS *but the ACC looks*

2

away. By now GODBOLT *is at the other end of the table, pouring
out a whisky for himself and for* ROSS.)
What are you trying to do? Discredit the union? Don't you
think there's enough people who want to do that?
(*He stands there with an empty glass in one hand and the bottle of
Bells in the other. He looks at* CRAVEN. *Almost imperceptibly,*
CRAVEN *shakes his head. Nevertheless* GODBOLT *pours whisky
into the glass and crosses to* CRAVEN *to give to him.*)
Come on, Ronnie, stop playing by the rules. They don't cover
this contingency . . .
(*He hands the glass to him. Fade in: the sound of the low-loader.*)

1:5 Outside the British Legion Hall, Craigmills. Night
*The low-loader breasts the rise and thunders past the hall, its cargo
covered by a tarpaulin.
As it goes by we see a man up on the hill standing beside the wet trees.
Camouflaged by his green anorak, his features are indistinguishable. All
we can make out are his wet, worn trainers – he is standing half in and
half out of the little stream which is rushing down the farm track.*

1:6 Inside the second car, British Legion Hall, Craigmills. Night
The older of the two DRIVERS, *who has been sitting in the front
passenger seat, slowly peers forward and rubs a hole on the fogged-up
windscreen. He peers through it.*
SECOND DRIVER: There's someone up there.
(*The* FIRST DRIVER *looks at him.*)
Up on the track, in the bushes.
(*The* SECOND DRIVER *leans forward and opens the glove
compartment. Inside is a pistol. He pulls it out.*)

1:7 Outside the hall, Craigmills. Night
*Both men get out of the car. They put their flat hats on. This confirms,
if we haven't already realized, that both are policemen. They move in a
determined way across the apron and the road, heading for the farm
track.*

1:8 Inside the hall, Craigmills. Night
GODBOLT *glances triumphantly at* ROSS. CRAVEN *sits, cradling the
empty whisky glass in his hands. Still stubborn and silent, he has the
look of someone who has given in.*

3

GODBOLT: All right? Are we agreed, then?

(CRAVEN *nods; it's a gesture of defeat.*)

Can we have a show of hands, then, brothers.

(*He laughs, his big, breezy, infectious laugh. He puts his hand on* CRAVEN's *shoulder but looks at* ROSS.)

You chose a good one here, Willy. He's stubborn, but he's OK. Not some star who's trying to get himself on *News at Ten*.

(ROSS *laughs.* GODBOLT *has made a joke. He's relieved. He puts his glass down, glad that the problem has been resolved.* CRAVEN *will not be taking his team of detectives to Blackpool; a nasty political wrangle has been averted.*)

1:9   Outside the hall, Craigmills. Night

GODBOLT *and* ROSS *appear, buttoning up their raincoats.* CRAVEN *follows, holding his case. Godbolt's* DRIVER *is waiting, the door of his car open.* ROSS *looks round to see where his* DRIVER *has gone. He comes hurrying back with Craven's driver,* ANDY.

ROSS'S DRIVER: (*Breathless*) There was someone up there . . .

(ROSS *grunts and gets into his car.*)

ROSS: Bloody reporter more than like.

(ANDY *looks at* CRAVEN *and shrugs. He walks with* CRAVEN *to their motor.*)

ANDY: It didn't look like a reporter to me.

(CRAVEN *gets in.* ANDY *gets in behind the wheel. Both cars drive out on to the road and accelerate into the wet dusk.*)

1:10   Inside Craven's house, Craigmills. Night

The room is open-plan and includes the stairway to the first floor, the front hall and door, the kitchen and the dining-room/living area. The furniture is informal, family-style; a chair is directed towards the television, which is tuned to the BBC nine o'clock news. On the mantelshelf are a number of snapshots, showing CRAVEN, *his dead wife Ann and his daughter* EMMA, *at random stages of their life.* CRAVEN *himself is in the kitchen preparing a meal. We now get a good look at him. He is a wiry, thin man in his mid-forties, of working-class origins. Although a policeman, he has all the nervous juices of an athlete. Instinctively, we think of him as a Conservative, someone who believes in capital punishment, Mary Whitehouse and the like.*

The television news is in progress – the item to be updated nearer production.

NEWSCASTER: (*Voice over*) The National Union of Miners came one step closer to an all-out strike when the Coal Board today announced its plan for the eighties. This includes the closing of a number of uneconomical pits. The Coal Board chairman Ian McGregor, introducing the plan, talked about the need to slim the industry to make it profitable, but Arthur Scargill, speaking for the NUM, said that this was unacceptable to the union. In Rome, the pope has warned of the growing danger of a nuclear war and has asked scientists engaged in nuclear research to refuse to work on projects which might contribute to a future holocaust. In London, Mr Reginald Rigg said that this was yet another example of CND hijacking the Christian Church.

(*The telephone rings.* CRAVEN *finishes preparing the food and then unhurriedly crosses the room, switches off the television set and answers the telephone.*)

CRAVEN: Craven?

(*On the other end it is* JONES, *his number two, speaking from the office.*)

1:11 The CID office, West Yorkshire police headquarters. Night

JONES: How did it go?

CRAVEN: (*Voice over*) He wants it put off.

JONES: Until when?

CRAVEN: (*Voice over*) Indefinitely.

(*Behind* JONES *a number of officers are working quietly. One is on the computer punching numbers. Two are by the wall map of the county; another is on the telephone.*)

JONES: Did you agree?

CRAVEN: (*Voice over*) No. We won't go to Blackpool, that's all I agreed.

JONES: What are you doing now?

CRAVEN: (*Voice over*) I'm picking up Emma . . . Why?

JONES: There was a geezer hanging round during the meet.

CRAVEN: (*Voice over*) Ross said he was a reporter.

JONES: Maybe. I think I'll go up and take a look.

CRAVEN: (*Voice over*) Don't catch pneumonia. It's pissing down outside.

5

1:12   Craven's house, Craigmills. Night

JONES *rings off.* CRAVEN *switches on the recording machine and returns to the kitchen, where he surveys the table set for two. He empties his glass, a vodka and orange – the policeman's drink (no alcohol on the breath) – and picks up his raincoat. As he reaches the front door, the telephone rings, but he ignores it and goes out, closing the door behind him.*

1:13   Outside Craven's house, Craigmills. Night

CRAVEN *comes out into the dark. It is still pouring with rain. Craven's home is mock-Tudor, a large house on the edge of Craigmills in a rambling 1930s estate, the roads of which are still unpaved. The house is double-fronted, with a short puddle-strewn drive which leads down to the unmade road. The rhododendron bushes in the garden are bending in the strong wind.* CRAVEN *puts his raincoat over his head and dashes for the road where his car is parked.*

1:14   The unmade road. Night

CRAVEN *gets into his car and turns on the lights. The rain drums down on the roof. Over this, we hear* CRAVEN'S *voice distorted as if it is coming through a machine.*

CRAVEN: (*Voice over*) Detective Inspector Ronald Craven is out at the moment. If the matter is urgent, please leave a message at Police headquarters, the number of which is Craigmills 0125. Otherwise, speak when the tone stops . . . Thank you.

(CRAVEN *starts the motor.*)

1:15   Inside Craven's house. Night

We focus on the recording machine at the telephone. We can see the tape going round, and the sound of the tone. When it stops silence emanates from the caller. It gets longer and then suddenly the telephone at the other end goes down and we hear the dialling tone.

1:16   In Craven's car on the unmade road. Night

CRAVEN *revs the engine. The car accelerates off.*

1:17   A suburban road. Night

Craven's car turns into a neon-lit street. Over this we hear a jingle on the radio overlaid by the voice of an American-style DISC JOCKEY.

DISC JOCKEY: (*Voice over*) Good evening and welcome once again to Radio Tyne. Following the news headlines we go south of the Red River to Georgia, where I am told on the undisputed authority of Waylon Jennings that Willie Nelson still is king. You can hear him and Waylon and other stars in our country show, *Blue Jeans*, following this message.

1:18   Inside Craven's car. Night
CRAVEN *drives, the radio still going.*

1:19   Inside the students' union, Teachers' Training College. Night
The room is full. It is difficult to get in through the door. The meeting is packed, although below stairs, a number of students are playing the pinball machines. We are listening to a POLITICIAN.* *There is a hint of Tony Benn in the calmness of the exposition, which belies the boldness of his ideas. On the platform beside him sits* EMMA, *the chairperson of tonight's meeting.*

POLITICIAN: We have reached a stage here in Britain where the rich and powerful have begun to draw back into their privileged Bailiwicks, and are starting to throw up trenches which will protect them from the rest of us when the crunch comes. Education and welfare, which were once the great equalizers of our society, are being cut down at their roots, to provide a greater field of fire, as it were, between those who man the citadel and those outside. Education in particular is seen as a threat –
   (*There is a roar of applause.*)

1:20   The car park, Teachers' Training College. Night
The applause continues as Craven's car comes into the car park by the gymnasium. His lights illuminate a piece of graffiti on the wall. It just says 'Gaia'. CRAVEN *switches off the lights, gets out and slams the door. Overlaid is the politician's voice.*

POLITICIAN: (*Voice over*) And schools and colleges such as this one, which do not contribute directly to the technological future of the nuclear state, face closure. This is done in the name of economy. But it is the mentality behind it which is suspect. It is a siege mentality. While the Government pays lip-service to freedom and opportunity, its ministers are busy

*Michael Meacher, the Labour MP and Shadow Minister of Health, played the part in the BBC production.

locking the doors and winding up the drawbridge on the open society and preparing themselves for a re-run, I fear, of the Middle Ages. For the nuclear state which they are engaged in constructing is a feudal state, and its effect on freedom of speech and association, upon democratic government and public accountability, cannot be overestimated. It will destroy them.

(*There is great applause.*)

1:21 Inside the college. Night

CRAVEN *enters the Students' Union and stands crammed with the others. He takes in what he has heard of the speech in a good-humoured way. He stands pleasantly squashed by the curvaceous bodies of the students surrounding him, who, like him, have not quite lost their sense of humour.*

POLITICIAN: And yet I feel that there are forces in society, new forces, new loyalties, new ideas barely articulated, which may yet come to our rescue. Some of them will come from the Labour Party (*cheers*), others from new associations not yet formed. But in whatever shape these forces manifest themselves, they will come from you, the despised students of the humanities. (*Cheers.*) Your future, the country's future, is at stake. You may save the nation yet.

EMMA: Comrades, sisters . . . I think we should now put the motion to the vote. As a result of this latest crisis in Western capitalism the Corporation is running a reduced bus service (*laughter*) . . . and the last bus has been brought forward by one hour. May the tellers please come forward and make themselves known.

(*The rest is lost in cheers and clapping and the banging of chairs.*)

1:22 Inside Craven's car, travelling at speed. Night

It is still raining heavily. CRAVEN *drives,* EMMA *beside him. His car is an ex-police vehicle and still retains the two interior mirrors.* EMMA *is looking into the lower mirror; her eye shadow has run in the dash to the car. She is beautiful, even dressed as she is for a cold, wet, autumn night.*

EMMA: Did you catch any of the speeches?

CRAVEN: I got stuck in a crowd of your sisters. It was difficult to concentrate.

EMMA: You think of nothing but sex these days, Dad.

8

CRAVEN: Do I?
(EMMA *still concentrates on the mirror.*)
EMMA: You should try and grow out of it.
CRAVEN: Why?
EMMA: Because there are other things. The whole world's falling
about your ears and you don't even care. What about the
union inquiry?
CRAVEN: We're making progress.
(EMMA *looks at him.*)
EMMA: Are you going to Blackpool?
CRAVEN: No . . .
(EMMA *considers this for some time.*)
EMMA: Good. The press would have had a field day.
CRAVEN: (*Nods*) I'm not sorry.
(*She kisses him, gratefully.*)
EMMA: Who's going to look after you when I'm gone?
(CRAVEN *tries to joke about it.*)
CRAVEN: I'll find some little number. Set her up –
(EMMA *looks at him sharply, disliking the sexism.*)
EMMA: That's not funny.
(CRAVEN *takes her hand, and, keeping his eyes on the road, kisses
it. She lets him do so and then brings it back to scratch her nose,
where a raindrop or a tear is trickling down her face.*)
CRAVEN: When are you going?
EMMA: Soon.
CRAVEN: Have you got someone?
EMMA: Yeah.
CRAVEN: (*Casually*) What's he like?
EMMA: You wouldn't like him.
(CRAVEN *nods again.*)

1:23 The unmade road outside Craven's house. Night
*It is still raining, the wind is getting up again, restlessly shifting the
trees and the bushes. Craven's car comes to a halt outside his garage.
The lights are dipped and then put out.* CRAVEN *gets out of one door,*
EMMA *from the other. Huddling together under Craven's coat, they
make their way up the steps towards the door of the house. They chatter
as they go.*
EMMA: What's for supper?
CRAVEN: *Ratatouille.*
EMMA: Bet it's tinned.

9

CRAVEN: No, it's not.

EMMA: It always is, Dad, and you always pretend that it isn't.

CRAVEN: You can't tell the difference.

EMMA: Yes, I can.

CRAVEN: I've discovered a new recipe. You take a tin –

GUNMAN: Craven! You bastard!

> (CRAVEN *and* EMMA *wheel in the rain. So wet is the intruder that he stands almost indistinct from the trees, a matt, damp blob.*)

GUNMAN: (*Screaming*) You bloody murdering bastard!

> (*The* GUNMAN *pushes his way clear of the bushes and on to the mole-infested grass of Craven's overgrown garden. He wears a service anorak with a hood, out of which we can just see the peak of a check cap. It is the same man we spotted earlier at the British Legion hall. He is screaming, rocking on the soles of his worn trainers.*)

GUNMAN: It's your turn now.

> (*Then* CRAVEN *sees the shotgun. But* EMMA *is already running towards the man, putting herself between the* GUNMAN *and her father.*)

EMMA: Don't!

> (*At the same moment the* GUNMAN *aims, and fires both barrels. The shots catch* EMMA *full in the chest. She is blown backwards off her feet. The* GUNMAN *turns away and runs.* CRAVEN *falls on his knees by* EMMA's *side and pulls her to him. Out of sight, a car bursts into life and revs and revs fast, again and again.* EMMA *tries to say something to* CRAVEN, *through the sound of the revving engine.*)

EMMA: Dad . . . you're hurt . . . (*Her eyes unfocus.*) Don't . . . tell . . .

> (*Almost as the last word trickles from her mouth, the revving car takes off.*)

1:24 Outside Craven's house, some time later. Night

A series of cars have pulled up higgledy-piggledy on either side of the road in response to telephone messages on the part of other householders. On the lawn EMMA's *body still lies in the rain, but covered with a groundsheet. On the unmade road a Jaguar pulls up and* ROSS *gets out. He makes his way up the path past the police photographer who has just arrived and is about to begin taking pictures; past the body of* EMMA; *past the uniformed constable squaring off the murder area with white tape. Barely glimpsing all this,* ROSS *makes for the front door. The photographer pulls the groundsheet off* EMMA's *face.*

1:25 Inside Craven's house. Night
A number of large, heavily built DETECTIVES *meander round the room. Potato crisps have appeared, plus half a dozen bottles of Bells and a case of Newcastle Brown. They talk over the incident, their conversation running something like this –*
DETECTIVES: I was in Bradford when I heard . . . She hadn't an enemy in the world . . . Guns everywhere these days . . . Someone he put away, I'd say . . . It could have been you, it could have been me . . . She was a lovely little thing . . .
(In the kitchen, one DETECTIVE *is slicing himself bread for a cheese sandwich.)*
FIRST DETECTIVE: I remember when Ronnie used to bring her in on the morning shift . . .
(In the living-room CRAVEN *sits in an upright chair, still dazed by what has happened.)*

1:26 The lawn outside Craven's house. Night
EMMA's *body is flash-photographed by the CID photographer. By the garage an ambulance now stands, its engine off, but its blue lights still turning. The lamps of the nearest police cars remain on full beam, illuminating the area.*

1:27 The kitchen, Craven's house. Night
The DETECTIVE *has finished making his cheese sandwich but has started on another for his friend.*
FIRST DETECTIVE: He used to sit her down on the desk and she'd answer the phone . . .

1:28 The hall, Craven's house. Night
Two DETECTIVES *are talking.*
SECOND DETECTIVE: All right, you're forty-five. You've got the opportunity of getting out now or staying on for another five years. But if you leave it till you're fifty, the chances of a job are not so good, are they? So what do you do?

1:29 The living-room, Craven's house. Night
ROSS *enters. He crosses to where* CRAVEN *sits, in a state of shock.*
ROSS: Jesus, Ronnie, this is bad . . .

(CRAVEN *nods.* ROSS *looks round the room.*)
They've been turning out as far as Newcastle. Everybody's out.
(CRAVEN *nods.* ROSS *gets down on his haunches and looks at him.*)
It was you he was after.
CRAVEN: (*With difficulty*) He called me out, but she ran forward.
ROSS: She was a brave lass.
CRAVEN: It was a shotgun . . . He fired both barrels.
ROSS: We'll get the buggers, Ronnie, I promise you.
(*He straightens and looks around the room.*)

1:30   The hall, Craven's house. Night
JONES *is on the phone.*
JONES: We have road-blocks all round the county, so the only way out would be by rail . . .

1:31   The living-room, Craven's house. Night
The door opens and a YOUNG DETECTIVE *comes in, his coat dripping wet. He speaks to* ROSS *apologetically.*
YOUNG DETECTIVE: The photographers are finished, sir.
(ROSS *nods;* CRAVEN *gets to his feet and goes into the hall, followed by* ROSS. *The men in the hall and the kitchen fall silent; the last person to notice is the* SECOND DETECTIVE, *the one who has been talking about pensions and jobs. Eventually he cottons on as the rest button up and follow* CRAVEN *to the door. The door is held open by a uniformed* CONSTABLE. *They exit.*)

1:32   The hall, Craven's house. Night
JONES *is the only man left inside. He is still on the phone.*
JONES: Yes, we have a description, but we're not releasing details.
REPORTER: (*Voice over*) Then how are my readers going to assist you?
JONES: We'll have the bastard before they're out of bed.
(*But when he puts the phone down his face does not carry the same strength of conviction.*)

1:33   Outside Craven's house. Night
CRAVEN *walks out on to the drive. The others trail behind him. Some of them are carrying torches.*

The ambulance backs up towards EMMA's body, which is lying under a transparent plastic sheet. From the ambulance a MAN rolls out a coffin.

1:34   Flashback. The lawn outside Craven's house. Night
EMMA is running towards the GUNMAN.
EMMA: Don't!
    (*The* GUNMAN *fires.* EMMA's *body is lifted into the air by the force of the shots.*)

1:35   Outside Craven's house. Night
CRAVEN *stands looking down at* EMMA's *body. The* MEN *with the coffin come into view beside him.*
AMBULANCE MAN: Excuse me, sir.
    (*They place the coffin on the wet grass and lift the body into it.* CRAVEN *follows the coffin as it is carried to the ambulance. He watches it being loaded on board then he steps away and allows the door to be closed.*)

1:36   The unmade road. Night
The ambulance slowly lurches off, then turns into the neon-lit wet main road and proceeds towards the town.

1:37   Outside Craven's house. Night
The departure of the ambulance is a signal for the others to think of going home too. ROSS *turns to* CRAVEN.
ROSS: I'll leave a man.
    (CRAVEN *shakes his head.*)
CRAVEN: I don't want anyone in the house. And it's too wet for him out here.
ROSS: The bastards may be back.
    (CRAVEN *looks at him. If only they would, he seems to infer.* ROSS *nods, satisfied that Craven's anger will prevent him from doing anything foolish – like killing himself.*)
I'll see you first thing in the morning.
    (*With that, he steps into his car which, chauffeur-driven, has arrived by the gate.*)

1:38   The living-room, Craven's house. Night
CRAVEN *comes back into the living-room through the open door. He shuts it, snibs it and locks it. He crosses to a cupboard by the wall. He moves like an automaton. He selects another key from his key-ring,*

opens a hefty padlock and pulls back the cupboard door. Inside are two shotguns, a handed pair. He takes them out and crosses to the desk. He pulls open the desk drawer. Inside are a number of shells in cardboard boxes. He takes one of them, opens it and allows the shells to tumble on to the desk. He breaks open the first gun and rams a cartridge into the breach. Outside it is still raining. Now to the telephone. He pushes down a button on the recording machine, and listens for the message which follows.

EMMA: (*Voice over*) Hello, Dad, it's Emma. I shall be at college till ten. If it's still raining, please pick me up . . . Love you, bye.
(*The machine clicks off, there is a dialling tone for one moment and then it switches off. There is silence in the room until it is interrupted by* EMMA's *voice.*)

EMMA: (*Voice over*) *Ratatouille?*
(*The voice appears to be coming from the kitchen.* CRAVEN *wheels round.*)

1:39   The kitchen, Craven's house. Night

CRAVEN *swings open the ranch-type doors.*

EMMA: (*Voice over*) And it's tinned, I bet . . .
(*The rain is lashing at the back door, which for some reason is unlocked.* CRAVEN *crosses the kitchen to the back door and bolts it. As usual, his movements are unhurried. He is too far gone for fear of any sort. He is just filled with a great emptiness A void in which he can hardly breathe. He returns to the table and sits down. Before him the* ratatouille *tin is opened, the table still set for two.*)

CHILD'S VOICE: Don't worry, Daddy. I promised Mummy that I would look after you . . .
(*He looks up. A little girl stands at the kitchen door, with a teddy in her hand. It is* EMMA, *aged ten.*)

1:40   Flashback. A funeral. Day

The funeral moves at a brisk pace over the hill behind a stately hearse. One of the men following the hearse is CRAVEN; he looks younger. It is summer and he is in his shirt-sleeves. Beside him is a ten-year-old girl, trying to keep up. She has a black ribbon tied round her arm, as has CRAVEN. Behind them a few relatives. EMMA catches hold of CRAVEN's arm for support.

14

1:41 Flashback. A hospital corridor. Day

Shining institutional lino. A NURSE *and* CRAVEN *stand outside the ward door.*

NURSE: What will you do with the child? In your job you don't
    have much spare time.

CRAVEN: We'll manage.

NURSE: Have you thought of boarding school?
    (CRAVEN *shakes his head. The idea does not appeal to him.*)

1:42 The kitchen, Craven's house. Night

CRAVEN *is sitting by the table, his head in his hands. The little girl standing at the door clutching her teddy is in a nightdress.*

EMMA: (*Gravely*) I think you should sleep with me tonight,
    Daddy.
    (CRAVEN *looks up.*)

CRAVEN: (*Voice over*) I guess so.
    (*But she has gone. Only the open door hints that she might have
    been there.* CRAVEN *picks up the shotgun. He stands, stretches and
    walks out of the room and across the hall.*)

1:43 Emma's room

CRAVEN *enters. He still carries the shotgun, which he puts down. He closes the curtains and switches on the side lamp. He looks around. A young woman had lived in this room. It is furnished in an art-nouveau junk style; there are flying birds zooming over three different walls. A women's movement poster is pinned above the mantelshelf. A battered OXO sign with the woman's chromosome cross attached to both 'O's stands on it. Magazines like* Time Out *and* New Society *sprawl out of a tall cardboard box; a picture of Billy Connolly, paperbacks stacked horizontally not vertically, and certificates for swimming at school and the odd snapshot of college friends are also on the mantelshelf. The dresser top is a mass of toiletry: about eighty items, most of them bottles, which stand on a large tin tray. On the other table dozens of records are stacked under an expensive Japanese music-centre. There is a single bed in which* EMMA *had slept since she was a child, with a battered old sleeping-bag as a duvet and an even more battered old teddy bear with its one eye, which always lay squashed between the pillow and the headboard. Over the bed, there is a big NASA poster of the earth as seen from the moon.*

Once again, CRAVEN *is struck by how little he knows of his daughter.*

He takes his time searching the room. What he is looking for is not specific. He examines the records. The one on top is country and western – Willie Nelson. The others are all soul/reggae, rhythm and blues, UB40 etc. Clumsily, he puts on the record player. He has not used it before and the old one – the one he'd given her at fourteen – lies behind the new one, discarded. The record begins – it is 'The Time of the Preacher'.

He looks behind the curtain which serves as a wardrobe. Besides the anorak and the jeans there are scarcely three dresses. Not like her mother Ann, who had a wardrobeful. He turns away and surveys the room again. Books, magazines, a junk jewellery box with her mother's wedding ring next to a chrome razor blade. He pulls open the top drawer. It is full of Marks and Spencer knickers and tights. The other drawer contains skirts, nightdresses and her mum's wedding dress. The bottom one is full of junk: school reports, letters, toys, boxes of postcards, film magazines, a small collection of Picture Post *and* Radio Times. *And then there is a large box marked 'Gaia'. He pulls it out, looks through it. It seems like a project. Rocks, maps, stones. And a Geiger counter.*

He crosses to the bed. It is still blowing outside; still raining hard. CRAVEN *hears the gate creak and swing. He crosses to get the shotgun. He puts it beside the art-nouveau bedside table and sits down again. He pulls open a drawer and takes out a Kleenex box first and then a cheque book, a passport and a wallet. He opens the wallet. It has some French francs in it; he puts it to one side, uninterested. He opens the passport, hoping to get one more glimpse of* EMMA. *It is* EMMA's *face all right. In the second drawer is a vibrator. He looks down at it, then kisses it gently. He puts it with the other things. The third drawer is empty except for an automatic pistol. He takes it out. It is a 9mm Hungarian Firebird. He is completely taken aback by its presence.*

He lies back on the bed, gun in one hand and the battered old teddy in the other. Above him is the round orb of the earth, with a string of Mexican beads attached on one side.

1:44   A country road, West Riding. Day

GODBOLT *is being driven to police headquarters. On the radio is the eight o'clock news.*

NEWSCASTER: (*Voice over*) . . . one of the biggest man-hunts in the West Riding was underway last night for the killers of Craigmill student Emma Craven. Emma, nineteen-year-old daughter of a West Yorkshire CID officer, was shot dead by a masked man outside her home in Chorley shortly before midnight. Road blocks were set up on all exit roads from the county and there were delays on British Rail as detectives searched . . .

1:45 Pendleton's flat, London. Day

NEWSCASTER: (*Voice over*) . . . trains. No motive has yet been put forward for the killing, but a statement is promised later in the day by Assistant Chief Constable Ross, who is leading the investigation.

(PENDLETON *is sitting at his mahogany breakfast table with a small leather-bound Home Office directory in front of him. He is dialling a number on the telephone, a number which is obviously unfamiliar to him. The number begins to ring. On the sideboard, two pieces of lightly browned wholemeal bread pop up in the toaster, causing him to wheel round, just as someone speaks at the other end of the line.*)

VOICE: (*Distort*) West Riding Police.

(PENDLETON *pushes the toast back down into the toaster.*)

PENDLETON: My name is Pendleton. I would like to speak to the Chief Constable.

1:46 Outside West Riding police headquarters. Day

A dull grey Tarmac quadrangle. A number of vehicles and motor cycles are parked under weather-worn boards denoting name and rank. Godbolt's Granada sweeps into the car park driven by his assistant. GODBOLT gets out, looks around. He shakes the hand of the first policeman who recognizes him. It is a politician's handshake. He engages in conversation.

GODBOLT: A bad do this. (*His voice echoes across the ground.*) I don't know what the world is coming to . . .

(*Meanwhile, his assistant gets the papers and books out of the car and locks it up. Then* GODBOLT *and his assistant make for the Chief Constable's office.*)

1:47 The Chief Constable's office, West Riding police headquarters. Day

ROSS *enters the Chief Constable's office in his shirt-sleeves. He has been up all night. The* CHIEF CONSTABLE, *Jack Elliot, who is sitting at his desk, puts down the telephone.*

ROSS: I have to stand down the night watch, sir. They're dead on
their feet.
CHIEF CONSTABLE: (*Nodding*) That was Whitehall taking an
interest. They want to be kept informed.
(*He hands* ROSS *a memo with Pendleton's name and number.*)
Who is Pendleton?
(ROSS *looks at it sceptically.*)
ROSS: There's nothing here for them.
CHIEF CONSTABLE: Are you sure?
ROSS: Yes.
(*He stands at the window watching* GODBOLT *cross the Tarmac
towards the office.*)
It was her dad they were after . . .

1:48   Outside West Riding police headquarters. Day
CRAVEN *powers his car into the car park and brings it to a halt where
he normally parks.*

1:49   Inside Craven's car. Day
For a few seconds, CRAVEN *sits at the wheel, gathering strength for the
ordeal that lies ahead.*

1:50   The Chief Constable's office. Day
GODBOLT: I were only told the news when I reached conference. I
came straight over.
(*The* CHIEF CONSTABLE *rises to greet him.* GODBOLT *shakes his
hand and the assistant, having delivered the briefcase, leaves the
room.*)
CHIEF CONSTABLE: I appreciate your coming, Jim.
GODBOLT: I lost a son down the pit at twenty; you never get over
it.
(*The* CHIEF CONSTABLE *nods.*)
CHIEF CONSTABLE: He'll be given a spot of leave, you know, to
sort himself out; which means he'll have to come off your
inquiry.
(GODBOLT's *eyes brighten momentarily* . . .)
GODBOLT: I'll be sad to see him go. It's a difficult thing
investigating a union: historically the police and the unions
have always been on opposite sides and what Ronnie has got is
a certain tact. It's a rare quality in a Yorkshireman.
CHIEF CONSTABLE: Yes, I know what you mean.

(*There is an uncomfortable silence.*)
GODBOLT: So, who's going to replace him?

1:51   Outside West Riding police headquarters. Day
CRAVEN *gets out of his car and locks the door. He sees Godbolt's Granada parked directly across the Tarmac and recognizes it. He turns and trudges towards the entrance to the building.*

1:52   The Chief Constable's office. Day
The CHIEF CONSTABLE *turns and looks at* GODBOLT.
CHIEF CONSTABLE: I think we'll just shelve it. Don't you? Let it go.
(GODBOLT *nods. He can't believe his luck.*)
GODBOLT: That's OK with me.

1:53   Ground-floor corridor, West Riding police headquarters. Day
CRAVEN *traverses the corridor looking neither to right nor left. Unless someone raises their arm in greeting, he does not acknowledge their presence. Those who know what has happened and don't want to intrude upon his grief stay well clear.*

1:54   The CID operations room, West Riding police headquarters. Day
JONES *is at a computer terminal. Beside him is a cup of coffee. Like* ROSS, *he has been up all night. He is retrieving dozens of names of people who* CRAVEN *has put away over the past fifteen years. He curses, wishing for the umpteenth time that there was a computer program that could make short work of this task. But there isn't.*
JONES: Meadows, McCroon, McCallum, Norris, Patterson, Pargiter, Robertson, Reilly, Rawlinson, Shaw, Stammers, Stone.
(CRAVEN *enters. He crosses over to* JONES. *There is background chatter of typewriters and telephones but most of it is emanating from the room next door.*)
CRAVEN: Any news?
(JONES *looks up.*)
JONES: No. Are you OK?
(CRAVEN *nods and indicates the printer, which is printing out a list of names at Jones's bidding.*)
CRAVEN: Yes. What's this?

JONES: Ross wants a list of your arrests. He's convinced it's someone you put away.
(CRAVEN *nods but doesn't quite buy it.*)
CRAVEN: It could be.
JONES: When you see him show him it, will you?
(CRAVEN *tears off the list from the printer.*)
CRAVEN: OK.

1:55 The Assistant Chief Constable's office. Day

CRAVEN *stands in front of Ross's desk.* ROSS *looks haggard. There are three or four half-empty cups of cold tea on his desk, and dozens of reports lie between them. Apart from the reports, two telephones and the cups, the only object on the desk is a handsome silver statuette of a golfer.*
ROSS: I had to stand them down, Ronnie –
(CRAVEN *nods.*)
They're away by now.
(*He looks up.*)
CRAVEN: (*Flatly*) In London, I reckon . . .
ROSS: (*Nodding*) The road blocks will stay till noon. Then I meet the press. Do you want to come?
(CRAVEN *shakes his head.*)
I've been working on the assumption that this was a grudge killing.
(CRAVEN *looks at him but his face is expressionless.*)
ROSS: She stepped out in front of the gun – that's what you said last night.
CRAVEN: (*nods*) Yes.
ROSS: But it was aimed at you.
(CRAVEN *nods.*)
ROSS: So it has to be someone on this list!
(CRAVEN, *anticipating what's coming, interrupts.*)
CRAVEN: Sir, I want to get down to the college . . . pick up her stuff before it goes astray . . .
ROSS: This list is important, Ronnie. We should go through it.
(*He looks up, sensing Craven's reluctance.*)
Unless you think it's a waste of time.
(*The silver golfer stands between them.*)
CRAVEN: This afternoon . . .
(*He begins to turn. He just wants out of the office. But* ROSS *is determined to hold him.*)

20

ROSS: Is there anything you want me to tell the media?
(CRAVEN *hesitates*.)
CRAVEN: Just get her age right. She was twenty-one, not nineteen, as the radio put it.
(ROSS *nods, and looks down at his notepad*.)
ROSS: There's also a note from Muntsey. The coroners here postponed their report pending your identification. Can you manage that?
CRAVEN: I'll go down now.
(ROSS *looks up anxiously*.)
ROSS: Are you sure you can cope with it?
CRAVEN: (*Irritably*) Yes. I'm sure.
(*He turns again towards the door. But* ROSS *again calls him back*.)
ROSS: Officially, you're nothing to do with this enquiry, but unofficially you can do what the hell you like. Just keep me informed.
(CRAVEN *nods*.)
CRAVEN: Thank you, sir.
(*He exits*.)

1:56 The corridor outside the ACC's office. Day

CRAVEN *stands outside Ross's door. He leans against a filing cabinet. He is trembling. The interview has proved more difficult than he had imagined.* SHIRLEY, *the canteen lady, comes along with a bacon roll.*
SHIRLEY: Here you are, Mr Craven. I took out all the fat.
CRAVEN: Thank you, Shirley.
SHIRLEY: It was such a shock. She was such a little beauty.
(*She suddenly bursts into tears*.)
CRAVEN: C'mon girl.
(*She is now leaning up against him, with her head buried in* CRAVEN's *chest, sobbing away.* CRAVEN *holds her with one hand and the sandwich in the other*.)
You'll have us all greeting* in a minute.
(*It is then that* GODBOLT *hoves into sight. He immediately sizes up the situation*.)
GODBOLT: Hey, lass, he's got troubles of his own. Let him be.
(*He prises* SHIRLEY *away from* CRAVEN. *She immediately puts her head on his chest*.)

*Crying.

21

GODBOLT: (*To* CRAVEN) It's a bad day, son. We all share your loss.
(CRAVEN *feels totally inadequate.*)
CRAVEN: Thanks . . .
(*He puts the sandwich on top of a filing cabinet and turns away.*)

1:57   The lobby adjacent to the mortuary. Day

CRAVEN *enters.* DOCTOR MUNTSEY *is at his side. He closes the door behind them.* CRAVEN *has the hospital and mortuary reports in his hand and he is scanning them.*
MUNTSEY: We bypassed casualty.
(*He walks down the shiny white-tiled steps towards the mortuary.*)
There's always some bright young spark looking for kidneys.
CRAVEN: She wouldn't have minded.
MUNTSEY: Yes, well, she's the property of the court now. But tell that to some guy out there with a kid on a dialysis machine.
(*They have reached the mortuary.* MUNTSEY *unlocks it and then hesitates.*)
Remember, Ronnie, you aren't the first dad who's been down here. This is an identification procedure; not a test in stiff-upper-lip –
CRAVEN: (*Coldly*) Get the trolley out.
MUNTSEY: I don't believe in the repression of feeling.
CRAVEN: Don't lecture me, Muntsey.

1:58   A cityscape with the through-route to the college clearly marked. Day

Craven's car flashes by.

1:59   Craven's car. Day

CRAVEN *is driving.*
CRAVEN: (*Voice over*) I didn't want to look at you. I knew if I did, it wouldn't look like you, and I knew I'd say to Muntsey, 'This is not my Emma, there's been some ghastly mistake.'

1:60   The mortuary. Day

The body is rolled out on a spring-loaded chrome table. CRAVEN *looks down at the corpse. The porter takes the cover off the corpse.*
MUNTSEY: (*Formally*) This is your daughter?
(CRAVEN *nods.*)
CRAVEN: Yes, sir, it is.

(*The porter makes to pull the sheet back over the face but* CRAVEN *interrupts. He shouts.*)

CRAVEN: Leave it. (*He stares at* EMMA *for a moment.*) What was the cause of death?

MUNTSEY: Shock, massive haemorrhaging, the heart . . .
(MUNTSEY *continues to talk but we lose sound. Instead we pick up* CRAVEN's *voice, in an interior dialogue.*)

CRAVEN: (*Voice over*) I wanted to kiss you but it would have embarrassed Muntsey, so I asked for scissors and cut off a chunk of your hair. It was still damp and despite the lycol, it smelt of rain and crushed grass.

1:61   The locker room, Teachers' Training College. Day

The CARETAKER *and* CRAVEN *walk past a wall of lockers. Occasionally they bump into someone who is changing. It is a unisex place and there seems to be no thought for privacy. Out of vision we can hear the thump of feet on the squash court and the clatter of parallel bars.*

CARETAKER: She was a nice lass.
(CRAVEN *grunts.*)
She had a nice smile.
(*They turn the corner in the locker room.*)
And she never complained.

CRAVEN: You get a lot of complaints?

CARETAKER: About everything. I open too late, the courts are not swept, the showers are cold . . .
(*They reach a dead end. A couple of lockers are open here with gear spilling out, but there is one between them which is locked.*)

CRAVEN: Is this one hers?

CARETAKER: That's right.
(*He hesitates, thinking that* CRAVEN *will produce Emma's key, but he doesn't.*)

CRAVEN: Open it.
(*The* CARETAKER *opens the locker with a master key. The moment he does so, lots of gear spills out: towels, a bottle of wine, biscuits, a squash racquet, books, trainers, a sweater, swimming costume, an old handbag, and a parcel of what feels like old clothes. Both men stand looking down at it.*)

CARETAKER: I'll get you something to put it all in.
(*He exits.* CRAVEN *crosses to the squash court. The sound of the*

players hammering the balls against the walls parallels what's going on in his mind. Reality seems to be slipping away . . .)

1:62 The kitchen, Craven's house. Day

CRAVEN *drops Emma's stuff on the table.*

EMMA: (*Voice over*) Into the washer.

(CRAVEN *hesitates. The voice is so clear – but it's all in his head, he concludes. He up-ends the big bag and Emma's gear falls on to the table. He crosses to the Bendix, opens its doors and begins to stuff her clothes into the machine.*)

EMMA: (*Voice over*) Not that!

(EMMA'S *voice is sharp.* CRAVEN *has a sweater in his hand.*)
The colours will run.

(CRAVEN *puts it to one side and is more selective with the rest of the stuff. He closes the door of the machine and switches it on. Immediately there is a small rumbling sound and vibration as the impeller begins to turn.*)
Put it on 'cold wash'.

CRAVEN: (*Irritably*) I've done that.

(*He up-turns the other plastic bag which he had taken from Emma's locker. This contains the parcel of old clothes. He unties the parcel and examines the damp, crushed, dirty, sticky overalls and shirt and gloves which lie entangled within. In the bag is also a length of nylon climbing rope and a pair of sodden trainers. He picks up a limp badge, its colour a mottled black. On its face it carries the IIF logo. He stares at it. Although he has never seen one before, he knows immediately what it is: a radiation monitoring badge, and somewhere it has picked up a massive dose of gamma rays. He crosses to the sink where he begins to wash his hands vigorously.*)

1:63 Craven's garden. Day

A bonfire: the recognizable remains of the overalls, the rope and the trainers blaze up, giving off a cloud of dense smoke. To one side, the radiation badge curls up with the heat and bursts into flame.

1:64 Emma's bedroom. Day

The table is bare except for Emma's Hungarian automatic on the left-hand side and on the right the box marked 'Gaia'. CRAVEN *very carefully takes the lock of Emma's hair from his pocket and lays it on the table. Then he opens the 'Gaia' box and takes out the Geiger*

24

counter. *He switches it on. He passes the lock of Emma's hair over the face of the Geiger counter. There is an alarming response.* CRAVEN *switches off the Geiger counter and stares at the radioactive hair.*

1:65   Craven's garden. Day
CRAVEN *stirs the still unburnt bits of clothing with a stick to make sure they are consumed by the bonfire.*

1:66   The CID operations room, West Riding police headquarters. Day
CRAVEN *dumps a dozen legal files on Jones's desk before going back to his own desk, to fetch some more.* JONES *looks at them with resignation.*
JONES: Don't worry, Ronnie. I'll just keep these warm for you.
    (*He pauses.*) How long will you be gone?
CRAVEN: A couple of weeks.
    (JONES *drifts back to the computer where he is still sifting through Craven's recent arrests.* CRAVEN *moves a second stack of files to Jones's desk.*)
CRAVEN: What about the union inquiry? Can you handle it?
JONES: It's been shelved.
    (*He looks at* CRAVEN, *who is a bit startled, but shrugs.*)
CRAVEN: Well, that's one less to worry about . . .

1:67   In the ACC's office
CRAVEN *stands before Ross's desk, which is twice as cluttered now with paper cups and reports.*
CRAVEN: I'm thinking of going to London –
    (ROSS *looks up, alert.*)
ROSS: Why?
CRAVEN: That's where they will have gone and I want to be around when they're picked up.
ROSS: Did Emma have a boyfriend?
CRAVEN: Yes. I don't know the latest –
    (ROSS *reads a name from his notepad.*)
ROSS: Terry Shields . . . Muswell Avenue, N10. The Met checked him over.
CRAVEN: And?
ROSS: They gave him a clean bill of health – but (*he glances down at his notes*) he is a dodgy character, nevertheless, a left-wing agitator, evidently . . .

(CRAVEN *says nothing.* ROSS *looks at his notes again.*)
Now, what about this list? I've narrowed it down from fifty
to –
CRAVEN: Supposing it's none of them?
ROSS: Are you saying that this was *not* an act of vengeance? That
there is some other aspect to it?
CRAVEN: I just don't know . . .
(*He stares at* ROSS. *The strain is beginning to show in both men.
The telephone rings.* ROSS's *hand hovers over it.*)
ROSS: If you are going to London, draw a firearm. Better safe than
sorry.
(CRAVEN *nods – and turns to exit.*)

1:68   Inside Craven's car, on the motorway going south. Day
CRAVEN *is driving. He is 'talking' to* EMMA.
CRAVEN: I've only been to London on two occasions not connected
with business . . . Both times with your mother . . . The first
time we went to Buckingham Palace, where I received a medal
from the Queen. On the second occasion we went to a hospital
on the Fulham Road, where she underwent an operation (a
tumour of the breast had been diagnosed). On that occasion
we stayed for six weeks and you were sent to stay with your
Aunty May.
(*There is a long silence from the back of the car. Then we see*
EMMA, *aged about nine, sitting in the back.*)
EMMA: What did the Queen say to you?
(CRAVEN *concentrates carefully on the road ahead.*)
CRAVEN: She said, 'You must be a very brave man, Inspector.'
EMMA: Did she ask you to stay for tea?
CRAVEN: No.
EMMA: All that way, and you didn't stay for tea?
CRAVEN: There was a reception, we did have tea, but not with the
Queen.
(*There is a long pause.*)
EMMA: Ann Soames's dad said the Queen is not a friend of the
miners.
CRAVEN: Ann Soames's dad is a Communist.
EMMA: What is a Communist?
CRAVEN: Someone who doesn't like the Queen.
EMMA: Ann Soames's dad says the Queen is a waste of money.

CRAVEN: Money doesn't come into it. What difference does money make? You would still be dead and so would Mum.
(*A tear begins to roll down his face.*)
EMMA: Don't cry, Dad.
CRAVEN: I'm not.
(CRAVEN *wipes the tear away. There is a silence from the back. We go slowly back to* EMMA. *But she is not there. The back seat of the car is painfully empty.*)

1:69 The ACC's office. West Riding police headquarters. Day

ROSS, JONES, *the* CHIEF CONSTABLE *and a number of other* OFFICERS *listen to the statement which* CRAVEN *has recorded.*

CRAVEN: (*Voice over*) The gunman was young, he held the gun square . . . Emma ran towards him. She shouted 'Don't!' then he fired, she fell back. She was running forwards and yet the blast checked her. When I reached her she was on her back, struggling to get up. She looked at me as if she had slipped.
JONES: (*Voice over*) What happened to the gunman?
CRAVEN: (*Voice over*) I was more concerned with Emma. For one moment, I thought, 'She's all right,' and then I heard her sigh. I heard this exhalation and I saw she was bleeding all over . . . then I heard a car start and I could hear it sliding in the mud, and I knew we'd get a caste of the tyres, and she said, 'Dad, you're hurt' . . . but it was her blood all over me.
(*There is a pause in the tape and then* JONES *can be heard asking a question.*)
JONES: (*Voice over*) You say, when she ran forward it was almost as if she knew him.
CRAVEN: (*Voice over*) Yes, I got that impression.
ROSS: (*Voice over*) But he called your name?
CRAVEN: (*Voice over*) Yes.
ROSS: (*Voice over*) Did she say anything else, Ronnie, before she went?
CRAVEN: (*Voice over*) She just looked at me once and said, 'Don't tell.'
JONES: (*Voice over*) Don't tell what?
CRAVEN: (*Voice over, weary*) I don't know.
(*There is another long silence.*)
ROSS: (*Voice over*) And those were her last words?
(*And there is another long silence and* CRAVEN'*s voice can be heard, very bitter.*)
CRAVEN: (*Voice over*) Yes.

1:70 A lay-by on the motorway. Day

CRAVEN *has pulled his car into the lay-by. He can be seen bent over the steering wheel. He is crying. It is the first time he has cried since he was a little boy, but we can't hear him actually sobbing. The noise of the motorway traffic is very loud and long convoys of trucks speeding along at over sixty miles an hour on the slow lane impede both our view of him and the sound of his tears.*

1:71 Inside Craven's car. Day

The tears come in long, sobbing gasps, as if his throat were rusty and dry. Outside the motorway traffic whizzes by without a pause; more and more trucks.
CRAVEN *stays in the lay-by for a long time. No one stops to ask him whether or not he is in trouble.*

1:72 The Shepherd's Bush Roundabout, London. Day

Craven's car comes to a halt at the roundabout and waits for a gap in the traffic before entering the flow. Quickly he moves into the main stream and wheels it left into Holland Park Road.
CRAVEN: (*Voice over*) I suppose it's only natural, but a city seems to reflect the memories one has of it.
(*The car, having entered Holland Park Road, pauses and then makes a right to cross the road into the forecourt of the Hilton Hotel.*)
CRAVEN: (*Voice over*) So Emma always connected London with that trip to Buckingham Palace. But I always associate it with cancer.
(*Craven's car draws up outside the hotel and* DINGLE *the man who has been standing to one side of the door, straightens and comes towards him.*)
DINGLE: Inspector Craven?
CRAVEN: Yes.
(DINGLE *puts out his hand.*)
Detective Inspector Dingle, C11. Welcome to the Monkey House.
(CRAVEN *shakes* DINGLE's *hand.*)

1:73 A studio room, Hilton Hotel, Shepherd's Bush. Day

DINGLE *opens the door. He is carrying a Sainsburys carrier bag. He ushers* CRAVEN *in.* CRAVEN *takes in the neat, expensive little suite.*

DINGLE *puts the carrier bag on the hall table, and then, one after the other, switches on the refrigerator, the bathroom heater and the cooker.*
DINGLE: Don't use the booze in the fridge.
(*He opens the fridge door and indicates ranks of miniatures: whisky, brandy, rum, etc.*)
This is cheaper.
(*He pulls out a fifth of Bells from the Sainsburys carrier bag. He uncorks it and, taking two glasses from the little kitchen cupboard – closing the door with his knee – puts them on the fridge top.*)
CRAVEN: (*Bluntly*) Who's paying for this?
DINGLE: We are. We could have put you up in a section house, but (*he grins*) what the hell –
(*CRAVEN puts his case on the bed.*)
CRAVEN: I want to make it clear – I'm on leave. I'm not part of the investigation . . .
(*DINGLE pours a measure of whisky.*)
DINGLE: Of course, but . . . (*He pours a second measure.*) My guv'nor would like to see you.
(*CRAVEN looks at him.*)
Straight away, he says. He wants to sort out a few ground rules . . . mainly about the press.
(*He hands CRAVEN a glass.*)
CRAVEN: I'm not giving interviews.
DINGLE: (*Doggedly*) Nevertheless, they are persistent buggers; you say no, and they think you're just raising the price.
(*CRAVEN contains his irritation. DINGLE senses his reluctance.*)
Well, here's to a quick result.
CRAVEN: It's in your hands.
DINGLE: Of course.
(*Placing his glass empty on the table, he leaves. CRAVEN unzips his case – Emma's gun lies on the top of the baggage, next to it the battered box marked 'Gaia'.*)

1:74 Craven's studio room, Hilton Hotel. Evening
It is dark. The television is on. It is the only illumination in the room, except for the flare of the sodium lamps outside in the street. CRAVEN *sits, idly watching a television interview. The* PRIME MINISTER, *Mrs Thatcher, is arguing with* ROBIN DAY *about Trident.**

---

*This particular item was dropped in during production as it seemed pertinent.

PRIME MINISTER: (*Voice over*) Now which question are you asking first?

DAY: (*Voice over*) Trident.

PRIME MINISTER: (*Voice over*) First Trident. It's 3 per cent over the lifetime of the project.

DAY: (*Voice over*) It's 6 per cent of the equipment budget?

PRIME MINISTER: (*Voice over*) Yes, 3 per cent of the defence budget; 6 per cent of the equipment budget . . . We could not get such good deterrent value as we get in Trident.

(*At this moment the telephone rings and* CRAVEN *looks round. It is by the bed. He crosses to it and picks it up.*)

Now should we have Trident? Yes. We must have an independent nuclear deterrent in the country.

CRAVEN: Room 7016.

(*There is a cheerful voice at the end of the line. It is* PENDLETON.)

PENDLETON: Detective Inspector Craven?

CRAVEN: Speaking.

PENDLETON: I'd like a word with you.

CRAVEN: Who are you?

PENDLETON: My name is Pendleton. Can you meet me?

CRAVEN: When?

PENDLETON: Now. In the car park.

(*He rings off.* CRAVEN *puts the telephone down thoughtfully. He gets up and goes to the cupboard.*)

PRIME MINISTER: (*Voice over*) To leave the world totally in the hands of a potential aggressor seems to be the height of absurdity . . . If we don't deploy our nuclear forces, the alternative would be surrender –

DAY: (*Voice over*) Supposing they threaten us with massive conventional forces – is our answer to rely on nuclear deterrence first?

(CRAVEN *opens the door of the cupboard and pulls out an army flak-jacket which he puts on and then buttons up. Then he pulls on his raincoat on top of it, which he also buttons up.*)

PRIME MINISTER: (*Voice over*) The nuclear deterrent is there to deter *all* war – and it has.

(CRAVEN *switches off the television and crosses to his bed. He takes his automatic from under the pillow and checks the action. He stuffs it into his right-hand pocket and, picking up the keys from the table, crosses and opens the door.*)

1:75 A hotel corridor. Night

CRAVEN *comes into the corridor and locks the door to his room behind him. Then he walks down the corridor towards the lift.*

1:76 A hotel lift. Night

The lift door opens and CRAVEN *gets in. He presses the car park button and the doors close. Once the lift is in motion, he very deliberately presses the foyer button.*

1:77 The foyer, Hilton Hotel. Night

The lift doors open. A lady Japanese TOURIST, *carrying six parcels from Harrods, is about to step in.*

TOURIST: Going up?

CRAVEN: No. Car park only.

(*He gets out. The Japanese* TOURIST *watches as the door closes and looks up at the indicator. She presses the button once more.* CRAVEN *crosses to a door beside the lift. It says 'Car Park'.*)

1:78 The car park, Hilton Hotel. Night

PENDLETON *watches as the lift reaches the basement with a clang. The doors open. There is no one there.* PENDLETON *gives off no feeling of surprise. He pushes himself off the bonnet of the big Mercedes and turns to see* CRAVEN *standing on the far side of the basement, the firestair door still swinging behind him. He has his hand in his pocket.* PENDLETON *calls out.*

PENDLETON: Mr Craven?

(CRAVEN *nods.* PENDLETON *opens the door of his car.* CRAVEN *crosses slowly towards it.*)

CRAVEN: We'll talk in my motor if you don't mind . . .

(*He indicates it.*)

PENDLETON: Yours is bugged . . . like your phone . . .

(*He holds open the door of the Mercedes with a grin.* CRAVEN *looks at him. He sees a tall, stringy man in his thirties, grammar-school type, maybe army background. Not a policeman. He gets into the Mercedes.* PENDLETON *gets in on the other side.*)

1:79 Inside the Mercedes. Night

PENDLETON: We're safe in here – Chobham plate I'm told.

(*He takes out a cigarette package and offers one to* CRAVEN. CRAVEN *shakes his head.*)

CRAVEN: Are you from Six?*

PENDLETON: Good guess, but no. We're attached to the Prime Minister's office.

CRAVEN: Any ID?

PENDLETON: (*Cheerfully*) No, but you can talk to Sir Maurice Witherspoon. He heads the office . . .

(*He picks an ivory phone off the centre armrest and hands it to* CRAVEN.)

CRAVEN: What's the number?

PENDLETON: 853 1199.

1:80   The car park, Hilton Hotel. Night

The big Mercedes wheels around the bend and steams up the slope towards street level.

1:81   The Hilton Hotel, Shepherd's Bush. Night

The Mercedes leaves the hotel apron and turns left towards the Shepherd's Bush Roundabout.

1:82   Inside the Mercedes. Night

PENDLETON *drives fast up Shepherd's Bush Green.*

PENDLETON: You mentioned Six. Where did you come across them?

CRAVEN: Northern Ireland.

PENDLETON: Thick on the ground?

CRAVEN: Like blazers at Henley . . .

PENDLETON: You don't like cloak and dagger, do you?

(*It's a statement. He has sensed Craven's hostility.* CRAVEN *avoids answering.*)

CRAVEN: Where are we going?

PENDLETON: The BBC.

CRAVEN: Why?

PENDLETON: Because that is where the Prime Minister is. I'm looking after her tonight.

(CRAVEN *grunts, he is completely at sea.*)

CRAVEN: You do this for a living?

PENDLETON: No, but this evening we're a bit short-handed. My brief's a bit wider in scope. Which brings me to your daughter . . .

*MI6.

32

CRAVEN: Emma?

PENDLETON: She was some sort of terrorist, wasn't she?
(*There is a long pause.*)

CRAVEN: Terrorist?

PENDLETON: According to her file.

CRAVEN: What file?

PENDLETON: There is a file. But it's difficult to get hold of.

CRAVEN: What is your interest in this matter?

PENDLETON: The safety of the realm.
(CRAVEN *is silent.*)
I presume you discount the idea of revenge . . . no one down here believes it.
(CRAVEN *looks at him coldly.*)

CRAVEN: If you have an alternative, I'd like to hear it.

PENDLETON: What's all this about investigating the miners?

CRAVEN: I was called in by their election officers. Someone had been rigging the ballot.

PENDLETON: Who stood to benefit?

CRAVEN: James Godbolt.

PENDLETON: Is there motive there for murder?

CRAVEN: No.
(PENDLETON *draws up outside the gates of the Television Centre, White City, then wheels the car around until it is facing the other way. He switches off the ignition.*)

PENDLETON: Look, I'd like you to meet my partner . . .

CRAVEN: Mr Pendleton, I'm down here in a very particular circumstance. I don't think I could be of any use.

PENDLETON: On the contrary, you could be of enormous help . . .
(*There is an outburst of static from the radio telephone and then a voice comes in.*)
The question is, were they after her or were they after you?

RADIO VOICE: Hello, Cole-Fox for Delta Two. Portman is coming through now.
(PENDLETON *picks up the receiver.*)

PENDLETON: Delta Two received.

RADIO VOICE: Cole-Fox, owing to traffic congestion NHG, use alternate route Charlie, Hotel, Bravo.

PENDLETON: (*Into radio telephone*) Received, please advise all cars.

RADIO VOICE: Wil-co.
(PENDLETON *looks at* CRAVEN.)

33

PENDLETON: You'll have to walk back, I'm afraid, we've been re-routed.

1:83 Outside the Television Centre, White City. Night
Mrs Thatcher's car sweeps through the gates, followed by two escorting police cars.

1:84 Inside the Mercedes. Night
PENDLETON *looks at* CRAVEN.
PENDLETON: Call me tomorrow.
>   (*He hands* CRAVEN *a card.* CRAVEN *pockets it.*)

1:85 Outside the Television Centre, White City. Night
CRAVEN *gets out of the Mercedes and closes the door.* PENDLETON *takes off towards Shepherd's Bush following the trail of flashing blue lights.* CRAVEN *watches him disappear and then, tired, begins to retrace his steps towards the hotel.*

1:86 The Shepherd's Bush Roundabout. Night
CRAVEN *reaches the pedestrian underpass which will take him under the roundabout. He hesitates and stops. Over the noise of the late night traffic, we can hear the insistent jangle of freight cars and the exhaust of a diesel locomotive.* CRAVEN *turns and walks a few yards up the road looking for an entrance to the railway which lies beyond the fencing.*

1:87 The railway, Shepherd's Bush. Night
The yellow locomotive hauling the nuclear cars ghosts out of the tunnel gouged beneath the concrete of the roundabout. Only the vibration of the rails and the hum of its motor denotes its presence. It comes to a halt in a siding, facing a red light. CRAVEN *stares at it, then turns and crosses the road, making for the hotel.*
Fade out.

Into the Shadows

2:1 Craven's room, Hilton Hotel. Day

CRAVEN *is out on the balcony. He walks into the room to listen to the news headlines.*

NEWSCASTER: (*Voice over*) The time is eight o'clock. Our story this morning: The murder hunt for the killer of the young scientist Emma Craven has moved from Yorkshire to London after the discovery of an abandoned get-away car yesterday evening. Police have yet to issue a detailed description of the man wanted in connection with the killing. All-London headlines in a moment, but first, the latest on London's roads now . . .

(CRAVEN *walks over to the bed and picks up a towel. As he goes towards the bathroom, the telephone rings. He answers it. Intercut with* ROSS *in his office.*)

CRAVEN: Yes.

ROSS: Ronnie, did you hear the news?

CRAVEN: You found the car?

ROSS: We found the car. Got Lowe's fingerprints all over it.

CRAVEN: Lowe?

ROSS: (*Voice over*) Fifth on my list. You put him away ten years ago, remember?

CRAVEN: You saying he killed her?

ROSS: I'm not saying anything until we've picked him up. The Yard says he's in London. They should have him by noon. (*Cut to* CRAVEN.)
I'm sending Jones down to make the arrest.* Are you with me, Ronnie?

CRAVEN: Yes.

---

*The arresting officer is traditionally from the police force where the crime took place.

ROSS: (*Voice over*) I say, I'm putting Jones on the train. When you see Elham, tell him our man's on his way.
(*There is a knock at the door.* CRAVEN *moves to open it. It is the* CHAMBER MAID.)

MAID: Good morning, sir.

CRAVEN: I'm seeing him this morning.

ROSS: Well, be nice to him, Ronnie. He's been very helpful, so far.

CRAVEN: I'm also seeing Pendleton. Does the name mean anything to you?

ROSS: What does he want?

CRAVEN: A chat, he says.

ROSS: Well, if he gives you any aggro, just refer him to me. Right? Bye now.
(ROSS *hangs up. The* MAID *exits.*)

MAID: Thank you, sir.
(CRAVEN *stares at the telephone thoughtfully. It gives the most imperceptible tinkle. He lifts it up gently and then presses the bar gently. He hears a recording of his last conversation.*)

ROSS: (*Voice over*) What does he want?

CRAVEN: (*Voice over*) A chat, he says.

ROSS: (*Voice over*) Well, if he gives you any aggro, just refer him to me.
(CRAVEN *gently puts the telephone down.* PENDLETON *was right. His telephone is bugged.*)

2:2 Hilton Hotel, Shepherd's Bush. Day
CRAVEN *exits from the hotel by the 'side' entrance (the main entrance by right) as a bus load of tourists arrive.*

2:3 Outside the Hilton Hotel, Shepherd's Bush. Day
As CRAVEN *crosses the road, a man gets out of the driver's seat of a nondescript car and follows him. He looks like a plain-clothes police officer.*

2:4 Shepherd's Bush Roundabout. Day
The MAN *follows* CRAVEN *towards the underpass amidst screaming children on bicycles and pedestrians.*

2:5 The underpass, Shepherd's Bush Roundabout. Day
CRAVEN *walks down the slope, not looking round, dodging between*

other pedestrians. As CRAVEN *walks along the underpass, the* MAN *can be seen behind him.*

2:6 The underpass, Shepherd's Bush Greenside. Day

CRAVEN *comes out the other side of the underpass and walks up the slope, closely pursued by the man.* CRAVEN *walks along the street towards the underground station. The* MAN *is still following him.* CRAVEN *suddenly starts running.*

2:7 Shepherd's Bush tube station. Day

The man dashes into the station showing his police card. He makes for the escalator. He frantically searches for CRAVEN, *whom he has lost sight of.*

CRAVEN *stands at the top of the escalators. He watches the* MAN *as he is carried down the escalator. He turns, smiles, and makes for the exit.*

2:8 Carlisle's office. Day

CARLISLE *fires a gun into a hole in the floor. Then he reaches down and begins to haul up, by rope, a bucket filled with sand.* CRAVEN *watches from the far side of Carlisle's desk.*

CRAVEN: I don't think it's been fired –

CARLISLE: I still want to check it against another round we had in a little while ago. It came from a similar weapon.

(CARLISLE *reaches into the sand and picks out the round he has just fired.*)

This is quite an unusual gun, this, you know. It's based on the Swiss Zig. It's called a Firebird.

(*By this time* CARLISLE *is walking next door, towards his desk.* CRAVEN *follows him.*)

The Egyptians had a few which they off-loaded on to the market about ten years ago. Some of them fell into the hands of terrorists like the Baader-Meinhoff.

CRAVEN: Emma wasn't a terrorist.

CARLISLE: I know that, old mate, but we've got to make sure, haven't we?

(*He sits himself down in front of the microscope and puts under the scope the two rounds.* CRAVEN'S *eyes fall on the gun.*)

CRAVEN: What I want are the prints on the gun, excluding hers.

CARLISLE: (*Not looking up*) Hers were on the Revlon bottle, weren't they? (CARLISLE *is still mesmerized by the two rounds.*) It's all in hand.

CRAVEN: Can you put them through the computer for me?

CARLISLE: I can try.

CRAVEN: What's today's magic word?

CARLISLE: In the bumf on my desk.

> (*While* CARLISLE *continues to examine the spent rounds,* CRAVEN *rummages through the papers which are piled on the desk. He finds a list of the week's passwords and crosses over to the computer keyboard. Meanwhile, he continues to probe* CARLISLE — *whom he has known since both of them served in Northern Ireland.*)

CRAVEN: What do you know about a man called Pendleton?

CARLISLE: Not much.

> (*He is still concentrating. A pause.*)

He drives a green Mercedes, and parks in other people's spaces, dines at the Special Forces Club in Knightsbridge and drinks with the SAS in Chelsea Barracks. The security boys hate him.

> (CRAVEN *has moved over to the VDU and is sitting in front of it.*

CRAVEN: Did you know him in Northern Ireland?

CARLISLE: No.

> (CRAVEN *punches Shields's name into the computer.*)

CRAVEN: Done any work for him?

> (CARLISLE *looks up, slightly surprised by Craven's unsubtle probing, but he nods.*)

Recently?

> (*Again* CARLISLE *nods.*)

CARLISLE: It was a weapon which had been found in water which he wanted tested – for radioactivity.

CRAVEN: And was it? (*He turns from the keyboard.*) Radioactive?

CARLISLE: Oh, yes . . .

> (*By this time the VDU has screened out the following:* 'Shields, T. AKA "Terry" or "Tel". PF 185962. Access restricted.')
>
> (CARLISLE *continues talking about* PENDLETON.)

His friend Harcourt is the one to watch.

> (CRAVEN *looks puzzled.*)

CRAVEN: Harcourt?

CARLISLE: His other half. Drafted in from Lloyds. Dangerous bugger.

CRAVEN: What's his background?

CARLISLE: The City.

CRAVEN: City . . .

> (CRAVEN *looks at the VDU.*)

CRAVEN: Can I get through to R2* on this?
(*It is the first time that* CARLISLE *looks fraught.*)
CARLISLE: MI5 you mean?
CRAVEN: Yes. The Registry.
(CARLISLE *shakes his head.*)
CARLISLE: That's more than my life's worth.
(CRAVEN *nods.*)
CRAVEN: What does the phrase 'access restricted' mean?
(*He points to the VDU monitor where Shields's name can still be seen glimmering in the dull light.*)
CARLISLE: It means you can't get it on that file because it's on another file.
CRAVEN: (*Ironic*) Thanks, Carlisle. That's really helpful.
(CRAVEN *stands and moves back to* CARLISLE.)
CARLISLE: Or it could mean that the guy's an informer. So his record is restricted.
CRAVEN: They don't match, do they?
(*He is referring to the rounds under the microscope.*)
CARLISLE: No.
CRAVEN: I told you. She wasn't into that sort of thing.
CARLISLE: You want the gun back?
CRAVEN: Yes. And any information you can give me on the prints.
(CRAVEN *exits.* CARLISLE *goes back to his desk and sits down.*)

2:9 Shields's house, Muswell Hill. Day
The taxi comes to a halt outside Shields's house. CRAVEN *gets out.*
CRAVEN: Wait here. I'll be about ten minutes.
(*The* TAXI DRIVER *pulls over to the side of the road and stops.* CRAVEN *walks across to the front door of the house. He rings the bell. While he is waiting he turns and scans the Avenue. He sees a derelict van parked half-way down the hill, which he registers thoughtfully.*
The door opens and a tall, thin guy stands looking at him. CRAVEN *addresses him.*)
Terry Shields?
SHIELDS: Yes?
CRAVEN: I'm Emma's dad.
SHIELDS: Come in.

The MI5 dossiers held at the Registry in Curzon Street are accessed through a computer called R2.

(CRAVEN *enters the house.* SHIELDS *picks up the milk bottles from the window ledge and closes the door.*)

2:10 The hall, Shields's house. Day

CRAVEN *walks in and looks about him.*

SHIELDS: Straight up.

(CRAVEN *follows* SHIELDS *up the stairs to his flat.*)

2:11 Shields's flat. Day

CRAVEN *follows* SHIELDS *into the living-room.* SHIELDS *continues a conversation on the telephone.*

SHIELDS: Hi. Sorry, there was somebody at the door. (*Pause.*) What? (*Pause.*) No, come on – we discussed this already. We'll talk about it at Julie's on Wednesday. (*Pause.*) Look, there's somebody here. Can you call me back later? (*Pause.*) Tonight. Yeah. (*Pause.*) No. You call me . . . OK!

(SHIELDS *puts the telephone down and turns to look at* CRAVEN. *There is a silence.*)

SHIELDS: Look, they've already been here.

CRAVEN: Who?

SHIELDS: The Yard. They looked around, interviewed me . . . it's all on record.

CRAVEN: She told me she was leaving home. (*He looks around the room.*) She was coming here?

SHIELDS: Well, we talked about it, but we didn't have much time for home-building . . . even for the relationship. Politics is a full-time business.

CRAVEN: I thought you were a lecturer.

SHIELDS: Yes I am, and Emma was a physicist. But life doesn't stop with the job . . . unless you're a policeman, I suppose.

(CRAVEN *ignores the jibe. He picks up a political magazine which has 'Socialist Advance' all over its cover.*)

CRAVEN: 'Socialist Advance', is that the name of your party?

(*He flicks through the magazine.* SHIELDS *goes into the kitchen.*)

SHIELDS: (*Voice over*) I'm the Assistant Secretary. Not your cup o tea!

CRAVEN: No. (*He picks up a photograph on the mantelpiece.*) Was Emma a member?

SHIELDS: (*Voice over*) Yes. But she directed most of her energy towards sexual politics, Greenham, and the ecology movemer . . . not exactly our priorities.

40

(SHIELDS *returns to the main living-room.*)

CRAVEN: It must have been difficult for you two to hit it off, having such a diversity of views, I mean.

SHIELDS: It was a physical thing.

(CRAVEN *looks down at the photograph. It shows a group of young graduates sitting behind a cut-out whale, spouting the word 'Gaia'.* SHIELDS*'s remark stings.*)

CRAVEN: How deeply was she involved in Gaia?

SHIELDS: She was committed.

CRAVEN: How did that show itself?

SHIELDS: I don't know much about it, but what I do know, I don't think she would have wanted me to tell you.

(CRAVEN *turns away from the mantelpiece but pockets the photograph.* SHIELDS *doesn't object.*)

CRAVEN: Perhaps you're right. Her last words were 'Don't tell'.

SHIELDS: What?

CRAVEN: It all happened very suddenly, rather like a car crash. If you've ever been in one, you'll know it's often quite difficult to remember the actual sequence of events. For instance, I sometimes think she said 'Don't tell' as she was running towards the gunman. Or rather, 'Don't! Tel!'
(*He looks at* SHIELDS.)
Your friends call you Tel?

SHIELDS: But she didn't.

CRAVEN: What did she call you?

SHIELDS: She called me 'Darling', 'Dearest', 'My love'. Tel's a nickname used by old school mates.

(CRAVEN, *cut to the quick, is silent for a moment.*)

CRAVEN: The gunman stepped out. She ran towards him. She shouted 'Don't'. She died in my arms. Her last words were 'Don't, Tel'.

SHIELDS: Look, I was at the City Institute in London. I was two hundred miles away.

CRAVEN: Yes. I know . . .

SHIELDS: So if you've come to intimidate me, you've picked the wrong man.

CRAVEN: I came for her things, Tel.

(*This silences* SHIELDS. *He nods.*)

SHIELDS: I'll get them.

(*He leaves the room and goes into the bedroom.* CRAVEN *catches a glimpse of a nightie on the bed.* CRAVEN *moves to the window*

41

and looks out at the derelict van down the street. SHIELDS *returns with Emma's things.*)

SHIELDS: This is all there is.

(CRAVEN *crosses and takes them from him.*)

CRAVEN: She travelled light.

SHIELDS: It pays to these days.

(CRAVEN *looks at him.*)

Look. It is possible that it was nothing to do with me, that she was trying to warn you, not to tell them, about what was going on, in her life.

(CRAVEN *looks at him.*)

CRAVEN: What was going on?

(SHIELDS *crosses to the mantelpiece.*)

SHIELDS: I made a point of not asking.

(*He faces the mirror and, picking up a broad marker pen, writes across it 'Azure'.* Then he turns and looks at* CRAVEN. CRAVEN *takes it in and then looks through the mirror at* SHIELDS.)

CRAVEN: Well, if you remember, call me.

(*He moves towards the hall.*)

SHIELDS: Craven!

2:12 The hall outside Shields's house. Day

SHIELDS *hands* CRAVEN *a typewritten piece of paper.*

SHIELDS: This is an obituary I wrote for our paper.

(CRAVEN *takes the paper, half glances at it, folds it and puts it into his pocket.*)

CRAVEN: I'll read it later.

SHIELDS: It's only a short piece, written in haste. I hope it does her justice.

CRAVEN: As I said, call me . . . I'm at the Hilton, Shepherd's Bush.

(CRAVEN *exits.*)

2:13 Outside Shields's house

CRAVEN *walks down the path.*

CRAVEN: (*Voice over*) That wasn't your nightie on the bed, was it

EMMA: (*Voice over*) No.

CRAVEN: (*Voice over*) I didn't think it was.

(*He walks out of the gate and along the street towards the taxi.*)

---

*The word 'Azure' is a police term for the bugging of rooms.

(*Voice over*) You're dead less than a week and already he's got another woman in his bed. Do you understand that?

(*As* CRAVEN *walks,* EMMA *joins him.*)

EMMA: Yes, I do. He has his good points.

CRAVEN: Such as?

EMMA: He was a good lover.

CRAVEN: I'm sure he was . . . And in that van down there, there was a man listening to every creak of the bed, every sound you made.

(*He nods at the derelict van down the street.*)

EMMA: You're jealous, Dad.

(*He reaches the taxi and gets in.*)

CRAVEN: New Scotland Yard.

(*The taxi moves off.*)

He's a bastard.

2:14   Flashback. Craven's house, Craigmills. Day

EMMA: (*Voice over*) What does the word 'Azure' mean?

CRAVEN: The word 'Azure' is a police intelligence term. It means a room is bugged or under some sort of electronic surveillance.

(*It is a rainy afternoon.* EMMA *is sitting on the floor leaning against the sofa, where* CRAVEN *is stretched out in front of the fire, relaxed.*)

CRAVEN: The word 'Cinnamon' denotes the use of microphones inside telephones or junction boxes. 'Towrope' is the raw material gathered by telephone intercepts at the post office. F Branch is the office in MI5 in London that analyses the material. R2 is the MI5 computer that logs the material. We have a link with R2, but it's difficult to get at.

EMMA: That's where all the Gaia stuff will be.

CRAVEN: Yes.

2:15   Telephone booth, Victoria. Day

PENDLETON: (*Voice over*) Pendleton here.

(CRAVEN *puts in the coin. Outside we can see the cab.*)

CRAVEN: This is Craven. When do we meet?

PENDLETON: (*Voice over*) When is your appointment at the Yard?

CRAVEN: 11.30.

PENDLETON: (*Voice over*) Meet me in the basement car park at 11.00.

CRAVEN: We keep meeting in car parks.

PENDLETON: (*Voice over*) That is because you are under
    observation.
    (*He puts the telephone down.*)
CRAVEN: (*Voice over*) 'My love', 'My darling', what was the other
    thing you called him?

2:16 Outside the telephone booth, Victoria. Day

CRAVEN *leaves the telephone booth.*
EMMA: (*Voice over*) 'Dearest.'
CRAVEN: (*Voice over*) His bed is bugged. He's probably an
    informer. And you called him 'Dearest'.
    (*As* CRAVEN *walks down the street towards a taxi he is joined by*
    EMMA.)
EMMA: It's not his fault.
CRAVEN: He told you that, did he?
EMMA: He was playing them at their own game.
CRAVEN: Who?
EMMA: The people who were after him.
CRAVEN: And who were they?
    (*He bends down and talks to the* TAXI DRIVER.)
    How much do I owe you?
TAXI DRIVER: Eight pounds seventy.

2:17 Reception, Scotland Yard. Day

CRAVEN *walks into the reception area and goes up to a uniformed*
SERGEANT.
CRAVEN: Detective Sergeant Jones, please, Yorkshire. I believe
    he's in Detective Chief Superintendent Elham's office.
SERGEANT: Your name, please, sir?
    (*He is already scanning the appointment book.*)
CRAVEN: Craven, Inspector.
SERGEANT: You can go up, sir. Eighth floor. Room 810.
CRAVEN: Thank you.
    (CRAVEN *walks over to the lift.*)

2:18 The underground car park, Scotland Yard. Day

*A Morris Minor comes whizzing down the ramp. It speeds through the
car park and comes to a halt where* CRAVEN *is waiting.* PENDLETON
leans across and opens the passenger door.
PENDLETON: Get in.
    (CRAVEN *scrambles in and* PENDLETON *screeches off.*)

2:19   Inside the Morris Minor. Day

CRAVEN: What happened to the Merc?

   (*The car speeds up the ramp and out on to the street.*)

PENDLETON: We only use it for posh occasions. We're trying to
   save on fuel.

2:20   Outside Pendleton's office, Whitehall. Day

The Morris Minor comes to a halt. Both PENDLETON *and* CRAVEN
get out.

PENDLETON: Not exactly Albany.* But it's home.

   (*They walk down the street towards a door in the middle of a row
   of shops.*)

   You're about to meet Harcourt. Double First at Cambridge
   and an authority on E. M. Forster, he tells me, but a
   complete twat, I think, when it comes to making
   connections.†

   (*They reach the door and go in.*)

2:21   Stairs to Pendleton's office. Day

PENDLETON *leads* CRAVEN *up a staircase.*

PENDLETON: I myself favour an Irish education. Anyone who has
   examined the Book of Kells cannot but be impressed by the
   labyrinthine coils of the Celtic imagination. Are you a Celt by
   any chance, Craven?

CRAVEN: No.

2:22   Pendleton's office. Day

CRAVEN *and* PENDLETON *enter the office.* HARCOURT *is sitting at a
desk in a separate office, dictating into a tape recorder.* PENDLETON
calls out to him.

PENDLETON: Henry.

   (*He goes over to the office and taps on the window.* HARCOURT
   turns the recorder off and comes out of his office.)

   Henry, this is Inspector Craven.

   (HARCOURT *shakes* CRAVEN's *hand. He is a plump man who,
   when he isn't looking cross, seems permanently pleased with
   himself.*)

The Albany is a posh block of service flats opposite Fortnum and Mason. Those who
live there usually drop the 'The'.

'Only connect': Forster's famous phrase.

HARCOURT: I was sorry to hear your news, Inspector.
  (*He calls to his* SECRETARY.)
  Letters, Ellen.
SECRETARY: (*Voice over*) Yes, sir.
  (HARCOURT *turns to* CRAVEN.)
HARCOURT: It must have been a great blow.
  (ELLEN *enters to take the letters from* HARCOURT. *She wears standard art-school punk clothes and make-up, which looks outrageous in this particular environment. She leaves again with the eyes of all three men on her.*)
  Bizarre, I know, but not the sort who posts things to the *Guardian*.
CRAVEN: Where did you find her?
HARCOURT: Art school.
PENDLETON: (*Tactfully*) I'll get Ellen to make us some tea.
  (*He follows* ELLEN *out of the office.*)
CRAVEN: (*To* HARCOURT) Pendleton said you wanted to see me.
HARCOURT: What do you know about Gaia?
CRAVEN: Only what my daughter told me.
HARCOURT: And what did she tell you?
CRAVEN: That it was an organization against nuclear power.
HARCOURT: Was she a member?
CRAVEN: Yes, I think she was.
HARCOURT: You agree with her views?
CRAVEN: No, but I enjoyed the conversations.
HARCOURT: Sit down, Mr Craven.
  (CRAVEN *sits down.*)
  Would you say that Gaia was a subversive organization?
CRAVEN: (*Cautiously*) They broke a few rules.
HARCOURT: Did you know that six of them broke into the Nucle
  Waste Plant at Northmoor eight weeks ago? And they were
  led by your daughter?
  (*This singular piece of news leaves* CRAVEN *blinking.*)
CRAVEN: No.
  (*In the background* PENDLETON *comes into the office.*
  HARCOURT *studies* CRAVEN, *watching his reaction. Eventually*
  PENDLETON *intervenes.*)
PENDLETON: What we want to find out is whether Emma's deat
  had anything to do with the break-in.
CRAVEN: Is there anything to suggest that it was?

46

PENDLETON: Circumstantial evidence. Everyone connected with the raid has either disappeared or is dead.

(*This information is almost as shattering as his first announcement.*)

HARCOURT: We've had a report from the coroner. Her body has been subject to massive doses of radiation consistent with her participation in the break-in . . . And there is this.

(*He produces the Firebird, wrapped in plastic. For the third time,* CRAVEN *betrays surprise.*)

How did she come to possess this?

CRAVEN: If I knew that, I wouldn't have given it to Carlisle.

(PENDLETON *ignores the reference to* CARLISLE.)

PENDLETON: I presume you haven't told Ross about it.

(*He indicates the gun.*)

CRAVEN: I presume you haven't told Ross about the break-in at Northmoor.

HARCOURT: You like to play things close to your chest, don't you, Craven?

CRAVEN: Yes. Till I know what's going on. For instance, I don't know who you are, or what your interest is.

HARCOURT: Surely Mr Pendleton explained that last night?

CRAVEN: He said something about 'the safety of the realm'. But no more.

HARCOURT: He didn't have to – we work direct to Cabinet Office, and as far as they are concerned, we have *carte blanche.*

(*He pauses, then speaks very carefully.*)

All I can tell you is that we are interested in anything that goes on at Northmoor. That is our brief. What concerns us at the moment is whether your daughter's death is as a result of the break-in or, as your police colleagues believe, a rather unfortunate accident. What do you think?

CRAVEN: I came here to discuss the file Mr Pendleton mentioned last night. A file on Emma.

HARCOURT: (*To* PENDLETON) We haven't got a file on her – have we?

PENDLETON: He's talking about Jedburgh's file.

HARCOURT: Oh! Well, I see no reason why Mr Craven shouldn't be put in touch with Jedburgh, providing he helps us first.

(*They both look at* CRAVEN.)

CRAVEN: Let's be clear about this. You want me to help you, but you won't tell me what all this is about.

HARCOURT: That's right. We have no intention of putting you in the picture.

PENDLETON: But we will return the gun to Carlisle without comment and we won't stop or hinder your own inquiry. That's the deal.

CRAVEN: (*Nodding*) OK.

(HARCOURT *goes over to a tape recorder and switches it on. A telephone conversation can be heard.*)

HARCOURT: Well, who does this remind you of?

GODBOLT: (*Voice over*) I'm not going to be able to open my mouth without some journalist ramming this fraud down it. Let alone give evidence on your behalf before some parliamentary sub-committee. So, in the present situation I'm no bloody use to you.

(HARCOURT *turns it off.*)

CRAVEN: It's Godbolt.

HARCOURT: You were investigating an election fraud involving Godbolt's union?

CRAVEN: Correct.

HARCOURT: Did you know that he had a close relationship with the people who run Northmoor?

CRAVEN: No.

HARCOURT: Had it occurred to you that someone might have been interested in trying to get him re-elected?

CRAVEN: Yes. It had.

PENDLETON: But not the Northmoor management?

CRAVEN: I didn't know there was any connection.

HARCOURT: Well, now that you do know, would you agree that it would have been in their interest to see that 'their' man got his job back?

CRAVEN: Yes.

HARCOURT: And that they would have had both the skill and the opportunity to execute the fraud?

CRAVEN: Yes.

(HARCOURT *draws the interrogation to a close.*)

HARCOURT: What time was your meeting?

CRAVEN: Eleven thirty.

2:23 Outside Pendleton's office. Day

PENDLETON *holds the door open.* CRAVEN *exits.*

PENDLETON: Sorry I can't run you back, old chap. But you know
   how it is.
CRAVEN: I'll find my own way.

2:24   A telephone box, Battersea Bridge. Day

CRAVEN *walks along the street. He enters a telephone box. He tries the*
telephone but it has been vandalized. He puts it down, fed up. He exits
from the telephone box and crosses the bridge, making for Scotland
Yard.

2:25   Reception, Scotland Yard. Day

CRAVEN *comes through the door and crosses the reception area in a bad*
mood. The uniformed SERGEANT *at the desk looks up as he shows his*
pass and hurries past. CRAVEN *walks over towards the lift.*

2:26   The lobby, Scotland Yard. Day

CRAVEN *walks into a lift. The doors close.*

2:27   A corridor outside Elham's office, Scotland Yard. Day

CRAVEN *walks down the corridor looking for Elham's office. He finds*
it. The door is open and he walks in.

2:28   Detective Chief Superintendent Elham's office, Scotland Yard. Day

CRAVEN *enters. He looks around. The office is empty. There is no sign*
of JONES *or* ELHAM *or* DINGLE. *He crosses to the desk, sits down at it*
and dials PBX.
CRAVEN: Could I have the Home Office, please – extension 2793.
   Thank you.
   (*As he waits for an answer he picks up a memo which is on top of*
   Elham's desk. He scans it. It says 'Where the hell is Craven?' and
   is signed 'Tom'. CRAVEN *supposes that this is Elham's Christian*
   name. He puts the memo down. Then he is through to the Home
   Office – and Carlisle.
   Intercut between Carlisle's office and Elham's office.)
CARLISLE: Carlisle.
CRAVEN: (*His voice is cold*) What happened?
CARLISLE: They were on to me before you were out of the
   building . . . I'm sorry.
CRAVEN: They're returning the gun . . . Let me know if anyone
   else shows an interest.

CARLISLE: Shall I complete the tests?

CRAVEN: Yes. Today if possible.

(*He puts the telephone down as the office door opens.* DINGLE *and* JONES *enter the office together.*)

DINGLE: Where the hell have you been? You're in demand here.

CRAVEN: I got lost.

DINGLE: The word was you'd disappeared.

CRAVEN: I thought you had me under observation.

DINGLE: So did I.

JONES: Are you OK?

(ELHAM *enters the office.*)

CRAVEN: Of course I am.

ELHAM: What the hell's going on? You checked in two hours ago. Where have you been?

CRAVEN: (*Snarling*) I changed my mind and checked out again.

(ELHAM *is slightly taken aback by this.*)

ELHAM: Do you realize there have been twenty-eight sightings of Lowe in various parts of London. I want you here when we get him. You've got a TV interview in twenty minutes. We're late. And I want to talk to you about Lowe.

CRAVEN: I said I wasn't giving any interviews.

ELHAM: I don't want to discuss it now. We'll talk about it on the way. Now, let's go.

CRAVEN: Have you got his file?

(ELHAM *looks at* DINGLE.)

DINGLE: I'll find it.

(CRAVEN *moves towards the door, where* ELHAM *is already standing.*)

ELHAM: You should change your tie.

(CRAVEN *looks down at the tie* ELHAM *is offering him.*)

CRAVEN: It's black.

ELHAM: You're in mourning, aren't you?

(CRAVEN *looks at it, takes it and walks out of the door into the corridor, slinging the tie around his neck.*)

2:29   The corridor, Scotland Yard. Day

JONES *looks at* CRAVEN, *who is tying his tie. Two strangers in a hostile land, they talk almost furtively.*

CRAVEN: (*To* JONES) How's it going your end?

JONES: Fine. We're almost there.

CRAVEN: No news on the other one?

JONES: Ross will fill you in himself. He's on his way down. He's changed his mind. He wants in on the arrest.
(DINGLE *arrives with Lowe's file as the lift door opens and they all get in.*)

2:30   The lift, Scotland Yard. Day
DINGLE *is holding a photograph of* LOWE.
DINGLE: You remember him?
CRAVEN: Yes, I do. (CRAVEN *stares down at Lowe's face on the record sheet.*) What's the purpose of this interview?
DINGLE: To show the kind of co-operation the public can expect between the Northern and Metropolitan police forces.
(CRAVEN *looks at him, surprised, but the man is serious.*)

2:31   A make-up room, BBC Television Centre. Day
CRAVEN *is sitting at a mirror being made up.* SUE COOK, *the interviewer, approaches.*
SUE: Hello! Inspector Craven? I'm Sue Cook. I'm going to be interviewing you today. Thank you very much for agreeing to come in. I know it can't be easy for you.
(CRAVEN *remains silent, simply staring ahead in the mirror.*)
But it's quite a short interview – I won't make it much of an ordeal, I promise you. Just a few questions about . . .
(*She continues chatting to him about the form the interview will take as they are rushed out of the make-up room into the studio.* ELHAM *is waiting in the corridor.*)
ELHAM: All right Ronnie? Now just take your time. And take it easy. Don't let her throw you.
(ELHAM *turns to talk to* SUE COOK, *as* CRAVEN *is led into the studio and over to a chair in front of the cameras.* ELHAM *moves to join* JONES *and* DINGLE, *who are standing behind the cameras.* SUE COOK *walks over to where* CRAVEN *is seated.*)

2:32   The studio, BBC Television Centre. Day
SUE COOK *joins* CRAVEN *in front of the cameras and sits down.*
SUE: Right. Is everything OK, Inspector Craven? Are you all right?
CRAVEN: Could I have a glass of water, please?
SUE: Yes, of course.
(*She calls to the assistant floor manager.*)

Scott, could we have a glass of water, please, for Inspector Craven? Thanks.

(*She speaks to the director up in the gallery.*)

Yes, Peter. I can hear you now . . . Yes . . . Right . . . OK . . . So it's now camera two . . . And three for the rest of it . . . And you'll give me one minute thirty second cues? . . . Yes? OK. Right.

(*She turns to* CRAVEN.)

Inspector Craven, would you uncross your legs, please? (*To the gallery.*) Yes, I'm telling him now. Inspector Craven.

(CRAVEN *uncrosses his legs.*)

It's just that it looks rather odd on camera. I know it's silly. I'm talking to the director upstairs, by the way.

(*There is a request by the floor manager to clear the studio and then the countdown to transmission: Ten, nine . . . five, four . . .*

(*To camera*) Well, now we turn to the hunt for the murderer of the young student, Emma Craven . . .

2:33   Outside a television store, Shepherd's Bush. Night

SUE COOK *can be seen on the televisions interviewing* CRAVEN. CRAVEN *is standing outside in the rain watching.*

SUE: (*Voice over*) . . . who was gunned down outside her Yorkshire home last Thursday evening. Her father – a police inspector – was with her as it happened. And he's in the studio now. Inspector Craven, can you tell us if you've got any useful leads?

CRAVEN: (*Voice over*) Yes, there was a car used in the incident, which has turned up in London. It has been traced and the inquiry has moved down to this area.

SUE: (*Voice over*) Can you describe exactly what did happen on that night?

CRAVEN: (*Voice over*) I had just picked Emma up from her college. It was about five minutes drive away. It was a rainy night . . . (*Cut to* CRAVEN, *tears rolling down his face as he watches himself on all the television sets in the window.*)

2:34   Flashback. Outside Craven's house, Craigmills. Night

EMMA *is thrown back as the bullets hit her.*

2:35   Outside the television store, Shepherd's Bush. Night

CRAVEN *turns and walks away down the street in the direction of his hotel.*

2:36   The railway cutting, Shepherd's Bush. Night

It is still raining. A huge yellow cabbed diesel comes to a halt at the red signal, with a mournful cry of brakes. Its rumbling and churning echoes in the tunnel behind it.

2:37   Craven's room, Hilton Hotel. Night

CRAVEN *is standing outside on the balcony. The telephone is ringing. He goes inside to answer it. It is an American voice on the line, sounding somewhat drunk.*

CRAVEN: Room 7016.

JEDBURGH: (*Voice over*) Craven? My name is Jedburgh.

CRAVEN: Who did you say you are?

JEDBURGH: Darius Jedburgh. I'm a friend of Harcourt's.

CRAVEN: I am not a friend of Harcourt's. I only met him today
    and I already don't like him.

JEDBURGH: Well, he speaks very highly of you, son. That's OK
    with me. Look. I'd like to meet you.

CRAVEN: When?

JEDBURGH: Well, now, for Christ's sakes. Look, I just saw you on
    television. The sight of you struggling in that sea of
    sanctimonious shit is still before my eyes.

CRAVEN: It's almost 11.30, Mr Jedburgh, and I am just about to
    go to bed.

JEDBURGH: Well, take a cold shower and get on down here, you
    bastard. I really want to meet you. I'm at the Tiberio on
    Curzon Street.

CRAVEN: The Tiberio. . . ?

JEDBURGH: On Curzon Street, Craven.

    (JEDBURGH *hangs up.* CRAVEN *replaces the receiver, and goes
    into the bathroom. He splashes his face with water.*)

2:38   The Tiberio basement. Night

A sweeper casts a long mop over the tiled floor. CRAVEN *comes down the stairs into the cellar. The chairs have been up-ended on every table but that occupied by two men. Both are drunk.*

CRAVEN: Mr Jedburgh?

    (*From behind him, he hears a voice.*)

JEDBURGH: Mr Craven.

    (CRAVEN *turns round and sees* JEDBURGH, *a big man, whose
    genial manner could conceal a dangerous streak. They shake
    hands.*)

Darius Jedburgh at your service, sir. Come and join us.
(*He walks over to the table and pulls up a chair for* CRAVEN.)
Here, pull up a chair and join the party.
(CRAVEN *looks round*.)

CRAVEN: No Harcourt?

JEDBURGH: Harcourt, hell. You'll find him over at Fulham with
his leg over some law student. (JEDBURGH *calls to the waiter*.)
Silvio!

CRAVEN: What about Pendleton?

JEDBURGH: Oh! It's past Pendleton's bedtime. You know he
returns every night to the Abbey, where they lock him up in
one of those tombs. They only let him out when the kingdom
is threatened. Now, Craven, I want you to meet a couple of
friends of mine. (JEDBURGH *introduces his two companions*.)
This here is Colonel Robert G. Kelly, known in the service as
Key Sanh,* and over here, you got Colonel Mike
Merryweather, also known as 'Mad Mike' . . . They just got
back from South America – having a little celebration dinner,
here. Silvio, a drink for our guest. Come on, Craven, have a
seat, take a load off. Enjoy yourself. There you go.
(CRAVEN *looks at the two drunken men and sits down*.)

MERRYWEATHER: Who's this?

JEDBURGH: That's Craven, Mike.

MERRYWEATHER: He showed up at last.

JEDBURGH: That's right, Mike.

MERRYWEATHER: I just want to say this Craven – I was damned
sorry to hear about your daughter.
(JEDBURGH *hands* CRAVEN *a whisky*.)

JEDBURGH: A Macallan. I hope it's to your liking.
(CRAVEN *nods*.)

CRAVEN: Your friends are stationed in London?

JEDBURGH: No, sir. Colonel Kelly, here, is from Dallas. Have you
been to Dallas, Craven?

CRAVEN: No, sir.

JEDBURGH: It's where we shoot our Presidents.† The Jews have
their Calvary, but we got Dealey Plaza. Mad Mike, here, is
from Austen. It's the home of country music.

---

*A notorious battleground of the Vietnam War.
†In November 1963 President J. F. Kennedy was assassinated in Dealey Plaza, Dallas.

CRAVEN: According to Waylon Jennings.
MERRYWEATHER: Jennings? Who the hell's Jennings?
JEDBURGH: The country singer, Mike. Mr Craven here is a
connoisseur of country music – that is, according to Harcourt.
You know 'Way out Willie' – Willie Nelson – 'A Regular
Outlaw' – if his friends are to be believed?
CRAVEN: He has just made a new record.
JEDBURGH: 'Cut a disc', Craven. They may make records here in
London, but we cut discs in Texas. Cheers!
(*They both drink.*)
What was that song that Willie had out about a year ago? 'The
Time of the Preacher'. Something about the year of 01. You
familiar with the words, at all?
CRAVEN: 'It was the time of the Preacher
In the year of 01
And just when you think it's all over
It has only begun . . .'
(JEDBURGH *interrupts.*)
JEDBURGH: No, no, Craven:
'Now the lesson's all over
And the killing's begun . . .'
(CRAVEN *interupts him.*)
CRAVEN: That comes later.
JEDBURGH: All right. You remember what comes in between?
Wait – here it goes: (*He begins to sing, out of tune.*)
'But he cannot forgive her Though he tried and he tried.'
CRAVEN: 'And he tried.
In the halls of his memories still echo her eyes
And he cried like a baby
And he screamed like a panther in the middle of the night
And he saddled his pony
And he went for a ride.
It was the time of the preacher
In the year of 01
Now the lesson is over
And the killing's begun . . .'
(*There is a silence. They stare at each other.*)
JEDBURGH: You know what the term 'preacher' signifies, don't
you, Craven?
CRAVEN: Gun.

JEDBURGH: A gun. The time of the preacher is the time of the gun, in the year of 01, and just when you think it is all over, it is only begun . . . It's quite a thought, something we ought to reflect upon.

(*At this moment,* MERRYWEATHER *lays his head on the table with a dull thud and goes to sleep.* JEDBURGH *contemplates this, then looks back at* CRAVEN.)

I think we ought to get these boys to bed, Craven. I guess they're all tuckered out.

2:39   Inside Jedburgh's Rolls-Royce. Night

The car is weaving somewhat unsteadily along Park Lane towards Knightsbridge. JEDBURGH *is driving.* CRAVEN *sits in the passenger seat. Behind them in the back seats are the two good old boys, out to the world.*

JEDBURGH: We used to have this gunsight in Vietnam with an image intensifier. Are you with me, Craven? That's how I saw you on that little screen tonight. Like a sitting duck . . . Harcourt asked me to give you sight of a file. I wasn't too keen on it, till I saw you on TV.

CRAVEN: You work for the CIA?

JEDBURGH: Yes, sir.

CRAVEN: I find that hard to believe.

JEDBURGH: Time was when this station was full of joggers in Brooks Brothers suits.* With Reagan in the White House, we got to keep a higher profile.

CRAVEN: White Rolls and stetsons?

JEDBURGH: We're just blending in with the surroundings, son.

(*He indicates the Americanization of Mayfair with a wave of his hand.*) Look around. Like Uncle Ho says, blend in with the surroundings.† (*He changes tack.*) Do you play golf, Craven? It's a great game. Closest thing I've got to a religion. I really believe that God is a golfer.

(*They turn into a square and come to a halt. He looks at* CRAVEN *with concern.*)

Does that upset you, Craven?

---

*An Ivy League outfitter on the East Coast of the USA.

†A maxim of Ho Chi Minh on guerrilla warfare – a gloss on Mao's 'fish in the water'.

2:40   The foyer, Jedburgh's apartment building. Night

JEDBURGH *comes through the door carrying 'Key Sanh'*. CRAVEN *follows carrying 'Mad Mike'. They make for Jedburgh's apartment.*

JEDBURGH: When I think of St Andrews and Carnoustie and Leith, I begin to realize that it is more than a coincidence that divine providence has brought forth oil from the depth of the North Sea. That oil will help to save the golf courses of Scotland.

CRAVEN: From what?

JEDBURGH: From the Communists, Craven. Can you imagine what would happen to the golf courses of this country if a Communist government ever got in power? God may not be a Communist, Craven, he may not even be a Republican, but I know damned well he's not a member of the Socialist Advance.

2:41   The bedroom, Jedburgh's apartment. Night

JEDBURGH *switches on the light and enters the bedroom carrying Key Sanh*. CRAVEN *follows with Mad Mike*. JEDBURGH *is still talking away.*

JEDBURGH: Do you have any experience with Communism, Craven?

CRAVEN: No, sir.

JEDBURGH: It's an anal disease. Marx had trouble with his bowels.
(JEDBURGH *dumps Key Sanh on the bed.* CRAVEN *lets Mike drop on to the bed next to him.* MERRYWEATHER *suddenly comes to.*)

MERRYWEATHER: If the White House should ring, just say I'm out in the field.

JEDBURGH: OK, Mike.
(JEDBURGH *leaves the bedroom but turns to* CRAVEN *at the door.*)
Oh, Craven, you'll find that file in the top right-hand drawer of my desk, in the living-room.
(*He exits.*)

2:42   The living-room, Jedburgh's apartment. Night

CRAVEN *enters the room. He turns on the light and crosses to the desk. He pulls out the report from the right-hand drawer.* CRAVEN *opens the report. On the first page it just says 'Plutonium UK'. On the second page is a list of headings of chapters.* CRAVEN *runs his finger down the list. He crosses the room, sits down at the table and begins to read.*

CRAVEN: (*Voice over*) One year ago the MOD test station at
Eskmills confirmed radioactivity of above normal background
level at the Corry Reservoir, Craigmills, Yorkshire. The usual
emergency procedures were activated under NAIR
arrangements and the reservoir was shut down. (CRAVEN *reads
the rest of the page in silence and then he turns to the next page.*)
An independent inquiry was initiated under the chairmanship
of Dr Anthony Marsh. Suspicion pointed to a secret
plutonium source hidden in Northmoor Nuclear Waste Plant,
ten miles from the city. Northmoor is a labyrinth of mines
which have been utilized by the British Army since World
War II. Recently the mines were sold to a private company,
International Irradiated Fuels, specializing in the storage of
low-grade wastes. IIF is owned by Mr Robert Bennett, a free-
wheeling entrepreneur with extensive connections in the
nuclear industry. There have been persistent rumours that
plutonium has been illegally stored there. These rumours have
always been denied. But in the summer of this year, a team of
scientists from the ecology group Gaia penetrated the mines in
search of the source. They were organized and led by a local
woman, Emma Craven. Since all those connected with this
adventure are now dead or have disappeared, it is difficult to
discover what their mission was, or whether it was successful.
(CRAVEN *has to stop for a moment. He finds it difficult to take it
all in.*)

2:43   Flashback. A laboratory in Emma's college. Day
CRAVEN *enters the laboratory and walks over to where* EMMA *is
standing.*
EMMA: Tony Marsh is dead. Car accident on the motorway.
(CRAVEN *nods.*)
CRAVEN: I know. I'm sorry.
(*They both sit down.*)
Is there anything I can do?
(EMMA *shakes her head.*)
EMMA: He'd just finished a report on the reservoir. It points
conclusively to Northmoor as a contamination source.
CRAVEN: That lets Sellafield off the hook.
EMMA: Yeah. They're jumping for joy up there. But what's going
to happen here?
CRAVEN: It's none of your business.

EMMA: The analysis suggests the source has to be a reprocessing plant. IIF deny they've got anything like that down there.

CRAVEN: Spent fuel rods have been known to leak.

EMMA: No, Dad. It was done by some sort of laser operation, which they also deny. The only way to find out is to go down there.

CRAVEN: (*Horrified at the idea*) Northmoor is a nuclear waste plant. Anyone who breaks in there will be met with ultimate force. It's the most dangerous business in Britain. Don't even think of it.

2:44 The living-room, Jedburgh's apartment. Night

CRAVEN *continues to read the report.*

CRAVEN: (*Voice over*) The location of plutonium at Northmoor raises doubts about the status of current agreements with the British government. While our own need for plutonium is at a premium and British reserves are already at an all-time high, evidence that they have further stocks is something of a blow to those who advised us to put faith in the UK.* Is it possible that these stocks are not the product of the British reprocessing plant at Sellafield? This raises the sinister question as to where that source might be and for what purpose it is being made. As a matter of priority we must find out what's going on at Northmoor. (CRAVEN *turns to the next page and suddenly finds himself faced with a large photograph of* EMMA. *He glances at the notes below it.*) Emma Craven . . . Aged twenty-one. Bachelor of Science, studied under Emily Threadwell at the Cavendish. Gaia's representative at Craigmills College. Relatively inexperienced in these matters, she was ordered to organize the raid on the mines. No one knows exactly what occurred, but one source indicates that the team was trapped in an underground tunnel below the cooling pools and that a large quantity of radioactive water was directed into it. Whether this was a calculated act on the part of the company is not known. Her boyfriend Terry Shields, a left-wing firebrand, is believed to have passed information to Scotland Yard's Special Branch on matters connected with Socialist Advance, the Trotskyite party to

---

*It should be remembered that this report was written by an American and it is American concern about the possible proliferation of British plutonium that is voiced here.

which he belongs. It is possible that Special Branch would have had foreknowledge of the raid and alerted the company accordingly. (CRAVEN *turns the page.*) Her father, a police officer in Craigmills, may also have known of his daughter's activities. It is difficult to conclude that he did not, yet he made no attempt to stop her going in. Why? (CRAVEN *puts the report down. The telephone rings. He gets to his feet and crosses to the telephone and picks it up.*) Yes? (*He listens.*) He's out in the field . . . (*He listens again.*) That's the message I got . . . (*He puts the telephone down and, picking up a pen, writes on the pad by the telephone in big letters: 'The White House called'.*)

2:45 A London square. Night

CRAVEN *leaves Jedburgh's apartment and stands for one moment outside the door. The square is deserted. In the distance he can hear an echo of the Gaia party trapped in the mine. It is soon overlaid by the sound of a taxi.* CRAVEN *crosses the road and, as it comes into view, hails the cab.*

2:46 Craven's room, Hilton Hotel. Night

CRAVEN *enters. He crosses to the table and pours himself a glass of vodka. He sits down on the bed. From his top pocket he takes the photograph of the group round the whale, which he picked up in Shields's flat. He looks at it. On the back are a number of names: Magnus, Jane, Elie and John, London '84, Imperial College. He drops it on the desk. Finally he takes out the piece of paper* SHIELDS *had given him and, returning to his bed, sits down and reads it.*

CRAVEN: Obituary – Emma Craven. Emma Craven, who died tragically at the hands of a gunman last week, would have been twenty-two today. For the past three years she has been a fully paid-up member of Socialist Advance, serving in a number of capacities, particularly on the Political Committee. It is not our practice to comment on the personality of party members but in this particular case Craven, despite her background, showed both courage and wit. She was, and always will be remembered as, a good comrade. (CRAVEN *lies down on the bed.*) Comrade!

EMMA: (*Voice over*) You don't understand, Dad.

CRAVEN: No, I don't.

EMMA: (*Voice over*) I loved him.

CRAVEN: You loved him.

2:47 A railway siding, Shepherd's Bush. Night
*The freight train, which has been waiting in the tunnel for an hour,
now slowly comes forward. Picking up speed, the train moves into the
night.*

2:48 Craven's room, Hilton Hotel. Night
CRAVEN *is lying on the bed, on his side, his eyes open.* EMMA's *voice
comes out of the darkness again.*
EMMA: (*Voice over*) Poor old Dad.

Burden of Proof

3:1 The bedroom, Lowe's flat. Day
It is early morning. LOWE *is still asleep in bed. He stirs as he hears his watch alarm go off and stretches over to switch it off. The* WOMAN *in bed with him groans and turns over.*

3:2 The bathroom, Lowe's flat. Day
LOWE *looks at himself in the mirror. He opens the cabinet and takes out a bottle of mouthwash. He gargles.*

3:3 A housing estate near the Edgware Road. Day
Two squad cars draw up slowly outside a block of flats. As they come to a halt we hear Elham's voice from the first car.
ELHAM: *(Voice over)* I want Lowe and I want him in one piece.

3:4 Inside the squad car. Day
JONES *and* ELHAM *sit in the back;* DINGLE *is up front with the driver.* DINGLE *stares at the face of one of the high-rise blocks.*
DINGLE: Sixth floor.
    (DINGLE *pushes open the door.*)
ELHAM: Good luck.
    (DINGLE *gets out of the car and looks up at one of the windows.*)

3:5 The housing estate. Day
JONES *and* ELHAM *get out of the squad car. The other men from the second car get out.* JONES *walks round the car to join* ELHAM.
ELHAM: Have you got a number for Craven?
JONES: Yes.
ELHAM: Call him.

3:6 The hall, Jedburgh's apartment building. Day
JEDBURGH *opens the front door to reveal* CRAVEN. *He is holding Jedburgh's report.*

63

JEDBURGH: It's seven o'clock, Craven.
  (CRAVEN *indicates the report.*)
CRAVEN: I brought your file back.
JEDBURGH: It was never meant to leave the god-damned apartment.
  (*He turns back into the room.* CRAVEN *follows closing the front
  door behind him.* JEDBURGH *walks along the hallway to the
  kitchen.*)

3:7   The kitchen, Jedburgh's apartment. Day
JEDBURGH *turns away from the stove with a pan of boiled eggs.*
CRAVEN *enters the kitchen.*
JEDBURGH: Did you photocopy it?
CRAVEN: No, sir.
JEDBURGH: Want some breakfast?
CRAVEN: Yes, please.
JEDBURGH: Merryweather won't be up till noon. Kelly got called out.
  (*He sits down.*)
CRAVEN: Out?
JEDBURGH: Athens. Somebody just shot the Station Chief.
  (*He hands* CRAVEN *some orange juice and a glass.*)
  Bad business, that. (JEDBURGH *holds out a bowl of eggs.*)
  Boiled eggs?

3:8   The housing estate. Day
Ross's car pulls up behind the other cars. ROSS *gets out.*
NEWBY: Jones is in a call box trying to locate Craven.

3:9   A call box on the housing estate. Day
JONES *pushes money into the slot.*
RECEPTIONIST: (*Voice over*) Good morning, Hilton International.
  Can I help you?
JONES: Detective Inspector Craven, please. Room 7016.

3:10   Block B, the housing estate. Day
*Several detectives run along the base of the tower block towards the
front entrance and in through the door.*

3:11   The bedroom, Lowe's flat. Day
LOWE *can be seen doing strenuous sit-ups. He stops and
takes a few deep breaths.*

3:12   The roof, Block B. Day
Two marksmen come out on to the top of the tower block and run across a bridge.

3:13   The kitchen, Lowe's flat. Day
LOWE *puts bread into the toaster and pushes it down. He wipes his face with a tea towel.*

3:14   The roof, Block B. Day
The two marksmen run on to a section of the roof and take up their positions overlooking the entrance to the block of flats. They take their rifles out of their cases.

3:15   A call box on the housing estate. Day
JONES *looks round towards Block B as he speaks into the phone.*
JONES: Did he leave a number where he could be reached. . . ?
RECEPTIONIST: (*Voice over*) One moment, sir. I'll just check.

3:16   The living-room, Jedburgh's apartment. Day
JEDBURGH *and* CRAVEN *are seated at the dining-table having breakfast.*
CRAVEN: To go 'into the shadows' – what does that mean?
    (JEDBURGH *pours himself some coffee.*)
JEDBURGH: It's an Italian expression much used by the Red Brigades. It means to abjure the world, to become a terrorist. Your daughter was a terrorist, Craven. You might as well get used to it.
    (CRAVEN *looks at him.*)
CRAVEN: It says here she went into Northmoor with half a dozen of her friends looking for plutonium. It doesn't say anything about being armed.
JEDBURGH: Plutonium is the key word here, Craven. People who mess with plutonium are terrorists.
CRAVEN: What do you know about Northmoor?
JEDBURGH: Only what I read in the report. Northmoor is a low-grade waste facility, run by a company with a very long name. There is no evidence of plutonium in Northmoor. Craven, why are you trying to convince me about your daughter? I was only asked to give you sight of the report.
CRAVEN: She was not a terrorist.
JEDBURGH: She sure believed in direct action.

CRAVEN: Cutting corners.

JEDBURGH: Breaking into offices, stealing files.

CRAVEN: The sort of thing we do every week.

JEDBURGH: But we have a licence to do it, Craven. She did not. Unless you gave her one. (*The telephone rings.* JEDBURGH *crosses to the desk and picks it up.*) Jedburgh? (*He listens to the caller at the far end.*) Yeah. He's here.

3:17 The landing, Block B. Day

In order not to alert LOWE, DINGLE *decides to bring his men out on the floor below Lowe's flat. When the lift door opens we see that the entire squad is jammed inside, including* DINGLE *and* JONES. *They get out with difficulty and walk along the corridor towards the fire stairs. One man stays with the lift, keeping the door jammed open.*

3:18 The kitchen, Lowe's flat. Day

LOWE *hesitates, his piece of toast hovering between his plate and his mouth. The fact that the lift door has not closed on the floor below registers in his subconscious, but he can't quite locate the source of his unease.*

3:19 The landing, Block B. Day

The men make their way up some stairs towards Lowe's flat.

3:20 The kitchen, Lowe's flat. Day

LOWE *listens. He continues to butter his toast. We now see that there is a gun on the table in front of him.*

3:21 A corridor, Block B. Day

Three of the men enter into the corridor outside Lowe's flat from the stairwell. A couple more approach from the other end.

3:22 The kitchen, Lowe's flat. Day

LOWE *sits at the table. He continues with his breakfast.*

3:23 The corridor outside Lowe's flat. Day

DINGLE *leads his men to the door of Lowe's flat. He pulls out his automatic. At the count of three they will charge the door down.* DINGLE *begins to count. Suddenly a woman and her child come out of one of the other flats. She cries out when she sees them. Quickly she and the child are led off by one of the detectives.*

3:24 The hallway, Lowe's flat. Day
The cry has confirmed Lowe's suspicions. He stands at the top of his stairs, gun in hand.

3:25 The corridor outside Lowe's flat. Day
DINGLE *counts to three again and they storm Lowe's flat, breaking down the door, yelling and shouting as they go in.* LOWE *retreats back up the stairs.*

3:26 A street near Hyde Park. Day
Jedburgh's Rolls-Royce hurries towards Marble Arch.

3:27 Inside Jedburgh's car. Day
CRAVEN *is holding the steering wheel while* JEDBURGH, *in the driving seat, runs his electric razor over his chin, his eyes on the driving mirror.*

JEDBURGH: You know, I like this city, even in the rush hour.

CRAVEN: I could have taken a cab.

JEDBURGH: Listen, Craven, I'm your magic helper.* I gave Pendleton my word I'd guide you through these difficult times.
(He finishes with the razor and resumes his responsibility as driver.)

CRAVEN: OK. Tell me what you know about Gaia.

JEDBURGH: It's an organization of scientists who believe it is their duty to save the planet from the human race, which they are convinced is doing its best to destroy it. They're very dangerous people, Craven, people who put trees and flowers before people – they're beyond reasoning with. And you can never appeal to their humanity 'cause they don't believe in humanity except as a form of moral pollution.

CRAVEN: My daughter never expressed such a view.

JEDBURGH: She probably did, Craven, a dozen times a day, but you never noticed it.

3:28 The road outside Block B. Day
Several men stand around while Lowe's body is loaded on to a stretcher. The two marksmen turn and walk away. JONES *turns and*

---

*Adlerian term denoting someone who 'helps' a patient unfold his story. Also a guide in many fairy tales (cf. *Morphology of the Folk Tale*). Both describe Jedburgh.

walks over to join ROSS, *who is standing by the ambulance. In the background Jedburgh's car approaches. It comes to a halt and* CRAVEN *alights.* JONES *walks over to meet him.* JEDBURGH *gets out the other side.*

CRAVEN: What happened?

JONES: The bastard jumped.

(JEDBURGH *is viewing the scene from a different angle.*)

JEDBURGH: How far did he fall?

JONES: Six floors.

JEDBURGH: From whereabouts?

(CRAVEN *looks up at the side of the high-rise and walks over to* ROSS *just as* LOWE *is being put in the ambulance.*)

ROSS: (*Grimly*) He's still alive – just.

(CRAVEN *looks into the ambulance as the doors are closed. He turns and looks up at the window through which* LOWE *jumped. He feels cheated.*)

3:29 The lobby, Middlesex Hospital. Day

The media are setting up their gear. An unmarked police car pulls up and parks. DINGLE *gets out and moves towards the hospital entrance. The press surge forward.* DINGLE *battles his way through them and is finally provoked by their insistence.*

REPORTER: Hey, Inspector, how is Lowe?

DINGLE: Not too well. He fell off a tower block.

REPORTER: Why?

DINGLE: Because he didn't want to be taken alive, that's why.

REPORTER: Nobody's going to believe that.

DINGLE: You arsehole – that's what happened. Now get in touch
  with the Press Bureau – you know the business.

3:30 A corridor, Middlesex Hospital. Day

CRAVEN *is sitting in the corridor.* ELHAM *is standing at the other end of the corridor with* JONES. *They appear to be arguing.* DINGLE *enters and goes up to* ELHAM. ROSS *joins* CRAVEN.

ROSS: I want you to talk to him.

CRAVEN: How is he?

ROSS: Not well. Not well at all.

(ELHAM *approaches from the other end of the corridor.* JONES *and* DINGLE *follow him.*)

ELHAM: We can go in now.

(ROSS *stands.*)

ROSS: I want Craven to talk to him alone.

ELHAM: One of our men has to be present. That's the law.

ROSS: We need the name of the other man, and we're not going to get it unless he sees him alone.

DOCTOR: If you wish to see him, you should go in straight away.

(*Following the* DOCTOR, *the four men walk towards one of the wards.* CRAVEN *remains seated for a moment before following.*)

3:31   A ward, Middlesex Hospital. Day

ELHAM, ROSS, DINGLE, JONES *and* CRAVEN *enter the ward slowly. The television set is on with a preview for the Saturday afternoon sports programme. There are a number of people in the ward, but none of them is watching it. Beside a curtained-off bed stands a policeman.* ELHAM *turns to* DINGLE.

ELHAM: Wait here.

(ROSS, ELHAM *and the* DOCTOR *enter the curtained-off area.* CRAVEN *stays by the window. As* ROSS *and* ELHAM *talk in low tones to the* DOCTOR, DINGLE *glances across at* CRAVEN. *Their eyes meet.* DINGLE *is left in no doubt how* CRAVEN *feels about the handling of Lowe's arrest.*

CRAVEN *glances back at the television.* DINGLE *sits down. The double doors of the ward open suddenly and a woman patient is wheeled through on a trolley by two* NURSES. *They are chatting amiably. The trolley is wheeled past* CRAVEN *and into one of the empty spaces in the ward.*

The NURSES *put the bed into position.* CRAVEN *is watching this and it reminds him of Ann and her operation. As we hear* CRAVEN's *voice we see the* NURSES *continuing to settle the patient in, chatting cheerfully as they work.*)

CRAVEN: (*Voice over*) I was driving Ann to the hospital at the time. Twice a week for radium treatment. There was something in her manner that told me not to talk about her illness. Every time I tried to discuss it she warned me off. The doctor, of course, told me nothing. I realized it was serious when I found she'd been buying clothes for Emma, but they were much too big. I volunteered to take them back, but she said, no, let it be. It was only later that it occurred to me that her choice had been deliberate. She knew she was dying and she wanted to stock up on things like clothes for Emma before she went.

I remember it clearly, dropping Ann off, seeing the pain in
her face, and then confronting Lowe a few minutes later.
(ELHAM *appears from behind the curtains*.)
ELHAM: Craven. You can come in now.
(CRAVEN *moves past* ELHAM *into the cubicle*.)

3:32   A cubicle, Middlesex Hospital. Day

CRAVEN *and* ELHAM *join* ROSS *in the cubicle*. CRAVEN *looks at the
bandaged body of* LOWE.
ELHAM: Take it easy.
(ELHAM *and* ROSS *leave the cubicle*. CRAVEN *walks over to the
bed and leans over* LOWE. *He looks at* LOWE *and talks in a
gentle voice*.)
CRAVEN: Lowe, this is Mr Craven. Can you hear me?
(*Lowe's eyes remain shut*. CRAVEN *leans forward*.)
You've been hurt, but you're safe now. No one can reach you
here.
(*As* CRAVEN *leans over* LOWE, *we hear* CRAVEN'S *voice*.)
CRAVEN: (*Voice over*) He had committed a brutal killing – in
pursuance of a theft and there was a sexual element. There
was no evidence to speak of, and nothing of a forensic nature,
so we needed a statement – an admission of guilt.
CRAVEN: (*To* LOWE) Lowe, this is Mr Craven. Remember? Ronnie
Craven. I'm here to help you.
CRAVEN: (*Voice over*) I developed a soft approach in interrogation
which with certain prisoners meant spending long periods of
time alone with them. It would involve holding hands and
being physically close. Sometimes I even kissed Lowe and it
worked.
CRAVEN: Lowe, can you hear me? This is Ronnie Craven.

3:33   The ward, Middlesex Hospital. Day

As we hear CRAVEN'S *voice, we see* ROSS *pacing up and down the
ward waiting for* CRAVEN. ELHAM *and* JONES *are standing patiently*.
DINGLE *is seated*.
CRAVEN: (*Voice over*) He was a brutal man. Though not without
resources. He knew what I was doing and the kind of pressur
I was putting on him.

3:34   The cubicle, Middlesex Hospital. Day

CRAVEN *leans forward*.

70

CRAVEN: Lowe, you're hurt, you're hurt badly. Who is it you're afraid of? I want you to tell me who you were afraid of.
(*There is no reaction from* LOWE. CRAVEN *drifts off.*)
CRAVEN: (*Voice over*) But driving Ann to the clinic each morning made it easy to share his torment. Soon we were like lovers and lovers have no secrets. Eventually he signed a statement and when it was produced in the High Court he was convicted.
(CRAVEN *looks at* LOWE *again.*)
CRAVEN: I want your help, Lowe. I've lost my daughter. I want to know who killed her.
CRAVEN: (*Voice over*) By which time, Ann was dead.
(CRAVEN *stares at* LOWE. *It's going to be a long wait.*)

3:35 Outside Salter's Court Restaurant. Day

JEDBURGH *slams the door of the taxi and pays the driver. He crosses the road towards the restaurant.*

3:36 Inside Salter's Court Restaurant. Day

JEDBURGH *enters and is greeted by one of the waitresses.*
JEDBURGH: Morning.
WAITRESS: Good morning, sir.
JEDBURGH: Mr Harcourt's table, please.
WAITRESS: Yes, of course, if you'd like to come with me.
(*She leads* JEDBURGH *through the restaurant towards a table where* PENDLETON *and* HARCOURT *are tucking into a huge English breakfast. Both are reading newspapers. They look up as* JEDBURGH *joins them, but don't waste their breath with 'good-mornings'.*)
PENDLETON: Breakfast?
JEDBURGH: (*To* WAITRESS) Yes, a large malt on the rocks, black coffee with honey.
HARCOURT: There's no need to play the Texan, Jedburgh. We can take it as read.
JEDBURGH: You're history, Harcourt. Heseltine is cutting Intelligence by 15 per cent.*

Michael Heseltine was Minister of Defence at the time, and Jedburgh implies that Heseltine's cuts in defence will effect the intelligence services and put paid to 'boutique' operations such as Harcourt's. Harcourt's tongue-in-cheek reply is that Pendleton has arranged for their funding to be independent of central government.

71

HARCOURT: We are not funded by the MOD but by the Prime Minister's office.

PENDLETON: And the Arts Council.

HARCOURT: Mr Pendleton has us down as a band of strolling players.

PENDLETON: And the Commonwealth Foundation.

HARCOURT: As professional historians.

PENDLETON: And the GLC.

HARCOURT: A lesbian co-operative.*

JEDBURGH: Frick and Frack.

HARCOURT: Well, what about Lowe?

JEDBURGH: The Met picked him up, then they dropped him again – from the sixth floor.

PENDLETON: Oh, dear!

JEDBURGH: Well, boys – I gave the report to Craven, like you asked me to. He read it.

HARCOURT: How did he react?

JEDBURGH: Stout defence of daughter. Doesn't see much beyond her death. He's under pressure but he's hanging in there.

PENDLETON: He knows a damned sight more than he pretends to, in my opinion.

JEDBURGH: So do you, Pendleton. Now, why don't you two just fess up and tell me what the hell's going on, huh?

HARCOURT: If we knew, you'd be the last to be told.

(JEDBURGH *squints at Harcourt's newspaper.*)

JEDBURGH: Grogan?

HARCOURT: He's flying in for the inquiry.

(JEDBURGH *takes the paper and reads it carefully.*)

He's going to buy IIF.

JEDBURGH: So he's going to own Northmoor.

HARCOURT: And what's in it.

JEDBURGH: Trouble, right here in River City.†

3:37 A small airport. Day

A jet drops on to the runway. Smoke billows off the tyres as they touch the hot tarmac.

---

*The GLC under its legendary leader Ken Livingstone had a much-maligned reputation for supporting only marginalized organizations.
†A catchphrase from the Superman comic strip. The line was contributed by Joe D Baker.

3:38 The runway. Day

GROGAN *moves down the steps of the aircraft.* BENNETT *walks towards him. They greet each other warmly.*

BENNETT: Jerry, how are you? I hope you had a pleasant flight?
   (*He ushers him towards the waiting limousine.*)
GROGAN: We had a 180 knot tailwind, which helped us along.
BENNETT: You piloted the plane yourself?
GROGAN: Yes. On the long hops, I like to take over. Flying exercises the right side of the brain. It can be very stimulating. Particularly since most of our days are spent in left-side activity.*
BENNETT: I'm afraid you've lost me, Jerry. We never got beyond the cortex at school.

3:39 A limousine. Day

The car is heading across the tarmac towards the airport gate.

GROGAN: Well, what's the situation?
BENNETT: The cave's down to 500 rads, but the chamber's still too hot.
GROGAN: So, a few more days, we can get in?
BENNETT: Yes.
GROGAN: That's OK. What about the sale?
BENNETT: That's making a few waves.
GROGAN: That's only to be expected.

3:40 The cubicle, Middlesex Hospital. Day

CRAVEN *leans over* LOWE. *He is in his shirt-sleeves now.*

CRAVEN: Lowe?
   (LOWE *murmurs. He is almost conscious.*)
   Lowe, who was the other man?
   (CRAVEN *watches* LOWE *intently.* LOWE *appears to subside again.*)

3:41 The ward, Middlesex Hospital. Day

A recorded interview with ROSS *is on television.* DINGLE, ELHAM *and* JONES *are gathered round watching with* ROSS.

ROSS: (*Voice over*) . . . surprised him, while he was at breakfast.

The point here is the habit that some modern American businessmen have of appropriating the gentle, hippie New Age philosophy as a part of their own ruthless code.

There was a struggle and, still struggling, he was brought out of the flat into the corridor. An attempt was made to take him down the emergency stairs. At this point he broke free and reached the window.

INTERVIEWER: (*Voice over*) From where he jumped?

ROSS: (*Voice over*) Yes.

INTERVIEWER: (*Voice over*) He wasn't handcuffed?

ROSS: (*Voice over*) No, it appears that none of the officers making the arrest was carrying handcuffs.

INTERVIEWER: (*Voice over*) How did that happen?

ROSS: (*Voice over*) An oversight, I presume.

(CRAVEN *appears through the curtains. He stands there.* ROSS *and the other officers turn to look at him.* CRAVEN *addresses* ROSS.)

CRAVEN: I've got a name.

3:42   Inside Elham's car, Hyde Park. Day

ELHAM: McCroon? Who is McCroon?

(ROSS, ELHAM *and* CRAVEN *are travelling back to the Yard.* DINGLE *is driving.*)

CRAVEN: He's a gunman. Ex-Provo. Part of the fall-out from Belfast.

ELHAM: You put him away?

CRAVEN: (*Nodding*) Eight years ago. But he had nothing to complain about.

ROSS: He must have had something, Ronnie, to turn up on your doorstep.

CRAVEN: If he did, he was paid to.

(*There is a silence, almost an embarrassing one.*)

Someone gave him a gun, a car, my address, details of my movements.

ROSS: There is not an ounce of evidence to support that notion, Ronnie, and you know that.

CRAVEN: Do you really think two misfits like Lowe and McCroon can turn up out of the blue?

ROSS: What else? They came looking for you, they shot her. It's just one of those things, Ronnie.

(*As the car is driving alongside Hyde Park,* CRAVEN *asks to be let out.*)

CRAVEN: Let me off here. I'll walk . . .

(*Surprised,* DINGLE *slows the car.* CRAVEN *opens the door.*)

74

ELHAM: Give us a chance.
CRAVEN: You've just killed the chief witness.
   (*As* CRAVEN *gets out he turns to* ROSS.)
   I'll call you later.
   (CRAVEN *walks away from the car across the park.*)

3:43 Hyde Park. Day
From the stationary car ROSS, ELHAM *and* DINGLE *watch* CRAVEN
walk towards the park.
ELHAM: (*Voice over*) He's got a point.
ROSS: (*Voice over*) I think he's cracking up.

3:44 Inside Elham's car, Hyde Park. Day
ELHAM *leans forward.*
ELHAM: Let's go.

3:45 Hyde Park. Day
CRAVEN *walks towards the Serpentine, past rows of empty deckchairs.*
EMMA: (*Voice over*) Are you angry?
CRAVEN: Yes, I am. I'm angry.
EMMA: (*Voice over*) Well, don't be angry at me.
   (CRAVEN *walks fast, then stops.*)
CRAVEN: What the hell were you up to? What the hell do you
   think you were doing?
EMMA: (*Voice over*) I knew what I was doing.
CRAVEN: Did you . . . like hell you did.
   (EMMA *comes into shot next to* CRAVEN. *He continues walking.*)
EMMA: Yes, I did.
   (*She tries to keep up with him.*)
CRAVEN: You took on some of the toughest men in the most
   dangerous business on this earth. God knows what they had
   down there.
EMMA: We nearly made it.
CRAVEN: They were waiting for you. You didn't stand a chance.
   (EMMA *doesn't reply.* CRAVEN *comes to a halt. An overwhelming
   feeling of fatigue comes over him. He buckles on to his knees.
   EMMA looks down at him and then crouches beside him.*)
EMMA: Come on, Daddy. Get up. This is no time to break down.
   You've got to be strong – like a tree – don't break, please,
   Dad, don't break, please.
   (CRAVEN *slowly drags himself to his feet.*)

CRAVEN: What I want to know is, who the hell let you in there? Who let you do it?

(*But* EMMA *has gone.* CRAVEN *shouts out.*)

Emma!

(*He expects an answer, but there is nothing. He shouts again.*)

Emma!

(*Again silence.* CRAVEN *slumps into one of the empty deckchairs.*)

3:46   Hilton Hotel, Shepherd's Bush. Day

A taxi pulls up outside the entrance. CRAVEN *gets out and pays the fare.*

SHIELDS: (*Voice over*) Craven!

(CRAVEN *turns. He sees* SHIELDS *leaning against his motorcycle.* CRAVEN *crosses over to* SHIELDS.)

SHIELDS: I want to talk.

(CRAVEN *nods.*)

3:47   Royal Crescent. Day

SHIELDS *and* CRAVEN *walk up Royal Crescent, leaving the Hilton Hotel and the traffic on Holland Park Road behind them.* SHIELDS *is uneasy.*

SHIELDS: You know I'm under surveillance. Ever since the break-in – they think I'm connected.

CRAVEN: Who is it?

SHIELDS: I don't know who it is. But whoever it is, they think I'm connected.

CRAVEN: And are you?

SHIELDS: Don't be stupid. I'm a political agitator, not a bloody environmentalist.

CRAVEN: You're also a police informer.

SHIELDS: That's the trade-off you have to make to keep them off your back. You ought to know. You worked in Northern Ireland. (*He goes off at a tangent.*) When I think of the dozens of dangerous nut-cases in this city –

(CRAVEN *interrupts him.*)

CRAVEN: What did you tell them about Emma?

SHIELDS: I told them what I knew. Sometimes it's better.

CRAVEN: What did you tell them?

(SHIELDS *stops, turns and faces* CRAVEN.)

SHIELDS: Emma thought there was a hot cell down there.

CRAVEN: Where?

SHIELDS: In Northmoor.
CRAVEN: What the hell is a hot cell?
SHIELDS: I don't know, but whatever it is, it turned her on.

3:48 Elham's office. Day

JONES *is on the telephone.* DINGLE *answers the other telephone which is ringing.*

DINGLE: Yeah?
CRAVEN: (*Voice over*) Craven speaking. Superintendent Ross, please.
(DINGLE *looks over to* ROSS.)
DINGLE: Chief Superintendant, it's Mr Craven.
(*He hands the telephone to* ROSS.)
JONES: McCroon. (*Spelling it out.*) MCCROON. Wanted in connection with . . . the . . . murder . . . of Emma Cra . . . ven. For further information contact the West Yorkshire Police on 3 . . .
(*Meanwhile* ROSS *has crossed to the telephone and picked it up.*)
ROSS: Ronnie.

3:49 Craven's bedroom, Hilton Hotel. Day

CRAVEN *is on the phone.*
CRAVEN: I'm sorry I lost my temper like that. But I really think that we should sort out the alternatives.
(*We intercut between Elham's office and Craven's bedroom.*)
ROSS: We've just matched McCroon's thumb print with the gun in the car – it fits.
(CRAVEN *is silent.*)
The feeling here is he's still in the North.
(*He presses on, not allowing* CRAVEN *to intervene.*)
I want you to come back with me, Ronnie. You can stay at my place till we've got this sorted.
CRAVEN: When are you leaving?
ROSS: The 7.15.
CRAVEN: Thanks, but I'll come on later.
ROSS: Ronnie, now that Lowe's dead, I want you back.
CRAVEN: Look, I'll see you at the funeral. I need a couple more days down here.
ROSS: OK, but no more.
(ROSS, *a paternalist, puts the phone down, not liking to be put off like this.*

77

CRAVEN *puts the phone down. Before him on the dressing-table is the box with the word 'Gaia' written in big Pentel strokes.* CRAVEN *ponders for one moment, and then puts it in the wardrobe.*)

3:50 The Star and Garter Home, Richmond. Day

CRAVEN *sits in the hall. He is waiting to see a resident, someone he has known in Northern Ireland.*

CRAVEN: (*Voice over*) Lesson Number One, when fighting terrorism, is – be ordinary. Show no distinctive features either of dress or behaviour. Wear nothing that attracts attention. That put Mac at a disadvantage, he had red hair. From Portadown to Ballymena he was known as Carrot Top. It was only a matter of time before they got him.

(*As we hear* CRAVEN's *voice, a* NURSE *approaches.*)

NURSE: Mr Craven? You can go up now.

3:51 Mac's room, Star and Garter Home. Day

The NURSE *enters followed by* CRAVEN. *The blinds are drawn. A man reclines on the bed surrounded by silence. The* NURSE *approaches the bed.*

NURSE: An old friend to see you . . . Ronald Craven . . . Do you remember him?

(CRAVEN *comes forward. He speaks in a relaxed manner.*)

CRAVEN: Hello, Mac.

(*He sits down on a chair by the bed.*)

How are you?

(MAC *answers slowly.*)

MAC: A bit like doing time. Worse, really. No remission for good behaviour. I don't feel forgotten.

CRAVEN: How are the grafts doing?

MAC: The worst are over. And the flesh is healing.

CRAVEN: Any of the boys been to see you?

MAC: Yes . . . lots of visitors . . . tell the truth, I don't need them. You get so involved in what's going on here. It's a whole world. You know, there are people here from the Somme. From the Falklands. I'm the only one from Northern Ireland at the moment.

CRAVEN: You should have got out, Mac. You were pushing your luck.

78

MAC: I know. But you know what it's like. Anyway, I had nobody to come home to . . . How's Emma?

CRAVEN: She's dead. She was killed, gunned down last week. They say he was looking for me.
(MAC *puts his hand out and finds* CRAVEN's *and holds it. They are silent for a moment.*)

MAC: Do I know him?

CRAVEN: McCroon.

MAC: What's in it for McCroon? Why would he do it?

CRAVEN: Revenge.

MAC: Life's too short. Even for a nutter like McCroon.

CRAVEN: There's another dimension to this. I want to get into the MI5 computer in Curzon Street.

MAC: They wouldn't let you through the front door.

CRAVEN: I wasn't thinking of using the front door. I need an unguarded terminal and tap straight into the Registry. But I need help.

MAC: You got funny in the last five years? Become a vegan or something?

CRAVEN: I'm serious, Mac. Emma's dead. Both barrels of a shotgun, straight in the chest. I was there, Mac. She died in my arms. I can't just sit back and watch them making all the wrong moves.

MAC: Leave it with me. I'll see what I can do.

3:52   A corridor, Hilton Hotel. Night

CRAVEN *walks along the corridor to find the door of his room ajar. Inside he can hear that the television set is on. Cautiously he pushes the door open.*

3:53   Craven's room, Hilton Hotel. Night

CRAVEN *enters.* JEDBURGH *lies sprawled in front of the television set, completely at home, the miniature whisky bottles from the fridge lined up on the table next to him.*

JEDBURGH: Well, come on in. Watch this. You want a drink?
(CRAVEN *recognizes* GODBOLT *on the television set, sitting between two* CLERGYMEN. *They are involved in one of those all-too-frequent religious discussions – this one about the question of 'purpose' in life.*)

FIRST CLERGYMAN: (*Voice over*) . . . Which is also a fundamental of Trade Unionism?

GODBOLT: (*Voice over*) Yes.

FIRST CLERGYMAN: (*Voice over*) Now can we get back to the gentleman who so tragically lost his daughter?

GODBOLT: (*Voice over*) Yes.

JEDBURGH: Sit down, Craven. Make yourself at home.

FIRST CLERGYMAN: (*Voice over*) What stopped you from reaching out to him?

GODBOLT: (*Voice over*) When something as shocking as this happens to someone – it happened to my friend whose daughter was murdered – his immediate reaction is, there must be some evil purpose behind it. It's not that such things are motiveless. Of course there was a motive. It's just that mistakes sometimes happen.

(*The television discussion goes on, but* JEDBURGH *talks over it.*)

JEDBURGH: This is the second time that guy's made a reference to you.

CRAVEN: It's Godbolt.

JEDBURGH: I know who he is. It's what he's saying I find so damned interesting.

FIRST CLERGYMAN: (*Voice over*) And you're saying that your friend's daughter's death was accidental?

GODBOLT: (*Voice over*) I'm trying to distinguish between an accident and a mistake.

FIRST CLERGYMAN: (*Voice over*) I don't understand. What is the difference?

SECOND CLERGYMAN: (*Voice over*) Isn't an accident the result of divine providence? A mistake the result of human error?

GODBOLT: (*Voice over*) Yes. But my friend prefers to think that some malevolent force took a hand in his daughter's death – whereas in reality it was simply a mistake . . . But you can't explain that to someone who is overcome by grief. You have to escalate the rhetoric the way you two do, and talk about God and Fate and Destiny.

(*They both laugh.*)

SECOND CLERGYMAN: (*Voice over*) So men make mistakes.

GODBOLT: (*Voice over*) Oh, yes.

SECOND CLERGYMAN: (*Voice over*) But God can't.

GODBOLT: (*Voice over*) In your terms, God. In mine, History. And as far as history's concerned, history cannot make mistakes.

(*The camera cuts to close-up of the* FIRST CLERGYMAN.)

FIRST CLERGYMAN: (*Voice over*) I think at that point we'll leave i

James Godbolt, thank you. John Parker, thank you. (*To the viewers.*) Next week, 'The Creation: Accident or – '

(JEDBURGH *switches off the set.*)

JEDBURGH: What the hell was that all about?

CRAVEN: I don't know.

JEDBURGH: That man had an irresistible urge to tell five million people that your daughter was murdered by mistake. The man's trying to tell you something, Craven. Unfortunately, you weren't here. So you missed it.

(*He gets to his feet.*)

CRAVEN: What is a hot cell? . . . Shields came by, told me that there is something called a hot cell in Northmoor, which is why Emma went down there.

JEDBURGH: (*Casually*) Shields told you that?

CRAVEN: Yes.

JEDBURGH: Get some sleep, Craven, you need it.

(*He picks up his hat and coat and an envelope.*)

Oh, by the way, Harcourt asked me to give you this. You're to meet him tomorrow – ten o'clock at the Commons – details inside and don't be late.

(JEDBURGH *throws the envelope on to the table.*)

About Godbolt . . . if I were you, I'd get to him before the other side does.

(*He exits, leaving* CRAVEN *more mystified than he was when he came in.*)

3:54   Near Shields's house, Muswell Hill. Day

Pendleton's Mercedes sneaks slowly into view and edges to a halt. As it does so we hear Pendleton's voice.

PENDLETON: (*Voice over*) Good of you to keep us informed. If Shields knows about a hot cell, he could come in useful. We're going to be quite busy, you know. The Parliamentary Inquiry into the Northmoor takeover starts today.★

PENDLETON *and* JEDBURGH *get out.*

I'll just check the van.

(JEDBURGH *walks over to Shields's front door and rings the bell.*

★This is the sort of line which is insisted on by directors. The idea is to clarify for the viewer what is going on. But dialogue like this is virtually useless, since the viewer's attention is focused on the action. The first line the viewer will register is Pendleton's 'I'll just check the van'.

The door is ajar. He pushes it open and enters. He can hear rock music coming from one of the rooms upstairs.)

3:55   The hall, Shields's house. Day
JEDBURGH *enters the house. He shouts out.*
JEDBURGH: Shields?

3:56   The road outside Shields's house. Day
PENDLETON *goes up to the van and peers in through the window. He walks round the back and opens the door.*

3:57   Inside the van. Day
The first thing we hear is the sound of a tape machine, the loose ends of the tape going round and round. We also see the reaction on Pendleton's face. He clambers in. The body of the operator is slumped across the equipment. He has been shot. PENDLETON *turns off the tape.*

3:58   The hall, Shields's house. Day
JEDBURGH *cautiously climbs the stairs. The rock music gets louder.* JEDBURGH *checks out one room and then the second room on the landing. He takes out his gun and ascends the stairs to the next level.*

3:59   The living-room, second floor, Shields's house. Day
JEDBURGH *walks in. He crosses to the record player and removes the needle. As silence falls, he can hear the sound of running water coming from the floor above. He glances out of the window at the van and sees* PENDLETON *closing the doors and hurrying back towards the house.* JEDBURGH *leaves the room and climbs the stairs to the top floor.*

3:60   The bathroom, top floor, Shields's house. Day
JEDBURGH *bursts into the bathroom. He then retreats on to the top-floor landing, turns off the power at the electric socket and pulls out the plug. He goes back into the bathroom.* SHIELDS *lies in the bath with an electric fire floating beside him. He has been electrocuted.*
PENDLETON *comes running up the stairs and* JEDBURGH *goes out on to the landing to meet him.*
JEDBURGH: We got a problem.

3:61   Outside the House of Commons. Day
A black Cadillac sweeps up to the front of the building, where it is besieged by a number of photographers and financial

journalists. GROGAN *and* BENNETT *get out. As they walk towards the Commons they are photographed and quizzed by the journalists.*

FIRST JOURNALIST: Mr Grogan, are you here for the Inquiry?
GROGAN: I'm in London to talk to Mr Bennett.
SECOND JOURNALIST: Are you going to buy IIF?
GROGAN: We have discussed it, yes.
THIRD JOURNALIST: Do you anticipate any problems with the Government, Mr Bennett?
BENNETT: No, I don't.
SECOND JOURNALIST: Is your bid an attempt to head off this Inquiry into IIF by the British Government?
GROGAN: I don't ascribe to the conspiracy theory of history.
FIRST JOURNALIST: Then what is your interest in IIF?
GROGAN: Emerging technologies, nuclear waste. The management of nuclear waste is going to be big business. And IIF is well ahead of the game.
   (GROGAN *glances up. Across the street he sees* JEDBURGH *leaning against the side of the Rolls.* JEDBURGH *smiles at* GROGAN *and salutes him.*)
THIRD JOURNALIST: What will be Mr Bennett's position if you do succeed in acquiring the company?
   (GROGAN *regains his composure.*)
GROGAN: I'm sorry?
THIRD JOURNALIST: What will be Mr Bennett's position if you succeed in acquiring the company?
GROGAN: I'm not planning on making any changes in the management structure of the company. Thank you.
   (GROGAN *and* BENNETT *move towards the hall, one or two reporters still in tow.*)

3:62   The first-floor hall, House of Commons. Day
It is the first day of the inquiry by the Commons Energy Committee into the privatization of the nuclear industry. A large number of people are in the hall, all talking to one another.
CRAVEN *stands alone, wearing a starched collar on a shirt which is a little too big for him. He looks like a new boy.*
The members of the Committee file into the hall on their way to the Committee Room which will serve the Inquiry. They are led by
BERNARD CHILWELL *and his chief civil servant,* ERIC CHAMBERS.
A number of people from the Department of Energy, the UKAEA and

NNI are also on hand with legal advisers. CRAVEN *watches as they pass into the Committee Room. A notice at the door states that the Inquiry will be held 'in camera' and that all visitors must have the necessary security clearance.*

CLEMENTINE: (*Voice over*) Mr Craven?
  (CRAVEN *looks round. He sees a youngish, fit-looking woman smiling gravely at him.*)
CLEMENTINE: Jedburgh sent me. He thought you might need some help.
CRAVEN: Do you work for him?
CLEMENTINE: No. I am just a friend, but we do have interests in common. Like Gaia.
  (PENDLETON *eyes her as he joins them.*)
PENDLETON: Hello, Clemmy.
CLEMENTINE: Hello, Guy.
PENDLETON: And how's my favourite tart?*
  (CLEMENTINE *ignores the pleasantry and indicates* CRAVEN.)
CLEMENTINE: He won't be needed today. I've seen the list.
PENDLETON: The fact that he's not on the list does not mean he's not needed.
CLEMENTINE: I stand corrected. (*To* CRAVEN.) When you're finished, I'll be by the door.
  (*She walks away.*)
CRAVEN: Who was that?
PENDLETON: Oh, she's just a friend of Jedburgh's.
  (*He turns away, rather excited, as if he were at a cocktail party with lots of clever people, one of whom he spots immediately.*)
  Polly!
POLLY: Hello, my darling. How are you?
PENDLETON: Come and meet a friend of mine.
  (*He turns to* CRAVEN.)
  This is Polly Pelham, the Honourable Member for Plowhill, and Shadow Energy Spokesman –
POLLY: – person.
PENDLETON: Mr Craven.
POLLY: Not, I trust, in the Intelligence Service?
CRAVEN: No, a policeman.
POLLY: A proper job.
  (*She indicates* PENDLETON.)

*An upper-class use of the word, denoting not a prostitute but an attractive woman, but still not very nice.

84

Guy, I'm afraid, has rather gone to seed and is keeping bad company.

PENDLETON: She is referring to the intelligence services.

POLLY: (*To* CRAVEN) He's being set up, you know – (*She glances at* PENDLETON *fondly*.) Aren't you, Guy? You and Harcourt. (*To* CRAVEN.) They're such babes in arms. My father, who was after all, a Cabinet Minister, told me 'Never have anything to do with the Intelligence.' He said they were either falling out of windows or pushing people under trains. And they were always short of cash.

(CRAVEN'*s attention has been caught by the arrival of* BENNETT *and* GROGAN. *They have been welcomed into the hall by* MABERLEY *and* CHILDS, *both of whom have been waiting for them.* POLLY *and* PENDLETON *continue to argue between themselves.*)

PENDLETON: (*Voice over*) Can't you understand it's because they are so grubby that we've been invited in . . .

POLLY: (*Voice over*) You're very naïve if you believe that, dear boy.

(CRAVEN *can't take his eyes off* BENNETT.)

PENDLETON: (*Voice over*) I do.

POLLY: (*Voice over*) The fact is, you couldn't put a dent in the SIS.* You're just a pimple on their bum.

PENDLETON: (*Voice over*) So why have we been brought in?

POLLY: To muddy the water. There's obviously something very subterranean going on.

PENDLETON: Look, Pol, if you've got information, I'd very much like to have it . . .

POLLY: You're the spy. Find out for yourself. I must go.

(*She turns to* CRAVEN, *who is still observing* BENNETT *and* GROGAN.)

Goodbye, Mr Craven. (*Then, indicating* PENDLETON.) Keep an eye on him.

(PENDLETON *looks at* CRAVEN.)

PENDLETON: Do you know that man?

CRAVEN: I know his face.

PENDLETON: He's the man we think had your daughter killed.

(*At the other end of the hall* BENNETT *catches sight of* CRAVEN *staring straight at him. He half recognizes him.*)

*Secret Intelligence Service (MI6).

85

BENNETT: What's he doing here?

(CHILDS *and* MABERLEY *turn. They look at* CRAVEN; CHILDS *recognizes him.*)

CHILDS: I'll find out.

(CRAVEN, *from his end of the hall, sees* CHILDS *slip away from* BENNETT. *His eyes wander around the room, then he looks at* BENNETT *again, to find* BENNETT *still staring at him.* PENDLETON *observes this exchange with some satisfaction. In the meantime* MABERLEY *is explaining to* GROGAN *the details of a Parliamentary Inquiry. This conversation is lost in the background.*)

GROGAN: What is the composition of the committee?

MABERLEY: Middle-of-the-road Tory. The only anti-nuclear person is Polly Pelham. She's in the Shadow Cabinet and a firm believer in coal.

(*As they talk,* BENNETT *and* CRAVEN *continue to examine each other in the most unnerving manner.* CHILDS *returns to* BENNETT.)

CHILDS: The rumour is, he's here to give evidence.

BENNETT: What the hell does he know?

(*He continues to stare at* CRAVEN.)

MABERLEY: It's time to go in.

(BENNETT *is loath to move. His eyes find* HARCOURT'*s, who has been observing the situation from another part of the hall.* HARCOURT *looks at him, amused.* BENNETT *stares at* CRAVEN *again.*)

GROGAN: What's going on, Bobby?

(BENNETT *shrugs off the question, but* GROGAN *is not fooled so easily. He glances at* BENNETT *anxiously.*)

MABERLEY: Come on, let's get in there. Time's pressing.

BENNETT: See you at the hotel.

(GROGAN *nods. The two of them walk to the door of the Committee Room.* PENDLETON *and* CRAVEN *watch them go. Just before he exits,* BENNETT *turns and gives* CRAVEN *one last glance. Then he is gone.*)

HARCOURT: Well, you've certainly upset Mr Bennett.

3:63   An ante-room, House of Commons. Day

HARCOURT, PENDLETON *and* CRAVEN *enter. The room is crowded. They are surrounded by civil servants drinking tea.*

CRAVEN: Is that why I was brought here – to upset Bennett?

HARCOURT: I want him to know that you're on to him.

CRAVEN: On to him?

HARCOURT: Well, aren't you?

(CRAVEN *stares at him*.)

PENDLETON: Cup of tea?

(*Tactfully he disappears, leaving* HARCOURT *to do the business.* CRAVEN *understands this*.)

CRAVEN: (*Wryly*) Is there anything else I can do for you?

HARCOURT: Yes, I'm looking for a witness. Well-spoken, of good character, a police officer if possible. And well-motivated. A daughter having recently been murdered would be useful.

CRAVEN: You want me to be a witness?

HARCOURT: We will provide all the information necessary to blast Bennett out of the water.

CRAVEN: Why me?

HARCOURT: Our intelligence is coming from people whose cover we can't afford to blow. But anything coming from you would look as though you'd picked it up in the course of investigating your daughter's death . . .

(PENDLETON *returns, with a cup of tea.* CRAVEN *looks at both of them*.)

CRAVEN: No thanks. (*He turns to go. Pleasantly*) Sorry.

3:64   The Committee Room, House of Commons. Day

The COMMITTEE MEMBERS *sit around a vast horseshoe-shaped table in the imposing room.* CHILWELL *opens the Inquiry*.

CHILWELL: The purpose of this particular session is to examine, at somewhat short notice, the consequences, if any, of the take-over of International Irradiated Fuels Limited by the Fusion Corporation of Kansas. For obvious reasons, this will be a closed session.

So, we will begin with our first witness, Mr Robert Bennett, the Managing Director of International Irradiated Fuels Ltd.

3:65   Outside the House of Commons. Day

GROGAN *exits from the House and moves to car. The driver holds the door open*.

3:66   Inside Grogan's car, Westminster. Day

As GROGAN *enters,* JEDBURGH *gets in the other side, sits down and closes the door.* GROGAN *stiffens, as does his driver, but then* GROGAN *signals for him to take a walk. The driver exits*.

JEDBURGH: Hi, Jerry – you look tired. You still on Houston time?

GROGAN: What are you doing here, Darius?

JEDBURGH: I'm an Energy Attaché at the embassy – regular diplomat. (*He shows his passport.*) See – *corps diplomatique*.

GROGAN: You're wasted in England, Darius. You should be back in the Third World killing communists. That was what made you a star, wasn't it?

JEDBURGH: This is the Third World, and communists are not the problem.

GROGAN: So what is?

JEDBURGH: You are – and I'm here to warn you. You're stirring up the natives. You're making them restless. We have our own interests on this island. Quite apart from the air-bases, there're the golf courses.

(GROGAN *looks at him aghast.*)

GROGAN: The golf courses?

JEDBURGH: Don't forget, Grogan, I'm a golfer. And when you and your friends are busy in the Stadiums,* who will look after the golf courses? That is the question I ask myself every time I address the ball.

GROGAN: You keep talking that way, you're not going to pass your next medical.

JEDBURGH: To know is to die† . . . Remember that, Jerry.

(*With that he gets out of the car.*)

3:67   The House of Commons. Day

CRAVEN *exits with* CLEMENTINE. JEDBURGH *calls out to them from his Rolls.*

JEDBURGH: Craven!

(CRAVEN *turns. He sees* JEDBURGH *in his car and walks towards him with* CLEMENTINE.)

Did you see Bennett?

(CRAVEN *nods.*)

(*To* CLEMMY) Look after him, Clemmy – we may need him.

(JEDBURGH *drives off.*)

---

*He is referring to the Pinochet coup in Chile in 1973, when the military used the football stadiums to hold (and execute) the supporters of the deposed President Allende.

†Jedburgh has pretensions to being a Zen master. This is one of his deeper thoughts.

CRAVEN: A man of few words.
CLEMENTINE: When he's sober.

3:68 The Committee Room, House of Commons. Day
BENNETT *is sitting in the witness chair.*
CHILWELL: Mr Bennett, you are the Managing Director of International Irradiated Fuels. Perhaps you can give us some idea of the philosophy behind the company?
BENNETT: Yes. The company was formed in response to the growing demand for permanent and semi-permanent storage facilities in the nuclear field. In particular, the need to store the low-grade wastes emanating from our nuclear installations, without contaminating the oceans, and also to find the answer to the question of the disposal of the high-grade wastes which emanate from our reprocessing plants. Now, this high-grade waste must be stored in such a way that it is impervious to accident, earthquake, flood and theft.
BEWES: Your charter calls for the storage of low-grade waste?
BENNETT: As a first objective – but of course we are aiming at the long-term solution to the disposal of high-grade waste.
POLLY: Mr Bennett, to what extent did you have government backing for your venture?
BENNETT: We had the full support of all the agencies. And very generous grants, particularly for our research facilities. For example, we are designing a vitrification plant,* which is not cheap. And we have had a generous measure of support for this project from the government.

3:69 St James's Park. Day
CRAVEN *and* CLEMENTINE *walk across the park.*
CRAVEN: Where did you meet Darius?
CLEMENTINE: Nicaragua, during the Revolution. He was photographing a Sandinista hide-out in the mountains and his plane ran out of gas. We found him in the village, trying to persuade the garage to let him pay for a tankful of fuel with a Diners' card. His Spanish is appalling.
CRAVEN: You rescued him?

---

*An industrial process in which high-level radioactive waste is encapsulated in glass in order to prevent seepage.

CLEMENTINE: Not quite. I was a liaison officer with the
Sandinistas at the time, so we took him prisoner. We kept
him for six weeks and ran up a huge bill on his card before
letting him go. Nothing personal. It was a CIA account.

CRAVEN: So, when did you two become friends?

CLEMENTINE: Later. In London.

CRAVEN: What does he know about Gaia?

CLEMENTINE: He helped to found the organization in '77.

CRAVEN: Jedburgh?

(*This fact astonishes him, and he shows it.*)

3:70 Craven's room, Hilton Hotel, Shepherd's Bush. Night

CRAVEN *sits at the cramped table by the window. He finishes penning
a report of the involvement of Northmoor and Gaia in the events which
preceded the murder. He puts it into a Hilton envelope. Scrubbing out
the Hilton logo, he writes across the top of it, 'Assistant Chief
Constable Ross'.*

At that moment the telephone rings. CRAVEN *completes the word
'Ross', allowing the telephone to ring. He then seals the envelope and
puts it in another, bigger envelope, which we see he has already
addressed to 'Assistant Chief Constable Ross, West Yorkshire Police
Authority'. He picks up the telephone.* JEDBURGH *is on the line.*

JEDBURGH: (*Voice over*) Craven, I'm at the airport. I have to
return to Washington.

CRAVEN: Washington?

JEDBURGH: (*Voice over*) Don't worry. I'll be back. Did Clementine
put you in touch?

CRAVEN: Not yet.

JEDBURGH: (*Voice over*) Stick with her, she's OK. But don't you
ever give her your Diners' card. Do you hear?

3:71 The cemetery, Craigmills. Day

*The little party moves briskly towards the freshly dug grave, the coffin
being hauled on a barrow along an unmade track. Once it has reached
the top of the slope, the route is downhill, so the hearse trundles fast and
everyone's pace quickens.* CRAVEN, *Sergeant* JONES *and a clergyman
and a dozen mourners hasten behind it. The mourners include* ROSS *and
there are some students at the back.* TERRY SHIELDS *is conspicuous by
his absence.*

The route of the cortège is the same as that CRAVEN *had taken for the*

burial of his wife Ann, and most of the people are the same, except that
then EMMA, *who was about ten, had held* CRAVEN'S *hand throughout the*
ceremony and had run beside him down the slope, which he now traverses
alone. CRAVEN'S *face is expressionless as the cortège moves on.*
Cut to gravestone. Emma's name has been added underneath Ann's:
'Aged 21 years'.

3:72 Flashback, British Rail, a sleeping car. Night
CRAVEN *and* EMMA, *aged eight, are squashed in the two-berth*
compartment.
CRAVEN: (*Determined*) Mummy will sleep on top. Emma will sleep
    on the bottom.
EMMA: What about Daddy?
CRAVEN: Daddy will sleep with Emma.
EMMA: What about Mummy? She'll be all alone.
CRAVEN: No, she won't.
EMMA: (*Stubborn*) Yes, she will. She will be up on the top bed all
    by herself.
CRAVEN: (*Irritated*) All right, you sleep with her.
EMMA: If I sleep with Mummy, you'll feel neglected.
CRAVEN: No, I won't feel neglected.
EMMA: Yes, you will feel neglected.
CRAVEN: No, I will not feel neglected, Emma, believe me.
EMMA: I think the best thing is for you and Mummy to sleep on
    the bottom and for me to sleep on the top.
CRAVEN: (*Getting more and more angry*) But you're the smallest.
EMMA: (*Determined and climbing*) What does that matter? We've
    got to get it right.

3:73 The cemetery, Craigmills. Day
CRAVEN *stares at the grave as earth is thrown on the coffin. He is*
thinking of EMMA.
CRAVEN: (*Voice over*) Emma sleeps on top – Mummy sleeps on the
    bottom.
    (*He comforts one of the tearful party. Then they gradually move*
    away, leaving CRAVEN *standing alone by the grave.*)

3:74 Ross's office, West Riding police headquarters. Day
ROSS *sits at his desk, staring at Craven's report. Eventually he looks*
up. CRAVEN *stands before him.*

ROSS: You know, Ronnie, you can't make allegations like this and expect to be taken seriously.

(CRAVEN *leans forward to take the report.*)

CRAVEN: (*Flatly*) Can I have that back, sir?

(*But* ROSS *retains it. He looks up at* CRAVEN, *exasperated. There is a limit to the amount of sympathy any man can give to someone who's undergone a bad experience.*)

ROSS: We know it was McCroon. We have Lowe's dying statement, we have his prints on the car. Doesn't that satisfy you? We know why he did it. It was revenge.

(ROSS *folds the report and puts it in an official-looking envelope, which he seals and dates.*) Does he have to put a bullet in you before you'll admit it?

(*But his last words are lost on* CRAVEN, *who seems to have distanced himself from the encounter.*)

(*Indicating the envelope*) Now, this is going in my safe, and it will stay there till you come to your senses . . .

(*When we pick him up,* CRAVEN *is in another corner of the room, looking at a statuette on the showcase by the wall. He examines it curiously.*)

CRAVEN: What I want is a warrant to get into Northmoor.

ROSS: It's out of the question.

(*He looks at* CRAVEN.)

Ronnie, you're not well. You're depressed. I think you should see a doctor.

(CRAVEN *ignores him.*)

CRAVEN: (*Calmly*) I would like the watch taken off my house.

ROSS: No.

CRAVEN: McCroon isn't going to come as long as it's there . . .

(ROSS *stares at him, suspicious, but wonders whether he can do a deal – trade the watch for the doctor.*)

ROSS: All right. If you agree to see a doctor, we'll take it off.

(*Cautiously.*) But not the telephone intercept, you understand.

(CRAVEN *nods.*)

CRAVEN: OK.

(*He exits.*)

3:75 The rear garden, Craven's house, Craigmills. Day

CRAVEN *starts the lawnmower and begins to cut the grass.*

3:76   The hill overlooking Craven's house. Day

MCCROON *is watching* CRAVEN. *He munches an apple, then turns and throws it away. On the ground there are the remains of a dozen apple cores.*★

★This last shot was cut from the final version.

Breakthrough

4:1   The rear of Craven's house, Craigmills. Night
It is raining. The lights are on in Craven's living-room.

4:2   The living-room, Craven's house. Night
CRAVEN *is sitting at his desk writing out cheques for household bills.*

4:3   The rear of Craven's house. Night
A view of CRAVEN *through the rain-raddled living-room window, sitting at his desk. Pan to a man with a shotgun standing in the rain at the end of garden observing* CRAVEN. *Close-up of man's face. It is* MCCROON.

4:4   The living room, Craven's house. Night
CRAVEN *puts his papers away in drawer of desk and stands up. The television news is audible in the background.*

4:5   The kitchen, Craven's house. Night
CRAVEN *walks into the kitchen and turns on the light. He opens the fridge and takes out a can of beer. He moves to cupboard and takes out a glass. Suddenly he looks up, hearing a noise outside.*

4:6   The rear of Craven's house. Night
Close-up of McCroon's trainers as he walks along the garden path in the pouring rain. They stop.

4:7   The stairs, Craven's house. Night
CRAVEN *moves to the stairs and ascends carrying a shotgun. He turns off the hall light and enters Emma's bedroom.*

4:8   Emma's bedroom. Night
CRAVEN *looks out of the window into the garden. He sees* MCCROON

appear from behind the bushes and walk to the centre of the lawn.
CRAVEN *stares at the figure and slowly raises his shotgun.*

4:9 Flashback. Outside Craven's house. Night
MCCROON *rushes forward screaming.*
MCCROON: Craven! You bastard! You bloody murdering bastard!

4:10 Emma's bedroom. Night
Close-up of CRAVEN *as he stares down at* MCCROON. *He raises the shotgun to his shoulder.*

4:11 The rear of Craven's house. Night
Close-up of MCCROON *as he stares up at Emma's window.*

4:12 Flashback. Outside Craven's house. Night
EMMA *screams and runs forward.* MCCROON *shoots* EMMA.

4:13 Emma's bedroom. Night
Close-up of CRAVEN *aiming the shotgun at* MCCROON.

4:14 The rear of Craven's house. Night
MCCROON *stands motionless in the centre of the lawn.*

4:15 Emma's bedroom. Night
Close-up of CRAVEN's *face.*

4:16 The rear of Craven's house. Night
MCCROON *stands in the centre of the lawn.*

4:17 Emma's bedroom. Night
Close-up of CRAVEN's *face.*

4:18 The rear of the Craven's house. Night
MCCROON *turns and walks away.*

4:19 Emma's bedroom. Night
CRAVEN *lowers the shotgun.*

4:20 The living-room, Craven's house. Night
CRAVEN *enters holding a glass of whisky. The television is still on and we hear the weather report in the background.* CRAVEN *puts some coal on the fire and sits down in the armchair.*

4:21 Outside Craven's house. Night
MCCROON *stands looking in at* CRAVEN. *He turns and walks away.*

4:22 The living-room, Craven's house. Night
CRAVEN *stands up and walks over to his desk. He picks up his address book from the table. He looks up as he hears a noise. Slowly he turns to see* MCCROON *standing in the doorway, his shotgun aimed at him at shoulder height.*
MCCROON: Remember me?
CRAVEN: I've been waiting for you.
(MCCROON *edges around* CRAVEN *towards the telephone. All the while the shotgun is pointed at* CRAVEN's *chest.*)
I've already made the call.
MCCROON: Then I hope you said goodbye.
(*He has reached the telephone, and, without taking his eyes from* CRAVEN, *he rips the telephone from the wall and hurls it into the corner of the room. On its trajectory, it takes most of the photographs off the mantelpiece with a shattering clatter. But* CRAVEN *does not flinch. He has turned inside the circle caused by McCroon's circumnavigation of the room and now stands with his back to the television.*)
Ten years, Craven, that's how long I've been waiting . . . ten years.
(*He hisses out the words.*)
CRAVEN: If you're talking about ten years, we're talking about Ireland.
MCCROON: We're talking about 1973. Three Brigade. We're talking about your job, Sergeant.* Turning good men into touts and traitors and when you had no further use for them, turning them over to the Provos to be shot.
CRAVEN: And for that you killed my daughter?
MCCROON: I was looking for you, Sergeant – she just got in the way.
CRAVEN: You fired *both* barrels – into her chest.
MCCROON: She was coming at me like a goalkeeper.
CRAVEN: You could have picked me off blindfolded, if you'd wanted to, you daft Irish pratt.
MCCROON: I was in no hurry. I knew I'd get you sooner or later.
(*As* MCCROON *talks, he searches the drawers and cupboards for*

---

*McCroon uses the army pronunciation of 'third', and Craven's old rank.

97

valuables, keeping an eye – and the shotgun – on CRAVEN *all the while. The newscaster on the television is now replaced by the smiling face of a linkman, outlining the next day's programmes. A list is flashed on the screen with the schedule.*)

CRAVEN: How long have you been out?

MCCROON: A year.

CRAVEN: You took a year before you came looking for me?

MCCROON: I told you, Sergeant, I was in no hurry.

CRAVEN: Someone gave you the gun and the car and told you where to find us. Who was it?

MCCROON: Why don't you make your peace with God?

CRAVEN: I want to know before you pull that trigger.

MCCROON: What's the use? You were both marked, both of you.

CRAVEN: It matters to me.

MCCROON: Ask her, Craven, next time you meet her.

CRAVEN: Please, I want to know.

(*All at once, out of vision,* MCCROON's *head explodes, his brains filling the air in a red haze.* CRAVEN's *face is splashed with blood, and it is some seconds before we realize that it is* MCCROON *who has been shot, not* CRAVEN. *By now* CRAVEN's *hands are in the air, his face a mask of anger.*)

No! No! No!

(*He falls to his knees in a state of shock and gives way to abject despair.*)

4:23 The psychotherapy room, Craigmills Psychiatric Hospital. Day

Close up of CRAVEN. *He is in a cell-like room, rather like an interview room in a police-station. The wall is spaced with photographs of rugby teams. He is looking into the camera – as if he were being interviewed on television. But his interlocuter is* OAKLEY, *an ex-rugby international, and the chief medical officer of the hospital.*

CRAVEN: She no longer speaks to me.

OAKLEY: Does that disturb you?

(CRAVEN *stares straight ahead.*)

But you still see her?

(CRAVEN *nods.*)

Did you see her this morning?

(CRAVEN *nods again, still staring straight ahead.*)

In some – (*he chooses his words with care*) – societies, the dead are thought to be reluctant to proceed on their way because they fear what might happen to them in the next world. Do you think Emma's like that?

(CRAVEN *doesn't comment.*)

So they are chased with threats and insults. Do you find such a notion fanciful?

(CRAVEN *shakes his head. We now see that he is sitting on a wooden chair, facing the wall, in the almost empty room.*)

CRAVEN: What worries me is not that she's gone. (*Pause.*) But that we parted on such bad terms.

OAKLEY: You quarrelled?

(CRAVEN *nods.* OAKLEY *looks at his notes.*)

CRAVEN: In Hyde Park. I felt myself disintegrating. She was telling me to hold on. She kept asking me to be strong – like a tree.

OAKLEY: A tree?

CRAVEN: That was how she saw me – just . . .

OAKLEY: And you became angry with her?

(CRAVEN *nods.*)

Why?

CRAVEN: Because she had allowed herself to be abused, got herself into such a mess. (*The thought of this brings tears to his eyes.*)

4:24   The entrance to the Craigmills Psychiatric Hospital. Day
ROSS *arrives in his car. He parks it, turns off the engine and gets out.*

4:25   The hospital foyer. Day
OAKLEY *walks towards the front door.* ROSS *is waiting for him.*

ROSS: How's the patient?

(OAKLEY *shrugs.*)

OAKLEY: Very interesting. He has what primitives call a bush soul. He identifies himself with a tree.

(ROSS *finds this fanciful.*)

ROSS: I mean, is he suffering from shock or depression or what?

OAKLEY: All three.

(*He begins to walk* ROSS *towards Craven's room.*)

ROSS: The 'what' being. . . ?

OAKLEY: Grief.

4:26   Craven's room, Psychiatric Hospital. Day
ROSS *enters.* CRAVEN *is sitting on the side of his bed, eating lunch. He looks up.*

ROSS: (*Heartily*) Hello, Ronnie. How are you?

CRAVEN: OK. Did you call into the house?

(ROSS *holds out Craven's razor.* CRAVEN *takes it.*)

ROSS: Yes, we tidied up a bit. Sorted things out.

(*He looks uneasily at* CRAVEN, *aware of the unspoken accusation.*)

Well, we got McCroon before he got you.

CRAVEN: Why did you leave the marksmen on site?

ROSS: Jesus Christ, Ron, he was going to kill you.

(ROSS *pulls out a small quarter bottle of Scotch and looks round for a glass.*)

CRAVEN: You gave me your word.

ROSS: Ronnie, I knew exactly what I was doing. We saved your life.

(*His sincerity is so patent that* CRAVEN *feels at a loss.*)

Perhaps you didn't want it saved?

CRAVEN: I was drawing it out of him. He wanted to tell me.

(ROSS *suffers in silence for a minute, too chagrined to argue. Slowly he takes Craven's report from his pocket. He hands it to him.*)

ROSS: I'm closing the case, Ronnie.

(CRAVEN *takes it.*)

Nothing is ever cleared up. You know that. We don't know how he got the gun. Or your address. We still don't really know why he did it. But I don't think we ever will know.

(ROSS *pours a thimbleful of whisky into the bottle cap and gives it to* CRAVEN.)

I know it sounds callous, but at least you have been spared the stress of a trial and the dirt that goes with it . . . Your health, Ronnie. And may she rest in peace.

(CRAVEN *drinks down the whisky.*)

4:27 Craven's room. Psychiatric Hospital. Night

CRAVEN *lies in bed. The hospital is dark and silent. He lies staring at the ceiling. His eyes close.*

4:28 Flashback. Hyde Park. Day

A girl on a bicycle cycles past CRAVEN. *She wears an orange kagoul. She turns her head. It is* EMMA. CRAVEN *shouts soundlessly, 'Emma'. He begins to run after her.*

4:29   Craven's room, Psychiatric Hospital. Night
CRAVEN *sleeps.*

4:30   Corrie Reservoir, Craigmills. Night
*A partially decomposed body of a young woman – wearing an orange
kagoul like Emma's – comes to the surface amidst a confusion of
bubbles and turbulence. It bobs on the water buoyantly.*

4:31   Craven's room, Psychiatric Hospital. Night
CRAVEN *wakes up, screaming.*
CRAVEN: Emma!

4:32   Corrie Reservoir, Craigmills. Day
An inflatable boat approaches the shore. In it are two POLICE
FROGMEN *and an orange bundle – a dead body.* PENDLETON *walks
down towards the water's edge, passing a number of policemen and
other onlookers.* ROSS *arrives in his car and gets out. The boat reaches
the shore and a group of* POLICEMEN *surrounds it.*

4:33   The shore, Corrie Reservoir. Day
The body is laid out on the pebble shore. PENDLETON *kneels beside it. He
has a small Geiger counter which he switches on and runs over the body. It
registers strongly. Uneasily, the crowd around the body shifts back to a
safer distance. They know what it means.* PENDLETON *looks up.*
PENDLETON: (*Quietly*) I want her taken to London.

4:34   Craven's room, Psychiatric Hospital. Day
CRAVEN *stands at the window.* OAKLEY *enters the room, in the breezy
mood he adopts while doing his morning rounds.* CRAVEN *looks up.*
OAKLEY: Tell me about Ireland.
    (CRAVEN *looks at him coldly.* OAKLEY *sits at the dressing-table-
    cum-desk and begins sorting through a number of letters and
    envelopes from* EMMA, *most of which bear some kind of drawing
    of a tree.*)
CRAVEN: It was my job to select and train informers. In those days
    you could only find them in jails. McCroon was one of them.
    You know how it is with informers – they grow to depend on
    you.
    (OAKLEY *looks up.*)
OAKLEY: You encouraged that?
    (CRAVEN *glances at him, guessing that the dependency between*

patient and shrink is not very different from that between the informer and his master.)

CRAVEN: You do, don't you?

(*But* OAKLEY *refuses to be drawn.*)

I had six or seven of them working for me. Then when Ann got cancer I came home. And they were all . . . let go. (*He stares out of the window.*) It was all out of my hands. Some of them were betrayed to the IRA. Some of them were used in dirty little schemes which meant their inevitable exposure. None of them received the money or the protection I had promised them. They were bad times. And they got a bad deal.

OAKLEY: And McCroon remembered that?

CRAVEN: Yes. But he . . . something else motivated him . . .

4:35 The shore, Corrie Reservoir. Day

The body is loaded into a truck. PENDLETON *watches it from the beach. He is still trying to scan the sand for traces of mud or sediment which might give an indication of where the body had come from.* ROSS *slowly walks into shot and stares at him.*

ROSS: I'm Assistant Chief Constable Ross. Who are you?

PENDLETON: I'm Pendleton.

(*He goes about his business.*)

ROSS: Craven mentioned the name.

(PENDLETON *looks up at him.*)

PENDLETON: I heard he was off his rocker.

ROSS: Not really. Just needs a bit of a rest, that's all.

4:36 Craven's house, Craigmills. Day

The shot is framed by the tree underneath which EMMA *died. In the distance we see a cab approaching the end of the drive.* CRAVEN *gets out and pays the fare. Then he trudges up the drive towards the house. Small flowers now grow under the tree and spring water emerges.* CRAVEN *comes and stands gazing at the stream. His shoes sound vaguely squelchy on the sodden turf. He kneels down, cupping his hands to the water, pulls it up to his mouth and drinks from it.*

4:37 The living-room, Craven's house. Day

CRAVEN *stands looking around the room. The furniture is covered with dust sheets. He walks over to the window and looks out. We hear the clock on the mantelpiece chime as* CRAVEN *walks over to the television*

He picks up a worn Radio Times *and begins to flick through it. There is a picture of* GODBOLT *on one of the pages.* CRAVEN *stares at it.*
GODBOLT: (*Voice over*) It's not that such things are motiveless. Of course there was a motive – it's just that mistakes sometimes happen.
　　(CRAVEN *looks round and sees* EMMA *standing in the doorway of the living-room. He drops the* Radio Times. *When he looks up again* EMMA *has vanished.*)
EMMA: (*Voice over, singing to the tune of 'Nuts in May'*)
　　　　Ra-ta-touille is my favourite food,
　　　　My favourite food, my favourite food,
　　　　I could eat it every day, every day, every day,
　　　　All I want is ra-ta-touille, ra-ta-touille, ra-ta-touille.

4:38　The kitchen, Craven's house. Day

CRAVEN *enters. Young* EMMA *is at the kitchen table making a cake.*
CRAVEN: Emma!
　　(*He looks again. She had disappeared. He walks to the window and starts humming 'Ra-ta-touille'. He goes to the bookshelf and takes out* French Provincial Cooking *by Elizabeth David. He finds 'ratatouille' in the index and turns to the recipe. Inserted between the pages is a piece of paper. He unfolds it and looks at it. It is a list of stations of the London underground, written in Emma's hand.* CRAVEN *immediately guesses that the list has something to do with Northmoor.*)
EMMA: (*Voice over*) I've been trying to tell you about this for ages.
　　(CRAVEN *looks up.* EMMA *is back again.*)
CRAVEN: Emma!
　　(*He looks at her.*)
EMMA: Don't lose it, it's important.
CRAVEN: Emma . . .
　　(*She is gone.* CRAVEN *sits down at the kitchen table.*)

4:39　Flashback. A laboratory, Craigmills College. Day

EMMA *leans forward.*
EMMA: (*Fiercely*) You could take us down there. You're one of the few people who could.
　　(CRAVEN *is equally vehement.*)
CRAVEN: Northmoor is a nuclear waste plant. Anyone who breaks in will be met with ultimate force. It's the most dangerous business in Britain. Don't even think of it.

4:40   The hall, Craven's house. Day

CRAVEN *dials a number which has a London prefix. A woman answers.*

CRAVEN: Mrs Mac?

MRS MAC: (*Voice over*) Yes.

CRAVEN: This is Ronnie Craven. I spoke to your husband three weeks ago. He gave me a name – Toby Berwick. But I need his number –

MRS MAC: (*Voice over*) I'm afraid he's going to be out till four o'clock, but the number's 472 1005.

CRAVEN: 472 1005 – I'll be in London tonight. I'll call him when I arrive.

MRS MAC: I'll pass it on.

CRAVEN: Thank you.

(He puts down the phone. EMMA *has been watching him from the stairs.)*

EMMA: Who was that?

CRAVEN: A friend of a friend.

EMMA: Can he help?

CRAVEN: I hope so.

(He decides to look at her – but she has gone.)

4:41   The motorway. Day

Craven's car is travelling at speed on the motorway.

4:42   Inside Craven's car. Day

CRAVEN *is at the wheel. The radio is on.*

NEWSCASTER: (*Voice over*) As the inquiry into the future of the nuclear industry continues, Jerry Grogan has stated once again his intention of buying IIF. IIF is a pioneer in the field of nuclear waste and there has been widespread concern at the prospect of the company being sold overseas. Whether the American take-over would have the blessing of the Department of Energy remains to be seen. Nevertheless, the Government remains determined to press ahead with its plans to privatize the industry. Abroad, the Gulf war . . .

*(*CRAVEN *turns off the radio.* EMMA *speaks from the back of the car.)*

EMMA: So what are you going to do?

CRAVEN: I'm going to go in.

EMMA: I thought you said it was the most dangerous business in
England run by the most dangerous men.
(CRAVEN *looks back at her*.)
CRAVEN: You're exaggerating again. (*He directs his eyes to the road.*)
But I'm glad you're back. I've missed you.
EMMA: Your doctor would say it was a terminal psychosis
preceding complete collapse.
CRAVEN: He doesn't use long words like that.

4:43   Outside a London teaching hospital. Day

*The truck from the Corrie Reservoir comes into the back of the hospital
and stops.* PENDLETON *gets out. He looks tired. He goes round to the
back of the vehicle. The doors are being opened by porters in protective
clothing.* HARCOURT *comes out into the courtyard.*
HARCOURT: Well?
PENDLETON: It was one of the Gaia girls.
HARCOURT: 'Women', Pendleton, even dead, would not like to be
known as 'girls'.
(*He follows* PENDLETON *into the hospital*.)
Well, is it radioactive?
PENDLETON: Oh, yes.

4:44   A pathology laboratory, London teaching hospital. Day

A glass screen separates PENDLETON *and* HARCOURT *from*
MENZIES, *the radiation-suited pathologist, who has been working on
the body. He now crosses from the body, which is surrounded by a
special anti-radiation screen, to the glass. He peers through it at*
HARCOURT *and* PENDLETON. *His voice is carried by two
loudspeakers set into the glass.*
MENZIES: So far, we have isolated four separation fission products
in the water in her lungs. In my opinion there were more but
the decay is so rapid that they've disappeared without trace.
HARCOURT: What was death by?
MENZIES: Drowning. But she'd been exposed to radiation
beforehand.
HARCOURT: What sort of radiation?
MENZIES: It's impossible to say. Radiation is radiation. Alpha
waves probably.
PENDLETON: Could it be connected with spent fuel rods?
MENZIES: The caesium might be, 137 is a beta-emitter thrown up
during reprocessing.

HARCOURT: (*Slowly*) So, what you are saying is, for that body to have been contaminated by caesium 137 it would have to have been exposed to a plutonium manufacturing process?

(MENZIES *looks wary but eventually nods.*)

MENZIES: All I'm saying is, it's possible.

4:45   The hall, Jedburgh's apartment. Day

The door is unlocked. JEDBURGH *pushes it open. He is carrying a golf bag and is in uniform. As he enters, he calls out.*

JEDBURGH: John!

(*He listens. All he can hear is the sound of a Hoover. He parks the golf bag in the hall and goes through the rooms looking for* JOHN, *the young Englishman who acts as a general cleaner and servant for the three men who share the apartment.*)

4:46   The living-room, Jedburgh's apartment. Day

JOHN *is hoovering the carpet as* JEDBURGH *creeps in. Mischievously,* JEDBURGH *tiptoes to the power plug and yanks out the plug.* JOHN *turns, surprised.* JEDBURGH *laughs like a school kid.*

JOHN: Jedburgh!

JEDBURGH: Where's everybody?

JOHN: Chasing ass all over Europe. Hank's in the Lebanon.

JEDBURGH: Are there any messages?

JOHN: They're on the machine.

(JEDBURGH *makes his way towards his bedroom.*)

JEDBURGH: You could say, 'Welcome home, Colonel,' or you could say, 'How was Salvador, Colonel?'

JOHN: Where's Colonel Kelly?

JEDBURGH: I had to leave him behind, John.

(JOHN, *sensing that something is wrong, follows* JEDBURGH *into the bedroom.*)

4:47   The bedroom, Jedburgh's apartment. Day

JOHN: What happened?

JEDBURGH: He got himself shot up a little.

JOHN: Badly?

(JEDBURGH *is silent.*)

(*Upset*) How badly?

JEDBURGH: I don't know, John. I got the word when I was leaving.

(JEDBURGH *puts his case on the bed. It is a travel-scarred, pigskin case. He opens it. On top lies his pistol – a Colt 45 automatic – and the police permit which allows him to bring it into the country. He takes both out and crosses to the bedside cupboard and puts them in the drawer. It is done as if an old habit. Then he upends the golf bag and out come his clubs, an M16 carbine and half a dozen clips of ammunition for both the rifle and the automatic. There are also some grenades – smoke, stun and fragmentation – another smaller, pearl-handled pistol (Key Sanh's), a small radio, a Red Cross pack, pills, two half bottles of Scotch (empty). While he is packing the things away and throwing the empty bottles out, JOHN begins to unpack the rest of the case. This, too, seems part of the old routine. He picks up the dirty, sweat-stained shirts and trousers which lie in the second strata of clothes in the suitcase.)*

JOHN: Blood.

JEDBURGH: It's not mine, pal . . .

(He looks into the mirror and sees JOHN's puzzled face.)

It's Colonel Kelly's.

(JOHN begins to cry.)

JEDBURGH: John, did you tape the *Come Dancing* finals?

(JOHN nods, tears streaming down his face, clutching at the shirt.)

JOHN: Yes.

4:48 The living-room, Jedburgh's apartment. Evening

Come Dancing is on the television. JEDBURGH watches this from the sofa. He is obviously a man content with life. He has a can of beer at his side and holds a pot full of freshly cooked popcorn. JOHN can be heard weeping somewhere in the background. The door-bell rings. JEDBURGH gets slowly to his feet. He crosses to the hall.

4:49 The hall, Jedburgh's apartment. Evening

JEDBURGH opens the door. CRAVEN is standing there.

JEDBURGH: Craven! I thought they had you locked away.

(CRAVEN enters the hall and walks through to the living-room.)

CRAVEN: I was in a hospital.

JEDBURGH: Are you crackers?

CRAVEN: No.

4:50 The living-room, Jedburgh's apartment. Evening

CRAVEN gestures at the television.

JEDBURGH: Do you like this programme, Craven?

CRAVEN: *Come Dancing?*

JEDBURGH: Yeah, it's my favourite programme. We don't have anything like that in the States. Want a drink?

(*He crosses to the video controls and thumbs down the sound.*)

CRAVEN: Vodka and ice.

JEDBURGH: All right.

CRAVEN: How was El Salvador?

JEDBURGH: Well, I spent the entire time playing poker with gangsters. One long round of gold chains and designer jeans. You know, those assholes, they figure they have to kill a half a million people to make the region safe for democracy. On top of that there's eight billion dollars worth of aid going down there and they all want a piece of it.

CRAVEN: How was the golf?

JEDBURGH: Well, bodies kept turning up in the bunkers, and you need air support to play out of the rough. Kind of puts you off your game.

(*We hear the door to the bedroom open and* JOHN *makes his way to the kitchen, still crying.*)

I heard they got the other guy – McCroon.

CRAVEN: They damned near got me too.

JEDBURGH: They shot up Key Sanh pretty good. Hence the weeping and rending of garments.

(*He turns back to* CRAVEN.)

What can I do for you?

CRAVEN: I want to know more about Gaia. Clementine told me you had a hand in founding it . . .

JEDBURGH: Oh, did she, indeed? Well, there's some truth in that.

CRAVEN: Why was the CIA promoting a British anti-nuclear ecology movement?

JEDBURGH: Because in 1977 Carter wanted to stop the worldwide spread of nuclear weapons. That meant stopping the manufacture of plutonium, and since the British were the largest manufacturers of the stuff, it meant stopping the Brits. So, I was sent over here with instructions to do just that. But when I got here and looked around for the anti-nuclear lobby there wasn't one. Out on the streets there was CND, but who gave a shit about them in those days? So I had to start from scratch. It took me about six months, but in the end I got some of the best scientists and professors in this country on

my side. Then lo and behold, Carter issued PD 59.* Now that
effectively started the new cold war. All of sudden America
wanted all the plutonium it could lay its hands on. So the
Brits were back on our side again. Then I got word from
Langley: 'Dismantle Gaia'. Good luck! Things like Banquo's
ghost just won't go away. What it did was go underground.

CRAVEN: So your involvement ended there?

JEDBURGH: Yeah, more or less, till Northmoor came along.

(CRAVEN *pulls his list from his pocket.*)

CRAVEN: I found this in Emma's things.

JEDBURGH: A list of subway stations . . .

CRAVEN: It's the route they took into Northmoor.

JEDBURGH: Are you planning on going down there?

CRAVEN: Yes.

JEDBURGH: What do you think is going to be waiting for you
down there, son? Snow White and the seven dwarfs? Because
as far as that list goes, I don't want to blow you out of the
water, but there's a hundred miles of tunnel down there on a
dozen different levels. You're going to need some sort of
three-dimensional map to find your way around.

(*On the television the final results are about to be given.*
JEDBURGH'*s eyes return to the screen.*)

Tell you what, you find a proper route and maybe I'll go
down there with you.

(CRAVEN *is silent for a moment.*)

CRAVEN: That's what I hoped you'd say.

(JEDBURGH'*s eyes stray back to the television.*)

JEDBURGH: Boy, nobody dances like the British. They deserve the
Falklands.

51   Outside Jedburgh's apartment building. Night

CRAVEN *walks towards a waiting car. He leans down and addresses
the driver.*

CRAVEN: Toby Berwick?

(BERWICK *nods.*)

---

*Presidential Directive 59 was issued by Carter in July 1980. It announced the so-
called 'countervailing strategy', which posited that nuclear war was winnable. It is
generally considered to mark the beginning of the new cold war that was to reach its
peak in President Reagan's first term of office.

BERWICK: Hop in.
　　(CRAVEN *peers into the back.*)
CRAVEN: Who's this?
BERWICK: My wife.
　　(CRAVEN *crosses round to the passenger side of the car.*)

4:52　Inside Berwick's car. Night
BERWICK *opens the car door.* CRAVEN *gets in. The car immediately
accelerates.* CRAVEN *looks at the woman in the back seat.*
CRAVEN: What's she doing here?
BERWICK: Ask her.
MIRIAM: If he's going down for ten years we might as well go
　　together.
　　(CRAVEN *stares at her bleakly.*)
CRAVEN: Can you operate a keyboard?
MIRIAM: Yes.
　　(*They turn at the next corner.*)

4:53　Chilwell's office, House of Commons. Night
CHILWELL, *the chairman of the Parliamentary Inquiry into the
privatization of nuclear energy, sits at his desk examining a report.*
HARCOURT *stands in front of him. There is an atmosphere of heavy
and bookish silence. Eventually* CHILWELL *speaks. But he doesn't
look up.*
CHILWELL: Who else knows about this, besides you?
HARCOURT: There's a Mr Jedburgh.
CHILWELL: Who's he when he's at home?
HARCOURT: He's an Acting Energy Attaché at the US Embassy.
　　But he's straight CIA.
　　(*There's a short but measured silence.*)
CHILWELL: Well, we can't expect to call him to give evidence.
HARCOURT: Then there's Craven. He's a Yorkshire CID officer.
CHILWELL: How did he get involved?
HARCOURT: His daughter. She was one of the Gaia team that we
　　down there . . .
CHILWELL: Did she survive?
HARCOURT: Not for long.
CHILWELL: Yes, I remember. I read about it. (*He puts the report
　　down.*) Well, you'd better have him called.
HARCOURT: If we can find him. He's skipped hospital.

4:54 Inside Berwick's car. Night

The car is travelling at speed through London streets. CRAVEN *pulls out a pair of thin gloves and puts them on.*

BERWICK: You'll have ten minutes at the most. And when I say go, we have to go. All right?

   (CRAVEN *nods.*)

   Here.

   (*He passes* CRAVEN *a couple of theatre tickets.* CRAVEN *looks puzzled but puts them in his pocket.*)

CRAVEN: Where is it?

BERWICK: It's a new place. It's not on stream yet, but the terminals are in. How was Mac?

CRAVEN: All right. Sent his regards. (CRAVEN *glances across at him.*) You know him well?

   (BERWICK *nods.*)

BERWICK: I wouldn't be here if I didn't.

4:55 Computer room, office block. Night

The room is in darkness. We hear the sound of a switch. The lights go on to reveal a gigantic office.

BERWICK: Ten minutes.

   (CRAVEN, BERWICK *and* MIRIAM *look around. The space is vacant except for dozens of empty desks, each with a computer keyboard and monitor in front of it.* MIRIAM *advances towards one of the desks. She sits down. She begins to switch on the equipment.* CRAVEN *crosses to the window.*

   We hear the tap of computer keys as MIRIAM *tries to raise the MI5 computer.*)

BERWICK: Ronnie . . . Ronnie?

   (CRAVEN *crosses towards him, weaving his way through the desks.* BERWICK *looks up, his face caught in the flickering light of the monitor.*)

   We're in.

   (CRAVEN *hands* MIRIAM *a piece of paper.* MIRIAM *looks down at it.*)

CRAVEN: Access Gaia. (*He spells it out.*) G, A, I, A.

MIRIAM: G, A, I, A.

   (*She keys the word into the computer. Immediately the high-speed printer beside the VDU begins to bash out a reply. Simultaneously there appears on the VDU screen:*

GAIA *(Description)*
a) *Aims*
b) *Organization*
c) *Membership*
d) *Finance*

CRAVEN *decides before the list is complete.)*
CRAVEN: Aims.
(MIRIAM *keys in 'a'). The VDU immediately flashes the following on to its screen: 'GAIA: Organization of scientific officers whose membership is critical of current government nuclear policy. Founded in* 1977.')

4:56 Lockett's Bar. Night
HARCOURT *has been called to the telephone. He walks across the bar to receive the call. The bar attendant hands him the telephone.*
HARCOURT: Thank you, Mark. *(Speaking into the phone)* Harcourt.
(PENDLETON *is on the other end of the line. We intercut between Pendleton's office and Lockett's Bar.)*
PENDLETON: I thought you ought to know that someone has broken into the MI5 computer. They're going through the Gaia file.
HARCOURT: Where are you?
PENDLETON: Office.
HARCOURT: I'll be right over.
(HARCOURT *puts the telephone down and hands it back to the bar attendant.)*
Thank you.

4:57 The computer room. Night
Information is coming up on the terminal. CRAVEN *watches it with a professional's eye.* MIRIAM *has the patient look of an operator who has been doing it too long to care about anything more than the job.*
BERWICK *is beginning to get concerned about the time.*
The VDU screen reads:

Actions:
    London Conference 1977 131/B
    Public Inquiry Windscale 1977 141/B
    Thorpe 1978 151/B

> *Operation Square Leg 1980* 161/B*
> *Windscale 1981 171/B*
> *Windscale 1982*
> *Hard Rock. Cancellation 1983 182/3*
> *Northmoor 1984 (International Irradiated Fuels) 192/B*

CRAVEN: Try the Northmoor reference.

MIRIAM: Northmoor.

CRAVEN: (*Nodding*) IIF.

> (*The report comes up on the screen:*
> *192/B Northmoor. On 5 May six members of Gaia penetrated*
> *the nuclear waste dump at Northmoor in an attempt to locate*
> *plutonium believed to be hidden at the deepest level. Four of the*
> *intruders were drowned when sluice water was released into the*
> *pipes down which they were crawling. Two escaped but have*
> *since died. The survivors were Martin Smith, SBRO 121973F,*
> *and Emma Craven, SBRO 1896561J.*)

CRAVEN: The Craven number.

> (MIRIAM *looks up.*)

MIRIAM: Craven.

> (CRAVEN *nods.* MIRIAM *begins to key in Emma's Special Branch*
> *Records Office number and the file reference.*)

4:58   Pendleton's office. Night

PENDLETON *looks up as* HARCOURT *enters.* PENDLETON *explains*
the sequence of queries on the monitor.

PENDLETON: First Gaia, then Northmoor, now Craven.

HARCOURT: Which one, Ronnie or Emma?

PENDLETON: Emma.

HARCOURT: Are they sure that it's an intruder?

PENDLETON: Absolutely.

> (*He falls silent as the information on Emma begins to come through*
> *on the VDU: 'Emma Craven. Recruited Gaia October 1980 by*
> *Mary Agnes Sillars. Initiated several actions including surveillance*
> *of NUM agent James Godbolt Oct. 1982–Feb. 1983.'*)

4:59   The computer room. Night

The monitor flickers on CRAVEN's *face as he watches the information*

---

*Operation Square Leg was a 1980 Home Office nuclear exercise, which aroused a
great deal of statistical controversy concerning how many warheads would be necessary
to flatten the UK.

come up on the VDU before him: 'Subject closely linked with attempt by Gaia to discover the existence of a secret stock of weapon-grade plutonium, which they claimed had been stored at Northmoor.'

4:60   Pendleton's office. Night
The telephone rings. As the information continues to roll off the screen, PENDLETON *picks it up.*
PENDLETON: (*Into telephone*) Yes?
> (*MI5 is on the line. In the meantime, the VDU continues to access information about* EMMA: *'Member of fatal Gaia probe into Northmoor 27.7.84 Murdered allegedly by IRA tout James McCroon CRO 1937195 10.8.85 . . .'*)

Well, the longer we let them operate, the more chance we have of finding out what they're after . . .
> (HARCOURT *looks up.* PENDLETON *shrugs.*)

Well, it's your computer. (*He puts the telephone down. Resigned.*) They've located the terminal.

4:61   Outside the office block. Night
A police car stops outside the entrance.

4:62   The computer room. Night
CRAVEN *is still staring at the VDU; the information about* EMMA *continues to scroll up the screen: 'Murdered allegedly by IRA tout James McCroon CRO 1937195 10.8.85, acting on orders of Northmoor Security.'*

4:63   Outside the office block. Night
A police Ford transit and several police cars pull up outside the entrance and a group of POLICEMEN *disgorge.*

4:64   The computer room. Night
BERWICK *turns away from the window.*
BERWICK: They're here . . .
> (*He crosses towards the monitor.*)

CRAVEN: (*To* MIRIAM) Go back to 'Northmoor'. Access 'Security'.
BERWICK: Time we left, Ronnie.
CRAVEN: Access 'Northmoor, Security'.
> (MIRIAM *keys it in.* BERWICK *wanders towards the window again, wondering how long they've got.*)

4:65 The foyer, office block. Night
The police have forced the door of the building and are pouring into the foyer and heading for the lift. The place is deserted and shows signs of not being fully decorated. Wires sprout from walls, etc. The lifts don't work either, or else they have been immobilized.

4:66 The computer room. Night
CRAVEN *looks at the screen:*

> Northmoor. Defence Systems.
> a) Below Ground
>   Alarms
>   Fields of Fire
>   Flood Zones
>   Gas Zones
>   Immediate Response Units
>   Perimeter Walls
>   Strong Points
>   Surveillance. Electronic
>   Weapons Utilization.

CRAVEN: Access 'Oxford Street'.
BERWICK: (*Firmly*) Craven, we must go now.
> (MIRIAM *looks up at* BERWICK, *but types in* 'Oxford Street'. *The screen remains blank.*)

BERWICK: They'll be here any minute.
CRAVEN: Access 'Oxford Street'.
> (*The VDU screen reads:* 'Command: Oxford Street. Command not recognized.')

4:67 The emergency stairs, office block. Night
The police are running up the stairs.

4:68 A corridor, office block. Night
The police run along a corridor towards the computer room.

4:69 The computer room. Night
CRAVEN: Access 'Oxford *Circus*'.
> (MIRIAM *deletes* 'Street' *and types in* 'Circus'. BERWICK *is trying to pull her away from the machine.*)

BERWICK: Come on, for Christ's sake.
> (*Immediately the machine begins to spew out a long intricate pattern of underground stations with alternative routes and 'no*

entry' signs. MIRIAM *and* BERWICK *head for the exit.* CRAVEN *waits as the print-out continues to spill from the printer. We can hear the police in the distance.)*

4:70 A corridor, office block. Night
BERWICK *and* MIRIAM *hare down the corridor.*

4:71 The computer room. Night
CRAVEN *waits for the print-out to unspool. A map gradually emerges: 'Plan of IIF Facilities at Northmoor'.* CRAVEN *rips it out of the computer.*

4:72 Another computer room, office block. Night
MIRIAM *and* BERWICK *run between the vacant desks.*

4:73 The computer room. Night
CRAVEN *runs towards the door, clutching the print-out.*

4:74 Pendleton's office. Night
PENDLETON *sits down and leans back looking at* HARCOURT.
PENDLETON: I'll give you three guesses as to who that was.

4:75 The other computer room, office block. Night
CRAVEN *charges between the desks, making for the exit.*

4:76 The bridge, office block. Night
One of the exits from the office block is an enclosed bridge leading from one building to another. BERWICK *and* MIRIAM *run across the bridge, chased by the police.*

4:77 A corridor, office block. Night
CRAVEN *halts. He tries to work out where the police are coming from and where* MIRIAM *and* BERWICK *have gone. Police tumble through a door at the end of the corridor.* CRAVEN *is forced to change direction. He exits, pursued by the police.*

4:78 Pendleton's office. Night
HARCOURT: I think we've got to get someone into that plant.
PENDLETON: Craven's the obvious choice. If he can get into that
    terminal, he can get into anywhere.

4:79 The first-floor bar, Barbican Theatre. Night
CRAVEN *enters from a side door and looks around, bewildered by the lights, the warmth and the chatter. There is no sign of* MIRIAM *or* BERWICK. *He mingles with the crowd.*
A SERGEANT *and* COLLEAGUE *enter the room and look around. They feel slightly out of place. The* SERGEANT *reaches for his telephone.*
SERGEANT: Assistance requested. Circle Foyer at the Barbican Theatre.
>(CRAVEN *shrinks into the crowd around the bar. He tries to avoid the eyes of the* SERGEANT, *who is sweeping the crowd with his gaze.*)
CLEMENTINE: Good evening, Mr Craven.
>(CRAVEN *turns to see* CLEMENTINE *smiling at him.*)
>What a pleasant surprise. I didn't know that you were a theatre-lover.
CRAVEN: You haven't seen a tall couple –
CLEMENTINE: Slightly out of breath? They went that-a-way . . .

4:80 A police van outside the Barbican. Night
A SECOND POLICE SERGEANT *gets into the van to answer a radio call.*
SECOND SERGEANT: Delta Two.
VOICE: I've covered the area, guv'nor. No sign of them up here.
SECOND SERGEANT: Where the hell are you?
VOICE: I'm on the roof.
SECOND SERGEANT: I told you to follow the exit signs.
VOICE: I did. And I'm on the roof.*
>(*An* MI5 OFFICER *steps into view.*)
MI5 OFFICER: I asked for thirty officers.
SECOND SERGEANT: They're all inside – totally lost.

4:81 The first-floor bar, Barbican Theatre. Night
Most of the theatre-goers are returning to their seats. CRAVEN *is left with* CLEMENTINE, *stranded, as it were, by the tide as it goes out.*
CLEMENTINE *calmly finishes her drink.*
CLEMENTINE: Have you got them?
CRAVEN: Got what?

---

*When the Barbican Theatre opened, its signposting was so confusing it became a by-word for inept design. Although this was a private joke, it is surprising how many people got it.

117

CLEMENTINE: The tickets. The ones Berwick gave you.
CRAVEN: Ah.
> (CRAVEN *pulls them out,* CLEMENTINE *takes them, puts her arm through* CRAVEN'*s and sweeps him towards the theatre entrance.*) What's it about?
CLEMENTINE: Incest.

4:82   Inside a taxi, Bayswater. Night

The cab draws up outside Craven's hotel. CRAVEN *looks at* CLEMENTINE.
CRAVEN: Thanks.
> (*He means it.* CLEMENTINE *is mock-embarrassed.*)
CLEMENTINE: I'm very sorry, but I'm afraid this isn't goodbye. I've been asked to look after you. Night and day.
> (CRAVEN *is pleasantly surprised.*)
CRAVEN: By whom?
CLEMENTINE: By Gaia.
CRAVEN: I'm under house arrest? Is that it?
CLEMENTINE: Protective custody. I'm very good at looking after people – ask Darius.

4:83   Craven's suite, Bayswater Hotel. Night

CRAVEN *opens the door to his small suite.*
CLEMENTINE *enters and gives the place a swift, professional once-over. She crosses to the bathroom.*
CLEMENTINE: (*From the bathroom*) I'll sleep on the divan, OK?
> (*By this time* CRAVEN *has entered the bedroom. He goes to the dresser, pulls out the print-out from his jacket and studies it. Then he begins to undress. The telephone rings and he picks it up.*)
CRAVEN: Craven.
> (PENDLETON *is on the line. We intercut between Craven's hotel and Pendleton's office.*)
PENDLETON: Sorry to ring you at this hour, but you were out earlier.
> (CRAVEN *looks at his watch. He answers wryly, since he guesses that* PENDLETON *knows exactly what he was doing.*)
CRAVEN: I was at the theatre.
PENDLETON: Were you? Harcourt and I stayed home and watched the telly. Interesting programme – called 'Shake up bits of information and reassemble all in the right order'.

(CRAVEN *looks over to* CLEMENTINE, *who is washing her face in the bathroom.*)

CRAVEN: What do you want, Pendleton?

PENDLETON: Well, you've been asked to give evidence before the House of Commons Energy Committee. Remember we discussed it some time ago?

CRAVEN: And I said 'no'.

PENDLETON: You don't say 'no' to the Commons, Craven, or they lock you up.

(CRAVEN *is silent, but* PENDLETON *takes it as submission.*)
Be at the Visitor's Gate by nine thirty. They'll have a pass made out in your name. And wear a tie – something regimental.

(CRAVEN *puts the telephone down.* CLEMENTINE *enters the room.*)

4:84   Craven's suite, Bayswater Hotel. Later that night

CRAVEN *lies awake in bed. He can hear the hum of the refrigerator. He gets out of bed and goes into the other room. The fridge door is ajar. He shuts it. Immediately* CLEMENTINE *is awake, with a gun in her two hands, not knowing what had triggered her reaction.* CRAVEN *freezes, knowing that in the darkness he could be mistaken for an intruder.*

CRAVEN: Fridge – keeping me awake.

(*The two of them stay frozen for what seems a long time, during which the tension of the intrusion seems to slip subtly into that of an unexpected sexual encounter.*

CLEMENTINE *puts the pistol down.* CRAVEN *stands there silently.* CLEMENTINE *indicates her divan.*)

CLEMENTINE: Come in – for a while.

(*She makes room for him.* CRAVEN *sits down and leans over to kiss her.*)

4:85   The House of Commons. Day

BENNETT *arrives in a cab. He pays off the cabbie and turns into the hall.*

4:86   The Great Hall, House of Commons. Day

There is the usual crowd of civil servants, lawyers and journalists waiting for the session to begin. BENNETT *is amongst the witnesses. He walks across the hall to confront* HARCOURT.

HARCOURT: Morning.

(BENNETT *gives* HARCOURT *a rather cold stare.*)

BENNETT: Was this your idea . . . bringing Craven in?

HARCOURT: My dear chap, why should I do something like that?

BENNETT: I hope you can rely upon his testimony. I'm told the man's deranged.

(BENNETT *moves away, past a number of civil servants from the Department of Industry, who shake his hand and wish him good morning. He comes across* CHILDS.)

What's the situation?

CHILDS: I've seen the report. The pathologist is going to mention radiation, but without any analysis of its source. He's simply going to say she was irradiated.

BENNETT: Well, we'll just have to front it out.

(BENNETT *notices* GODBOLT. *He crosses to him.*)

BENNETT: Hello, James.

GODBOLT: Hello.

BENNETT: Has Childs briefed you?

GODBOLT: Yes . . . the union isn't going to like it.

BENNETT: You won't let me down, will you?

GODBOLT: I'll try not to.

BENNETT: Good.

4:87 An ante-room, House of Commons. Day

CRAVEN *is shown into the room by* PENDLETON.

PENDLETON: This is better than hanging around in the hall. (*He nods at the telephone in the corner.*) I'll ring you when your name's called.

(*He exits, closing the door behind him.*)

4:88 A committee room, House of Commons. Day

The Inquiry is examining MENZIES, *the pathologist we have seen in an earlier scene with* PENDLETON *and* HARCOURT.

CHILWELL: Doctor Menzies, you were the pathologist who examined the body. What was the cause of death?

MENZIES: Drowning. But she had been exposed to a great deal of radiation.

CHILWELL: Are you able to confirm the source of the radiation?

MENZIES: No. But I am able to say that activation products from fast neutrons identifies her as having been exposed to a criticality accident.

CHILWELL: And what does that mean exactly?
MENZIES: It means that she was in proximity to concentrated
    fissile material.
CHILWELL: And where would you find that?
MENZIES: In a reprocessing plant.

4:89 An ante-room, House of Commons. Day

There is a knock on the door. CRAVEN *turns.* GODBOLT *enters the
room.* CRAVEN *looks at him.* GODBOLT *smiles nervously.*
GODBOLT: Waiting to be called?
    (CRAVEN *nods.*)
    Mind if I join you?
    (CRAVEN *shakes his head.*)
    All politics, isn't it?
    (CRAVEN *looks up.*)
    I suppose that's why they call it the Mother of Parliaments.
    (*He walks to the window and looks down into the courtyard.*) Lot
    of people down here got Northmoor in their sights.
CRAVEN: I'm one of them.
    (GODBOLT *waits for clarification. But* CRAVEN *has nothing to
    add.*)
GODBOLT: Why would they want to call you?
CRAVEN: They know about Emma breaking into the plant. And
    they think I can shed some light on it.
    (GODBOLT *is visibly jolted.*)
GODBOLT: And can you?
CRAVEN: I can tell them what I've found out since she died. (*He
    looks at* GODBOLT.) Which is quite a lot.
    (GODBOLT *swallows.*)
GODBOLT: It's the end of the road for me . . . when this gets out.
CRAVEN: How did you ever get involved in the first place?
    (GODBOLT *stares at him.*)
GODBOLT: It started back in the sixties. The Ministry of Defence
    took over the mines, started building storage facilities.
    Needed miners to maintain them. And someone in the union
    to look after the miners. I were picked. Signed the Official
    Secrets Act and that part of my job wasn't mentioned outside
    of the Executive Committee. Over the years Northmoor
    became an underground city. Then came the defence cuts.
    Changes in strategy. The MOD didn't need Northmoor any

more. So they leased it to Bennett. I were part of the deal. I suddenly found myself dealing with a nuclear waste plant.

CRAVEN: That must have made life difficult.

GODBOLT: (*Nodding*) We had a National Executive paranoid about nuclear power and I were now wading knee-deep in the stuff.

CRAVEN: Was it Bennett who rigged the last union vote?

(GODBOLT *nods*.)

GODBOLT: He needed me. He knew he'd never get another leader so compromised.

CRAVEN: Why didn't you tell me this at the time?

GODBOLT: How could I?

4:90 A softball game, Hyde Park. Day

A softball game is going on near Knightsbridge Barracks. JEDBURGH *approaches it across the fields.* SCHUMAKER *drifts away from the game, where he has been a spectator. As he approaches* JEDBURGH, *we see that he is a CIA functionary. Amicable, East-Coast-educated, he is one of the top three on the London station.*

SCHUMAKER: Hi, Darius.

(JEDBURGH *grunts*.)

JEDBURGH: Well, where is he?

SCHUMAKER: He'll be along. You play this game?

(*He nods in the direction of the pitcher.* JEDBURGH *shakes his head.*)

JEDBURGH: I'm a golfer, Schumaker. I happen to believe that the game is sanctified. I cannot in my wildest imagination see the same thing being said for softball, can you?

SCHUMAKER: I never give it that much thought.

JEDBURGH: That's the story of your life, Schumaker, the story of your life.

(SCHUMAKER *glances at him shrewdly. We can see that* JEDBURGH *is in fact overwrought.*)

SCHUMAKER: How was Salvador?

JEDBURGH: A pain in the ass.

SCHUMAKER: What were you doing out there?

JEDBURGH: Clearing up your mistakes.

(*Through the softball game, we see* WAGNER *approaching.*)

SCHUMAKER: It needed a field man like you there.

(JEDBURGH *ignores Schumaker's flattery and nods towards the approaching* WAGNER, *a younger version of* SCHUMAKER *himself.*)

JEDBURGH: Who is he?

SCHUMAKER: Kurt Wagner. He's a White House staffer.

(JEDBURGH *glances at* SCHUMAKER.)

JEDBURGH: (*Suspiciously*) I thought this was Company* business.

SCHUMAKER: (*Mildly*) We can't exclude the President, Darius. If he wants to take an interest.

JEDBURGH: Since when? Anybody else involved?

SCHUMAKER: No.

(WAGNER *approaches the two men and greets them cheerily*.)

WAGNER: Hi, guys.

SCHUMAKER: Kurt, this is Darius Jedburgh.

WAGNER: Glad to meet you.

(*They shake hands.*)

This is for you.

(*He hands* JEDBURGH *a letter.* JEDBURGH *tears open the envelope and takes out the note.*)

JEDBURGH: (*Reading*) Dear Jed. Get into the ball park and steal the ball. Signed Cord.

(*He looks up at* WAGNER.)

You guys . . . in the fifties it was football. In the sixties it was surf. In the seventies it was tennis. Now it's baseball. When are you guys going to grow up?

WAGNER: We need the plutonium, Colonel.

JEDBURGH: This is a friendly nation, pal. You know the rules – somebody's got to sanction this operation. The State Department, for a start . . .

WAGNER: We'll take care of the paperwork, Colonel.

4:91   The ante-room, House of Commons. Day

The conversation between CRAVEN *and* GODBOLT *continues.*
GODBOLT speaks haltingly, while it just stops short of being an interrogation on Craven's part.

GODBOLT: All this waiting gets to you . . .

CRAVEN: Do you remember that television programme you made two or three weeks ago?

GODBOLT: Just about.

CRAVEN: In it you said that Emma was murdered – by mistake.

GODBOLT: I don't remember, Ronnie. I were half-pissed at the time.

*i.e. CIA.

CRAVEN: You were trying to tell me something.

GODBOLT: I can't remember.

CRAVEN: She was killed by mistake. That's what you said. Was it McCroon who made the mistake?

GODBOLT: No, it weren't McCroon. It were the people who paid him. They made the mistake.

(CRAVEN *gets to his feet.*)

CRAVEN: They? Who are they. . . ?

GODBOLT: You know damn well who 'they' are, Ronnie.

CRAVEN: How did they make a mistake?

GODBOLT: They knew that someone had led the Gaia team under the Northmoor defences. They asked me to make a list of possible leaders . . . As an old caver your name were there. Someone who knew the shafts and vents of the old pits. Someone whom Emma could persuade . . . and they thought it were you.

(CRAVEN *is surprised.*)

CRAVEN: Me?

GODBOLT: Yes. You.

(PENDLETON *enters.*)

PENDLETON: They're ready for you, Mr Godbolt.

CRAVEN: They got it wrong.

GODBOLT: Like they always do. It were me.

CRAVEN: You? *You* took them in?

GODBOLT: Yes, I took them down there. I hadn't completely sold out.

CRAVEN: Why didn't you tell me!

GODBOLT: You're a police officer.

CRAVEN: She was my daughter.

(HARCOURT *enters the room.*)

HARCOURT: You've been called, Mr Godbolt.

(GODBOLT *exits.* CRAVEN *calls after him.*)

CRAVEN: Godbolt!

(HARCOURT *looks at* PENDLETON *and then at* CRAVEN.)

HARCOURT: I don't think they're going to let you speak.

(*He turns to* PENDLETON.)

PENDLETON: You're not serious.

HARCOURT: Well, evidently our friend here signed himself out of hospital. Bennett got hold of his psychiatric report – it could undermine his testimony.

CRAVEN: There's nothing wrong with my mind.

124

HARCOURT: You have a fixation with trees, Craven. An arboreal passion. That can be made to sound very odd in the hands of a skilled interrogator. Anyway, there's something better for you to do.

4:92   The Tiberio restaurant. Night

A pianist is playing in the corner. JEDBURGH *sits alone at a fairly low-lit table. He looks up as* CRAVEN *approaches.*

JEDBURGH: Still in one piece, I see.

(CRAVEN *sits down.*)

CRAVEN: What's that supposed to mean?

JEDBURGH: People have a habit of dissolving into their constituent parts these days. The political climate does not favour homogeneity . . . Key Sanh died – he died peacefully in bed . . . of gunshot wounds.

(*He laughs, but can't disguise his anguish.*)

CRAVEN: I'm sorry to hear that.

JEDBURGH: That makes me and old Mad Mike the last survivors of the 'Nam team.

CRAVEN: I wondered if you had made up your mind – about our little trip?

4:93   Craven's suite, Bayswater Hotel. Night

The telephone rings. CRAVEN *is in bed.* CLEMENTINE *is with him. It is* PENDLETON.

PENDLETON: I hear you're taking Jedburgh?

CRAVEN: What?

(CRAVEN *is half surprised that* PENDLETON *knows already.*)

PENDLETON: Will you be armed?

CRAVEN: Yes.

PENDLETON: Well, if he gets out of hand, shoot him. Remember he's an American, so not basically on our side. Goodnight, Craven. Give my love to Clemmie.

(CRAVEN *puts the phone down and lies back in bed.*)

CLEMENTINE: Who was that?

CRAVEN: Pendleton.

CLEMENTINE: Oh.

(*It is as if it is the most natural thing in the world that* PENDLETON *should know where they are and what they are up to.* CLEMENTINE *goes back to sleep.*)

Northmoor

5:1   The hills around Craven's house, Craigmills. Dawn
A view of the landscape. We hear the sound of JEDBURGH *snoring.*

5:2   The living-room, Craven's house. Dawn
JEDBURGH *is asleep on the sofa. He stirs. It is morning.*

5:3   Outside Craven's house. Dawn
There is a van parked in the driveway. All is quiet.

5:4   The kitchen, Craven's house. Dawn
JEDBURGH *is sitting in the kitchen in his dressing-gown. He is stirring honey into his tea. He sees someone walk past the window outside.*

5:5   The bathroom, Craven's house. Dawn
JEDBURGH *is shaving. He stops. There is the sound of someone hammering outside.*

5:6   The rear of Craven's house. Dawn
JEDBURGH *walks across the lawn in his pyjamas towards the shed at the end of the garden.* JEDBURGH *enters the shed. Inside* GODBOLT *is nailing up an old map.*
JEDBURGH: What the hell's this?
　　(*He peers at the map.*)
GODBOLT: It's an old map of the mine – painted on linen – nearly
　　a hundred years old, but accurate to an inch.
　　(JEDBURGH *examines it.*)
JEDBURGH: Where is it we're going?
GODBOLT: All the way from here (*Points at one end*) to there
　　(*Points at the other*). Ten miles.
　　(JEDBURGH *takes a closer look.*)
GODBOLT: I suppose you would've preferred a computer print-out.

JEDBURGH: No, sir. This here's just fine.

   (JEDBURGH *smiles and walks out of the shed and down the garden.*)

5:7   Craven's garden. Dawn

JEDBURGH *walks over to the tree near where* EMMA *had been shot. Below it a spring now trickles. Around it are some wild marsh flowers. Here* CRAVEN *sits.* JEDBURGH *continues to lather his face.*

JEDBURGH: Is this where she died?

CRAVEN: He was over there. (*He points.*) We were standing here. He stepped forward. Shouting my name.

   (*He lapses into silence.* JEDBURGH *looks down at the little stream.*)

JEDBURGH: Is this stream a permanent feature?

   (*He glances at* CRAVEN, *who shakes his head.*)

CRAVEN: No. (*He turns back towards the house.*) It's new.

   (JEDBURGH *follows him back into the house.*)

JEDBURGH: (*As he enters*) 'O Jephthah, judge of Israel, what a treasure hadst thou!' 'What a treasure had he, my lord?' 'Why – one fair daughter, and no more, The which he loved passing well.'*

5:8   The front of Craven's house. Day

JEDBURGH *and* CRAVEN *approach the van parked outside the house. They are arguing amiably with each other. They get in.* GODBOLT *is at the wheel. They drive off.*

5:9   A first-class suite, London hotel. Day

There is a knock at the door.

GROGAN: Come in.

   (BENNETT *enters. He sees that* GROGAN *is about to have breakfast – a* WAITER *is preparing the table.*)

   Morning, Bobby.

BENNETT: Morning, Jerry.

GROGAN: Have you had your breakfast?

BENNETT: Yes, thank you.

GROGAN: Well, there's some coffee over there if you want some.

---

*Jedburgh refers to Emma and her father by quoting *Hamlet* II.ii. Hamlet refers to Polonius by invoking Jephthah.

(GROGAN *moves over to the table with* BENNETT *and signs the bill the* WAITER *is holding out.*)

WAITER: Thank you, sir.

GROGAN: Thank you. I had a call from Washington a few moments ago. Somebody's about to break into your plant.

5:10 A moorland track near Northmoor. Day

Four Landrovers move in convoy up the single track. They reach a cattle grid and charge over it.

5:11 Single-track road near Northmoor. Day

Godbolt's van pulls up under some trees. CRAVEN, JEDBURGH *and* GODBOLT *get out and unload their gear.*

5:12 The front gates of Northmoor. Day

The guards can hear the Landrovers. They begin to push open the mesh gates. The Landrovers appear and swing through the gates heading for the compound.

5:13 The compound, Northmoor. Day

The Landrovers make their way across the level ground towards the entrance to a tunnel. Over the tunnel the IIF logo stands out proud.

5:14 The tunnel, Northmoor

The guards raise a red-and-white barrier and the Landrovers drive through. They trundle along the tunnel and veer right towards the lift shafts.

5:15 The lifts, Northmoor

They come to a halt. The doors open and a dozen men dismount. They gather around CONNORS, *an ex-army type, who addresses them tersely.*

CONNORS: OK. You know what you've got to do.

(CONNORS *walks towards the Guard House, where he is met by the Operations Manager,* CHILDS. *Together they move towards the open lift, followed by the men.*)

CHILDS: All we got is Bennett's phone call.

CONNORS: How many men?

CHILDS: Three of them. Coming in the same way as last time.

CONNORS: That's not much use.

(CONNORS *enters the lift.* CHILDS *follows him in.* CONNORS *speaks to one of the men who is about to follow him into the lift.*)

Gas gear. Protective clothing. Firearms.
(CONNORS *presses a button. The door closes.*)

5:16 A waterfall adjacent to the mine.* Day
Over the sound of the waterfall, we hear the sound of a generator.
GODBOLT *and* JEDBURGH *make their way down a path to the*
waterfall.

5:17 A stream adjacent to the mine. Day
Led by GODBOLT, CRAVEN *and* JEDBURGH *move upstream towards*
the mine.

5:18 The underground cooling ponds, Northmoor
CONNORS *and* CHILDS *exit from the lift and walk towards the*
Operations Building beside the ponds. An orange inflatable boat is
moored on the water near by.
CONNORS: Can we flood the lower levels?
CHILDS: Not without exposing the flasks. There's been a drought,
    don't forget. The reservoirs are drying up.
    (*They come to the door of the Operations Room.*)
CONNORS: This is what we do. We lay gas at the end of each level.
    Then we flood them. The pressure of the water will push the
    gas through every tunnel in the plant.
    (*They enter the Operations Room.*)

5:19 The Operations Room, Northmoor
A large plate-glass window overlooks the ponds. In front of it there is a
console with a number of VDUs and an electronic map of the main
tunnels showing their criticality alarms. There are also flood control
warnings, speakers and radios. CHILDS *looks at the water levels,*
troubled. To flood the levels means draining the ponds and hence
exposing the flasks.
CHILDS: If we expose the flasks, we're going to have a bigger
    problem on our hands than last time. Go and see for yourself.
    (CONNORS *crosses to the window and studies the ponds with their*
    ranks of yellow flasks, their tops just breaking surface.)
    You see, we just don't have the water
    (CONNORS *turns to* CHILDS.)
CONNORS: Give me what you've got.

*These scenes were shot in and around a gold mine in Wales.

5:20 The waterfall adjacent to the mine. Day
GODBOLT, CRAVEN *and* JEDBURGH *clamber their way up towards the bridge over the waterfall.* GODBOLT *hears a train of mining trolleys approaching with their cargo of ore. He signals for the other two to lie low.* JEDBURGH *and* CRAVEN *wait for* GODBOLT *to give them the OK before resuming their trek.*

5:21 The underground cooling ponds, Northmoor
CONNORS *exits from the Operations Room.* CHILDS *follows him. At the water's edge, two guards are standing in the orange inflatable dinghy. It is being loaded to the brim with gas cylinders by two further guards.* CONNORS *and* CHILDS *cross to the water's edge and look down at the flasks shimmering under the water.*
CHILDS: I can give you fifty thousand litres – no more.
CONNORS: That's enough.
   (CONNORS *goes back into the Operations Room, leaving* CHILDS *kneeling at the water's edge, staring at the lethal flasks.*)

5:22 The generator for the mine. Day
The three men, having crossed under the bridge, are making their way up the slope to the generator. As a large vehicle crosses the bridge, GODBOLT *shouts.*
GODBOLT: Get down!
   (*They climb up the slope past the generator and come to a barbed wire fence, where they pull off their equipment and begin assembling their climbing gear.*)

5:23 The Committee Room, House of Commons. Day
The members of the Committee enter the room to prepare for the morning session. HARCOURT *is having a quiet word with* CHILWELL. POLLY ELHAM *is with them, as is another member,* HAROLD BEWES, *who tends to support the IIF position.*
HARCOURT: Whatever Bennett says, I don't want you to adjourn. I
   want him kept on that stand as long as possible.
CHILWELL: I'm the chairman of this committee, old boy, and I
   have to tell you we have a great deal of business to get
   through.
POLLY: Do we have the pathologist's report on this body?
BEWES: No, I haven't got that report.
CHILWELL: There is one. It's on its way.

5:24 The entrance to the mine. Day

CRAVEN *lowers himself down a rope into the mine, watched by*
JEDBURGH *and* GODBOLT *from above. He reaches the bottom and
looks around him. He hears the sound of a siren and a train of mining
trolleys comes towards him. He ducks out of sight. When the train has
passed, he looks up the shaft and signals.*

5:25 The hall outside the Committee Room, House of
Commons. Day

There are a few moments before the doors open. PENDLETON *enters.
There is a tense atmosphere. He sees that* BENNETT *has* GROGAN *in
tow. He crosses towards them.*

BENNETT: Morning, Guy.

PENDLETON: Hello, Bobby. You about to hit us for six?

BENNETT: I think so. Do you know Jerry Grogan?

(GROGAN *comes alongside.*)

PENDLETON: No. How do you do?

(*He holds out his hand.* GROGAN *is about to shake it.*)

BENNETT: Guy's a friend of Jedburgh's.

(GROGAN *hesitates momentarily before grabbing* PENDLETON's
hand firmly.)

GROGAN: A great soldier in his day.

PENDLETON: Sounds like an obituary.

BENNETT: Has Harcourt read my statement? He's looking a bit
sick.

(*They turn towards* HARCOURT, *who has just left the Committee
Room.*)

PENDLETON: No, he always looks like that this early.

GROGAN: Jedburgh isn't here today?

PENDLETON: No, he rarely pokes his nose in this place.

GROGAN: What about Craven?

PENDLETON: He's taking the day off.

(*Both* BENNETT *and* GROGAN *take this in with the faintest hint
of amusement.* PENDLETON *watches as the two of them walk
towards the Committee Room door.* HARCOURT *joins him.*)

HARCOURT: Well, they look very chipper.

PENDLETON: They know. Someone's told them.

5:26 A tunnel in the mine

GODBOLT *reaches down and opens one half of a big iron flap to reveal*

a gaping abyss. As he opens the other half, CRAVEN *and* JEDBURGH
appear behind him, pushing a trolley.
GODBOLT: Right. This is where it begins.

5:27 The Committee Room, House of Commons. Day

The room is crowded. BENNETT *makes his way to the witness chair
and sits down on it. There is a murmur as both MPs and the members
of the audience recognize him. Eventually,* CHILWELL *looks up and
addresses* BENNETT, *at which point the murmur ceases.*

CHILWELL: A few days ago, Mr Bennett, a body of a young
woman was discovered in the Corrie Reservoir, Craigmills.
The pathologist's report suggests that, although she died from
drowning, she had suffered a radiation accident only an hour
before her death. Now, since your Northmoor site is the
nearest nuclear site to the reservoir, and since it shares with
the Corrie the local water table, I wonder whether you have
any evidence which might throw light on this occurrence.

5:28 The tunnel in the mine

JEDBURGH *seizes the pulley, which is looped to an old gantry above
the shaft and tests it for weight. Then he slowly drops down through the
hole, paying out the line as he does so.* CRAVEN *meanwhile takes the
equipment off the trolley.* GODBOLT *turns to help him.*

CRAVEN: How deep does this go?
GODBOLT: Eight hundred feet. Then we hit water.
JEDBURGH: This rope is not eight hundred feet long, Godbolt.
GODBOLT: There is a gallery sixty feet down. That's our way in.
JEDBURGH: Sixty feet. I'm counting.

5:29 The Committee Room, House of Commons. Day

BENNETT: In July this year, my plant at Northmoor was broken
into by terrorists, who stole a quantity of plutonium we had in
store. We had to take the necessary action to stop them
getting away.
(*There is silence in the room. They wait on every word of*
BENNETT's.)
CHILWELL: What action?
BENNETT: I gave orders to flood the lower gallery. As far as I can
determine they were all drowned.
CHILWELL: Was there no alternative?
BENNETT: None. If we had not acted promptly they might have

got away with it. And the consequences . . . I leave that for you to judge.

POLLY PELHAM: I'm afraid this raises more questions than it answers. Why was plutonium being stored in Northmoor? Who were these terrorists? And why, why was the AEA not notified of this incident?

5:30 The tunnel leading to 'Deep Throat', the mine

GODBOLT, CRAVEN *and* JEDBURGH *make their way along the tunnel.* GODBOLT *leads. He ducks under a low overhang and clambers down a steep slope.* JEDBURGH *and* CRAVEN *follow. They stop when they see the drop below them. The ground seems to cave away into the darkness.*

JEDBURGH: Look at this.

GODBOLT: When I were a kid they called it the Tonsils. Now it's Deep Throat.
(*They begin to negotiate the loose shale, sliding down to the bottom.*)

5:31 The Committee Room, House of Commons. Day

POLLY: Under the NAIR* scheme, you should have informed the police. Did you?

BENNETT: No. We did not inform the police.

BEWES: Under the Site Licence issued by the Nuclear Installations Inspectorate you should have informed both the AEA and the Health and Safety Executive.

BENNETT: We did not inform either of those bodies.

POLLY: Then whom did you inform?

BENNETT: We informed the Ministry of Defence. The plutonium we were storing was the property of the MOD and we felt they were the only people we were authorized to communicate with.

5:32 A long tunnel, the mine

GODBOLT, CRAVEN *and* JEDBURGH *trudge along a long, flat, low tunnel, walking in step. It is as if a rhythm has developed over a period of time. In the distance they hear the rumble of water. They stop and listen. The rumble continues and then disappears.*

---

*National Arrangements for Incidents Involving Radioactivity, administered by the police. Under the NAIR rules the police will call out various experts to deal with a leak of radioactivity.

CRAVEN: It sounds like a train.

GODBOLT: They're dumping water.

JEDBURGH: Is that normal?

GODBOLT: No. They're expecting us.

> (*This startling announcement is greeted with silence. Ever since they negotiated 'Deep Throat', CRAVEN has been more than usually uncommunicative.*
> *They hear a second rumbling noise. This time closer. It sounds like an underground train.*)

JEDBURGH: What you thinking, Craven?

CRAVEN: That Emma went through all this and never said a word.

GODBOLT: Odd, isn't it? How you can be close to someone for years and still not know what's going on inside their heads.

JEDBURGH: Don't knock it, Godbolt. It's our capacity for deception that distinguishes us from the animals.

GODBOLT: You should know, Mr Jedburgh – you have made a profession out of it.

JEDBURGH: Yeah, that's right.

5:33 The Operations Room, Northmoor

CHILDS *sits before half-a-dozen television monitors, punching up different pictures as he checks the various caves and tunnels which are due to be inundated. At the moment he is assisting in the flooding of the lower levels. And the monitor which holds his interest is a picture of just a mass of swirling water.*

CHILDS: That's K-2 flooded.

CONNORS: (*Voice over*) Is it holding?

CHILDS: Seems to be.

CONNORS: (*Voice over*) What about G-2?

> (CHILDS *flicks a switch and turns another. He looks up at the monitors.*)

CHILDS: No. I'll need about ten minutes to adjust the surge.

5:34 The 'Cathedral' cavern, the mine

The three men traverse the last few yards of the tunnel and find themselves in an underground slate quarry.

GODBOLT: (*Sharply*) Hold it. There's a two-hundred-foot drop.

> (JEDBURGH *splays his torch above him. The roof vaults high above him.*)

JEDBURGH: What's this place called?

GODBOLT: They call it the Cathedral. Hand-drilled by miners who had to buy their own candles.

CRAVEN: You'd have been out of a job then.

GODBOLT: Victorian values, Mr Craven.

JEDBURGH: I feel like Jonah in the belly of the whale.

CRAVEN: We absail down here?

GODBOLT: In the next cavern. That's where I leave you. At the bottom is a ventilator shaft. Beyond that – Northmoor.

5:35   The single-track road adjacent to the mine. Day
The view is from the little ravine that carries the river down to the valley. A Landrover carrying the IIF logo stands beside the Ford van belonging to GODBOLT. *Two guards, wearing ordinary mountain gear, are in touch with Northmoor by radio. They are trying to get some information on the van. They are armed with shotguns.*
While the FIRST GUARD *stays with the radio, the* SECOND *has begun to search the back of the van. He jumps out of it holding a gas mask.*

SECOND GUARD: Terry, gas mask.

FIRST GUARD: Alpha One.

RADIO VOICE: Alpha One receiving.

FIRST GUARD: Get me Connors.

5:36   A tunnel adjacent to the 'Cathedral' cavern
CRAVEN *and* JEDBURGH *are now preparing to go over the edge. They don their back packs.* JEDBURGH *disappears over the the edge.*

JEDBURGH: So long, sunshine.

> (*As* JEDBURGH *absails down the sheer drop.* CRAVEN *turns to* GODBOLT.)

CRAVEN: Thanks.

GODBOLT: Good luck. I hope you make it.

CRAVEN: You too.

> (CRAVEN *is about to go over the edge.*)

GODBOLT: Craven!

> (CRAVEN *looks up.*)

Watch that big lad!

> (CRAVEN *smiles at this reference to* JEDBURGH *and, taking the rope in his hands, disappears from view.*
> GODBOLT *waits till he gets to the bottom, hears him shout up 'OK' and then gets to his feet. He watches them stumble and slide across the uneven floor of the cavern towards the ventilation shaft. Then he turns to go back the way he has come.*)

136

5:37 The hall adjacent to the Committee Room, House of Commons. Day

The door of the Committee Room opens and the audience and committee begin to exit. BENNETT *comes out followed by* POLLY, *then* PENDLETON. BENNETT *is surrounded by people who want to talk to him, including parliamentary lobby correspondents.* GROGAN *gets up from his chair and tries to get an eye-contact reaction from* BENNETT. *He does.* BENNETT *is looking confident.* GROGAN *joins him.*

BENNETT: I think we're winning.

GROGAN: Good.

> (POLLY *and* PENDLETON *stop to watch* BENNETT *with the reporters.*)

POLLY: Well, at least he's admitted that the plutonium was down there. And that the Gaia team were drowned . . . on his orders.

PENDLETON: They'll probably give him a medal for it.

5:38 The outer circle, Northmoor

With a crash the wire mesh falls away from the wall and CRAVEN *pitches forward on to the cement floor. He finds himself in a narrow cement corridor, which is lit by a string of electric lights. Immediately, he starts coughing.* JEDBURGH, *already half-masked, follows him through, carrying Craven's bag. He opens the bag to pull out the mask as* CRAVEN *curls up on the floor of the corridor, coughing. He pushes the mask over* CRAVEN'S *face. For one moment* CRAVEN *lies there dormant, then he begins to recover.*

JEDBURGH: (*Shouting through his mask*) Come on Craven.

> (*At this moment they hear a rumble in the distance, which grows louder more rapidly than before, as if the water this time is heading directly for them at breakneck speed. The immediate stiffening of* JEDBURGH's *body betrays his fear that they are about to be overwhelmed. He grabs at a bar in the wall and hangs on to the still-curled up* CRAVEN *with the other hand. He does not want to see him swept away. But the water rumbles through on a level just overhead in a fury of sound and vibration, shaking dust and stones from the roof and starting a dozen high-pressure leaks. As the water flows down on* JEDBURGH *and* CRAVEN *from above the two men, covered in dust and streaked with water, look at each other in gratitude. Their particular level appears to have been spared.*)

5:39 The Operations Room, Northmoor

CHILDS *leans over and speaks into the radio mike.*

CHILDS: Connors, no more water.

CONNORS: (*Voice over*) I need everything you've got.

CHILDS: We'll expose the rods.

CONNORS: (*Voice over*) I need everything you've got.

5:40 An antechamber, the outer circle, Northmoor

It is almost pitch dark.

JEDBURGH: What the hell's this place?

> (*The two men enter through a door.* JEDBURGH *finds a switch and suddenly the room is filled with light. He exits into the adjoining chamber.* CRAVEN *finds himself facing a notice which has been placed in big letters behind the hatch.*
>
> > *Warning. Following onset of Nuclear War, no member of the condominium will be permitted beyond this point. By order. The Management. October* 1962.)

JEDBURGH: (*Voice over*) Craven!

> (*Puzzled by the notice,* CRAVEN *turns to join* JEDBURGH *in the next chamber.*)

5:41 A vaulted chamber, Northmoor

JEDBURGH *is triumphantly holding up a bottle of claret.*

JEDBURGH: Craven, a first growth St Julien '63. I think we got the whole vintage here.*

> (*He is standing by a dusty table in the middle of a vaulted chamber. The chamber itself is divided crudely into a number of sections, each of which seems to be stacked with wine, paintings, books.* JEDBURGH *turns the corkscrew in the bottle and begins screwing it tight.*)

This is the Doomsday equivalent of Harrods.

> (*He pulls out the cork.* CRAVEN *moves away to explore the sections of the chamber.*)

5:42 A section adjoining the vaulted chamber, Northmoor

The sound of Mozart drifts through the dry air. CRAVEN *stands in front*

---

*There are two errors here, which were pounced on by the critics of the posh Sunday papers. First, there is no such thing as a first growth claret. Second, the year is a particularly bad one for Bordeaux wines, but I chose it to coincide with the Cuban Missile Crisis (this would have been the first harvest to become available after the crisis).

*of a pre-war class photograph of boys at Eton. It hangs above a
campaign chest, which is filled with shotgun cartridges, old socks and
bottles of malt whisky.*

Looking around, CRAVEN *feels as if the artifacts of an aristocratic
family had been condensed to fit the size of a cabin – not much bigger
than that of a cross-channel ferry. There are pictures of débutante balls,
a royal garden party, a society wedding, and a Battle of Britain
Spitfire. A bust of Churchill stands next to a Lalique lamp, and an
aluminium Second World War fighter. A couple of Gainsboroughs are
stacked against the wall, beside half-a-dozen cases of Cockburn's port.
On the bed is a leather hat box and three worn cases. The cave gives
the impression of having been filled carelessly with whatever came to
hand, and should be saved for the future.*

It looks as if the occupants' heyday was in the forties.

5:43 The vaulted chamber, Northmoor

CRAVEN *returns to find* JEDBURGH *whisking eggs over a copper pan
which is sizzling over a small blue flame on a table-side trolley. The
table itself is laid with damask and silver and crystal and a bottle of
Chablis lies in a chrome ice bucket.* CRAVEN *is astonished by the
change.*

CRAVEN: What's for lunch?

JEDBURGH: For lunch we've got a lobster omelette with asparagus
tips and french beans and wine and coffee and cigars and
dessert, to be announced.

> (CRAVEN *smiles as* JEDBURGH *pours the whisked eggs into the
> pan.*)

5:44 The vaulted chamber, Northmoor. Some time later

JEDBURGH *and* CRAVEN *are dining at the table with relish.*

JEDBURGH: You know what's the most interesting thing about this
place?

CRAVEN: No locks?

JEDBURGH: No clocks. Time stands still. Real freaky feeling, huh?

CRAVEN: There is a plaque on the wall says it was built by a
condominium in 1962 – whoever they may be.

JEDBURGH: The year of the Cuban Missile Crisis. Lot of people
got shit-scared that year.

5:45 The hall outside the Committee Room, House of Commons. Day

HARCOURT *sits reading the* Financial Times, *when the* USHER *calls his name.*

USHER: Mr Harcourt.

> (HARCOURT *rises to his feet. He walks across the hall and into the Committee Room.*)

5:46 The Committee Room, House of Commons. Day

HARCOURT *crosses the room and sits down on a chair opposite the table at which the committee members sit.*

[CHILWELL: Mr Harcourt, it says here that you are on
> secondment from Lloyds and are at present attached to the
> Cabinet Office . . .

HARCOURT: Yes.

CHILWELL: Perhaps you could tell the committee exactly what
> your present function is?

HARCOURT: I'm what might be called a troubleshooter.

POLLY PELHAM: Does that mean you are in Intelligence?

HARCOURT: No ma'am. I'm a lawyer.]*

BEWES: Mr Harcourt, who or what first drew your attention to the
> present situation at IIF?

HARCOURT: The Treasury. They had heard that the company was
> about to be taken over by one of the big American energy
> corporations and they wanted a fix on it.

BEWES: How long ago was that?

HARCOURT: A year.

CHILWELL: And what was your reaction?

HARCOURT: Surprise. I wasn't able to understand what an
> industrial giant like the Fusion Corporation of Kansas would
> want with a low-grade storage plant in Yorkshire.
> (*After such a disparaging answer,* BEWES *feels forced to defend
> Bennett's company.*)

BEWES: They hold the Queen's Award for Industry . . .
> (CHILWELL *swiftly cuts in.*)

CHILWELL: So, what, on reflection, made this company so
> interesting to the Fusion Corporation?

HARCOURT: Well, it had to be something quite unique, and I

---

*Sections in square brackets were omitted in the final edit of Episode Five.

narrowed it down to one possibility – the ability to
manufacture plutonium . . . illegally.
[POLLY PELHAM: So you and Gaia came to the same conclusion?
HARCOURT: We both read the Marsh Report.]

5:47   The vaulted chamber, Northmoor
JEDBURGH *and* CRAVEN *have finished the meal.* JEDBURGH
unscrews the cap of a big cigar tube. CRAVEN *contemplates him and
suddenly gives voice to his suspicions that* JEDBURGH *is playing a
double game.*
CRAVEN: They know we're down here, don't they?
JEDBURGH: Yes.
CRAVEN: Who told them?
JEDBURGH: It could've been anybody.
    (CRAVEN *backs off from accusing him directly.*)
CRAVEN: What exactly were your orders?
JEDBURGH: To get into the ball-park and steal the ball.
CRAVEN: The plutonium?
JEDBURGH: That's right.
CRAVEN: (*Curtly*) You should have told me that up there – now
    let's get going.
    (*He is angry.*)
JEDBURGH: You're a driven man, aren't you, Craven? Here we are
    on the floor of Plato's cave,* with food from Harrods and a
    whole hillside of wine, and all you can think about is 'let's get
    going'.
CRAVEN: That's right.
    (CRAVEN *stands and trudges towards the exit.* JEDBURGH *follows
    him.*)
CRAVEN: Well, what will you do with it, when you've got it?
JEDBURGH: Hand it over to my superiors.
CRAVEN: What will they do with it?
JEDBURGH: Beats me. But Grogan won't get it. That's what
    counts.
CRAVEN: Why do you hate Grogan so much?
JEDBURGH: Because of who he is.
CRAVEN: And who is he?

*The reference is to Plato's discussion of illusion and reality in Book VII of *The
Republic*. Like his prisoners held in a cave who mistake the shadows on the wall for
reality, in this nuclear world it is hard to tell what is real and what is an illusion.

JEDBURGH: He's part of the Dark Forces who would rule this planet.

CRAVEN: You believe in all that stuff?

JEDBURGH: Yeah, sure. Why not? Look at yourself. You think of yourself as an English provincial detective . . . whose daughter died in tragic circumstances. Yet where she fell a well sprang, flowers grew. Now what kind of power is that?

(CRAVEN *is silenced for a moment.*)

CRAVEN: I don't know.

(*At the door of the chamber there is a large statue of Jesus. Both their torches focus on it before they disappear into the tunnel.*)

JEDBURGH: (*Voice over*) Mind you, I do have a personal grudge against Grogan – his great, great, great-grandfather killed my great, great, great, great-grandfather. We Jedburghs never forget . . .

(*As his voice fades, we pan up to the figure of Christ.*)

5:48 The Committee Room, House of Commons. Day

HARCOURT *is still in the witness chair, facing the somewhat sceptical committee, but he continues to answer the questions with an imperturbable air.* PENDLETON *enters discreetly, sits down, and writes a brief message which will be passed to* HARCOURT *as the scene progresses.*

HARCOURT: My first suspicions were aroused when I read the Marsh Report . . . which suggested that certain radioactive isotopes were found in the Corrie Reservoir. Now, I feel that that report motivated the Gaia organization into planning their raid.

CHILWELL: The Marsh Report, if I remember correctly, discounted Northmoor. It believed that Sellafield was responsible for the emissions.

HARCOURT: I think you will find if you read between the lines, that that was not the case with Northmoor. It was simply assumed that since no plutonium was being reprocessed, it could not be held responsible.

BEWES: Mr Chairman, this line of argument is getting us nowhere. The Marsh Report on the Corrie Reservoir has been completely discredited, not least by Friends of the Earth. This witness's evidence does not stand up. It has been introduced simply to discredit Northmoor and to scupper the take-over

by the Fusion Corporation of Kansas, which is in the interests
of the whole country as well as of the nuclear industry itself.
(HARCOURT *reads the note which has been handed to him:*
'Confirmation from Godbolt – they're in.')
We are all looking forward to a great deal more privatization
of this sector and it's a great pity to see so many obstacles
being put in the way of this process.

CHILWELL: I must ask you, Mr Harcourt, do you have any prima
facie evidence, apart from the body in the Corrie Reservoir,
which suggests the existence of any kind of illegal reprocessing
at Northmoor?

HARCOURT: Not at this precise moment, no.

CHILWELL: I'm afraid, Mr Harcourt, we really can't take all this
on board without it. You may be perfectly right, but as long
as the evidence remains purely circumstantial, I regret we
cannot act upon it. However, your views will be noted.

5:49   A tunnel, the outer circle, Northmoor

CRAVEN *and* JEDBURGH *move cautiously forward. It is very dark.*
CRAVEN *shines his torch round and catches sight of something on the*
wall. He calls to JEDBURGH.

CRAVEN: Jedburgh!

JEDBURGH: Yeah!

(JEDBURGH *moves over to where* CRAVEN *is standing.* CRAVEN
shines his torch on the wall to reveal the word 'GAIA' in big
chalked letters.

JEDBURGH *and* CRAVEN *quicken their step. The sound of water*
is audible. Ahead they see a sluice gate. Their torches focus on it.
They walk towards it and peer through. Behind the mesh they see
the remains of a body. JEDBURGH *finds the handle that opens the*
gate.)

JEDBURGH: Craven, watch yourself.

(CRAVEN *moves away and* JEDBURGH *turns the handle. As there*
is a gush of water and as the gate rises the remaining bodies of the
Gaia expedition are carried out in the tide. CRAVEN *turns to look*
at one of the bodies which is already decomposing. He looks at
JEDBURGH.

They climb under the sluice gate, where they find yet another body.
CRAVEN *switches on his Geiger counter which immediately*
registers radiation.

CRAVEN *moves ahead.* JEDBURGH *follows. The Geiger counter is*

143

*working overtime. They proceed along the tunnel until a vast
cavern opens up ahead of them.)*

5:50   The hot cell cavern, Northmoor
*They halt at the end of the tunnel. The Geiger counter now registers
intense radiation. Below them on the floor of the cavern is the building
which houses the hot cell. The body of a worker can be seen lying on the
platform outside. They stare down at the sinister building and then*
JEDBURGH *slowly begins to descend towards it.*
JEDBURGH: It's pretty, isn't it?
(*Both men are ignoring the danger posed by the radiation, although
they are clearly conscious of it.*)
Oh, oh, look at this!
(CRAVEN *follows* JEDBURGH *down towards the platform. On the
way they stumble across another dead body – that of a guard.*
JEDBURGH *crosses to examine it.*)
There's been a hell of an accident here . . . Gaia – they must
have blown the whole cell.
(*He hesitates.* CRAVEN *looks at the guard, at the building, and
then at* JEDBURGH.)
CRAVEN: I want to go on.
JEDBURGH: You're crazy, you know that?
(*They continue their descent towards the building.*)

**5:51   The hall outside the Committee Room, House of
Commons. Day**
GROGAN *sits by himself, listless and uneasy, listening to the murmur of
argumentative voices in the Committee Room.* PENDLETON *is the only
other person with him. He looks at* GROGAN *curiously.*
PENDLETON: Still running on Houston time?
GROGAN: Not quite. I just get the feeling I'm in the wrong place.

5:52   The hot cell cavern, Northmoor
JEDBURGH *and* CRAVEN *reach the platform outside the hot cell
building. They clamber on to it. For one moment they just stand looking
at the desolation. Then* JEDBURGH *walks to the corner of the building.*
JEDBURGH: Come on.
(CRAVEN *looks up. He catches sight of a camera.*)
CRAVEN: Jedburgh, camera.
(JEDBURGH *turns and aims his automatic at the camera. He
blasts it with one shot.*)

JEDBURGH: Let's go.
> (CRAVEN *follows* JEDBURGH *round the corner of the building*.)

5:53 The Operations Room, Northmoor
CHILDS *and* CONNORS *watch the monitor as* JEDBURGH *destroys the camera in the hot cell cavern.*
CHILDS: I don't believe it. They're through to the hot cell.
CONNORS: How long can they survive?
CHILDS: Twenty minutes at the outside.
CONNORS: Good.

5:54 The antechamber, hot cell building, Northmoor
CRAVEN *and* JEDBURGH *enter. The noise in the antechamber is deafening – every alarm and buzzer in the building is going. They have been sounding since the accident.* CRAVEN *makes straight for the window overlooking the cavern, aware that their cover is now blown.* JEDBURGH *glances through another window and then enters a side room. He selects a radiation suit and walks back to* CRAVEN *with the suit.*
CRAVEN: You going in here?
JEDBURGH: Yeah. That's where they keep the plutonium. Look, go outside and hold them off – they'll be here in a minute.
CRAVEN: I'm staying here.
JEDBURGH: What for? Look, I don't need you in here. I need you out there.
CRAVEN: How long do you need?
JEDBURGH: As long as it takes.
> (CRAVEN *takes his automatic and goes back out into the cavern.*)

5:55 The hot cell cavern, Northmoor
CRAVEN *closes the door of the hot cell building and turns round to look up into the cavern. He has a feeling he is being watched. He walks along the platform to the end and surveys the cavern again. It is very quiet.*

5:56 The antechamber, hot cell building, Northmoor
JEDBURGH *makes his way towards the hot cell chamber. He pulls his helmet over his head.*
JEDBURGH: (*To himself*) To know is to die!

5:57 The hot cell cavern, Northmoor
CRAVEN *lines up large drums in an attempt to form a barricade. He knows the guards will be coming for them.*

5:58 Inside the hot cell chamber, Northmoor
JEDBURGH *approaches the hot cell bunker. Peering through the glass he can see the plutonium bars lying in separate little compartments.*

5:59 The hot cell cavern, Northmoor
CRAVEN *rolls another drum towards the barricade. He pauses and removes his helmet to wipe the sweat from his brow.*

5:60 Inside the hot cell chamber, Northmoor
JEDBURGH *smashes the glass covering the plutonium bars.*

5:61 The hot cell cavern, Northmoor
CRAVEN *has up-ended another drum to form part of the barricade. He kneels down behind it and looks up into the cavern, checking angles of fire. Then he stands and returns to the side of the building to fetch another drum.*

5:62 Inside the hot cell chamber, Northmoor
JEDBURGH *opens a cupboard, where he finds a stack of plutonium containers.*

5:63 The hot cell cavern, Northmoor
As CRAVEN *rolls another drum across the platform he hears a voice from above.*

CONNORS: Craven!
> (CRAVEN *looks up into the cavern. He sees* CONNORS *standing against the rock dressed in a radiation suit and carrying a gun. Several more suited and armed guards move into view. As* CRAVEN *looks round he sees the rim of the cavern is studded with masked and radiation-suited guards, who seem to occupy every vantage point.*
> CONNOR's *voice booms out over the loudspeaker.*)

CONNORS: (*Voice over*) Stay where you are!
> (CRAVEN *ducks behind a steel drum. A fusillade of shots echoes round the cavern.* CRAVEN *pulls out his automatic.*)

146

5:64   Inside the hot cell chamber, Northmoor

JEDBURGH *carries the empty plutonium containers over to the hot cell.
He puts them down on top of the hot cell, puts his hand through the
broken glass and extracts a bar of plutonium. This he carefully puts into
one of the containers. Outside, there is an exchange of gunfire.*

5:65   The hot cell cavern, Northmoor

CRAVEN *sits behind the drums, re-loading his automatic. The guards
begin to move slowly and awkwardly down the shale towards him.*
CONNORS's *voice booms out.*

CONNORS: (*Voice over*) Craven! The radiation in this cave is
     deadly. Your chances of survival are slim. Give up before it's
     too late.]
     (*At this point one of the guards makes a dash across the bridge
     towards the first-floor platform.* CRAVEN *turns towards him and
     fires, bringing him down. The guards continue to advance down
     the shale towards the plant.* CRAVEN *looks towards the hot cell
     door. He dives along the corridor and flattens himself on the floor
     beside the only bit of cover.*)

5:66   Inside the hot cell chamber, Northmoor

JEDBURGH *opens a Harrods bag and puts the containers into it.*

5:67   The hot cell cavern, Northmoor

The guards descending the terraces bear down upon CRAVEN. *There is
a wild exchange of gunfire.* CRAVEN *makes for the door to the hot cell
building.*

5:68   The hot cell chamber, Northmoor

CRAVEN: Jedburgh, they're here.
     (JEDBURGH *is loading the last of the bars of plutonium into the
     Harrods bag. He looks up.*)
JEDBURGH: Get out of here – the lifts!
     (*He points towards the service lift foyer.*)
     The lifts!
     (CRAVEN *makes for the lifts while* JEDBURGH *finishes removing
     the plutonium.*)

5:69   The foyer, hot cell chamber, Northmoor

CRAVEN *reaches the entrance to the foyer and is confronted by the open
service lift. On the floor is the body of a technician, lying half in and*

half out of the lift. The lift door, obstructed by the body, moves back and forth. CRAVEN *puts his shoulder against the lift door and wedges it open while he begins to haul out the corpse.*

JEDBURGH *appears at the door of the foyer carrying his rucksack and the Harrods bag. He steps into the lift which* CRAVEN *is holding open for him and the door closes.*

5:70 The Operations Room, Northmoor

CHILDS *watches the action on a monitor.* CONNORS *speaks from the hot cell cavern.*

CONNORS: (*Voice over*) They're both inside. We've got them.

CHILDS: They've got the plutonium, for Christ's sake. They're in the service lift.

CONNORS: (*Voice over*) I thought it was jammed.

CHILDS: They've moved the body. They're on their way up.

CONNORS: (*Voice over*) You'll have to cut the power.

CHILDS: I can't cut the power. There's no back-up system.

CONNORS: (*Voice over*) Leave it to me.

5:71 Inside the service lift, Northmoor

CRAVEN *helps* JEDBURGH *to remove his helmet.*

JEDBURGH: Craven, I'm letting you out at the next floor. I want you to make a run for it.

CRAVEN: Where are you going?

JEDBURGH: To the top.

CRAVEN: With the plutonium?

JEDBURGH: I'll give you one bar. That's all you need for evidence.

CRAVEN: What happens to the rest?

(JEDBURGH *loses his temper.*)

JEDBURGH: What do you keep asking that question for? I told you, I don't know. We're both on the same side, so what the hell does it matter?

(*The lift stops and the doors open.* CRAVEN *and* JEDBURGH *stand back against the sides and look out cautiously.*)

CRAVEN: It matters.

(*There is an ominous sound as* JEDBURGH *cocks his automatic.* CRAVEN *looks down at the gun, then up at* JEDBURGH.)

You'd do that? Wouldn't you?

(*It is obvious from* JEDBURGH'*s eyes that he would.*)

JEDBURGH: Run like hell, Craven. Keep them busy.

(JEDBURGH *hands him one bar of plutonium.* CRAVEN *steps o*

148

of the lift. In the distance he can hear the yells of approaching guards. JEDBURGH *presses the button. The lift door begins to close.*)

Craven, if we make it, I'll see you in Scotland.

CRAVEN: Where?

JEDBURGH: You're the detective, find me.

(*He disappears from view as the lift door shuts.*)

[5:72   The Operations Room, Northmoor

CONNORS: (*Voice over*) Where are they now?

(CHILDS *follows* CRAVEN *on the monitor.*)

CHILDS: Second level. Craven's just got out. No sign of Jedburgh.

CONNORS: (*Voice over*) Which way is Craven heading?

CHILDS: G2. Loading bays.

CONNORS: (*Voice over*) Right.]

5:73   A tunnel, level G, Northmoor

CRAVEN *runs along the tunnel clutching the plutonium.*

5:74   The loading bays, level G, Northmoor

The tunnel widens into a cavern and CRAVEN *finds himself in the loading bays. He dives through a door marked 'Danger. Critical Zone'. Red lights are flashing. Gun in hand,* CRAVEN *edges his way round the corner and into a larger tunnel. Suddenly there is a flood of light as two Landrovers behind him switch on their headlights.*

5:75   The tunnel, level G, Northmoor

CRAVEN *runs along the tunnel pursued by the two Landrovers. Turning a corner, he sees a small brick building. He dashes inside.*

5:76   The Fire Control Centre, level G, Northmoor

CRAVEN *shuts the door and bolts it. He fumbles for the light and switches it on. He looks around the room. It looks like a TV control room, with dozens of telephones covered in cobwebs and lots of abandoned equipment. He can hear the guards banging on the door outside. He stumbles across the room and feels suddenly sick.*

5:77   The tunnel, level G, Northmoor

The Landrovers come to a halt at the end of the tunnel. CONNORS *and his* MEN *get out.* CONNORS *flicks on his radio telephone.*

CONNORS: He's in MOD 109.

5:78 The Operations Room, Northmoor

CHILDS *tries to find a monitor which covers* 109.

CONNORS: (*Voice over*) Is there another exit?

> (CHILDS *looks at a chart.*)

CHILDS: MOD 109 . . .

> (*The clerk already has the right chart and is looking it up.*
> CHILDS *quotes from it.*)
> War office. Fire Control. Northern Command Rocket Sites.
> Dismantled 1958.

CONNORS: (*Voice over*) Exits?

CHILDS: Just the one.

CONNORS: (*Voice over*) Got him.

5:79 The Fire Control Centre, Northmoor

Abruptly we hear the power cut off and the fan which pumps air into the room whines down till the room is silent. One by one the six bulbs which light the room also go out, till only two remain. Meanwhile, CRAVEN hunts the room, desperate to make contact with the outside world. He picks up a telephone and rattles the prongs. But he gets no dialling tone. He tries another, then another.

5:80 The tunnel, level G, Northmoor

Two Landrovers drive up and stop. The men jump out and begin to unload gas equipment.

5:81 The Fire Control Centre, Northmoor

CRAVEN *continues to look for a phone with an outside line. He picks up one phone after another but they are all dead.*

CRAVEN: Come on!

5:82 A basement corridor, Downing Street. Night

A telephone is heard ringing in one of the offices.

5:83 The Fire Control Centre, Northmoor

CRAVEN *has picked up a telephone that is connected. Then he sees the gas coming in through a vent in the wall. He dashes across to it and shuts it. But the gas has already begun to affect him. He coughs, and staggers back to the desk to try the telephone again.*

5:84 A basement corridor, Downing Street. Night

A DUTY OFFICER *is doing her rounds. She hears the telephone ringing* in one of the offices. *She makes her way down the corridor looking for the source of the noise. The sound of the telephone gets louder and louder.*

5:85 **The Fire Control Centre, Northmoor**
The room is filling with gas. CRAVEN, *still coughing, holds on to the phone. He can hear the number ringing at the other end.*

5:86 **A basement office, Downing Street. Night**
The DUTY OFFICER *opens an office and enters. She switches on the overhead light and sees a telephone on the desk. She walks over to it and picks it up.*
DUTY OFFICER: Downing Street?
    (*But the ringing continues and she realizes there must be another phone. She puts down the receiver and finds a second phone behind her, under a pile of papers.*)

5:87 **The Fire Control Centre, Northmoor**
CRAVEN *holds on to the phone, desperately waiting for someone to answer.*

5:88 **The basement office, Downing Street. Night**
The DUTY OFFICER *finally uncovers the telephone and picks it up.*
DUTY OFFICER: Hello, Downing Street.*

5:89 **The Fire Control Centre, Northmoor**
CRAVEN, *knowing that* HARCOURT *and* PENDLETON *are employed by the Cabinet Office, yells down the line.*
CRAVEN: Get me Pendleton!

* It is presumed that the Fire Control Centre at Northmoor formed part of a 1950's defence set-up and that when it was dismantled, this direct line was overlooked. In the transmitted version of the series the words 'Downing Street' were accidentally omitted, making nonsense of Craven's response in the next scene.

Fusion

6:1 Craven's room, radiation ward. Day

PENDLETON *walks up the hospital corridor and enters the ward where*
CRAVEN *is lying alone.*

PENDLETON: Where's the plutonium?

CRAVEN: With Jedburgh.

PENDLETON: Where's Jedburgh?

    (CRAVEN *looks up at* PENDLETON.)

CRAVEN: I don't know.

    (PENDLETON *crosses to the window and looks out. The room is*
    on the ground floor of the hospital. Outside he can see the police
    car parked on the drive and HARCOURT *pacing around.*)

PENDLETON: What happened?

CRAVEN: We found the hot cell.

PENDLETON: And?

CRAVEN: Where am I?

PENDLETON: You are at an American Air Force hospital.

CRAVEN: I feel sick.

PENDLETON: Radiation, Craven. Nausea's the first of its
    symptoms.

    (PENDLETON *crosses to the table and pours him a glass of water.*)

CRAVEN: How bad is it?

    (PENDLETON *cradles* CRAVEN's *head in his arms.* CRAVEN *looks*
    up at him.)

PENDLETON: It's bad.

    (*He puts the glass to* CRAVEN's *mouth.*)

    It's important, old chap, that you tell me everything you know.

    (CRAVEN *takes a sip of water.*)

6:2 Outside the radiation ward. Day

PENDLETON *leaves the hospital and walks down the path to where*
HARCOURT *is waiting in the Mercedes.*

PENDLETON: They found the hot cell. It had been sealed off. Apparently there had been some sort of explosion, resulting in massive radiation. Anyway, Jedburgh went in and located the plutonium and carried it out in a Harrods bag.
    (PENDLETON *gets into the car.*)
HARCOURT: Has Craven got any idea where Jedburgh went?
PENDLETON: He says his last words were something about 'meeting Moriarty at the Falls'!*
HARCOURT: If there is an Irish component to this, I shall retire.†

6:3   Craven's room, radiation ward. Day
CRAVEN *lies back in his bed. He feels exhausted. His eyes close. He falls asleep.*

6:4   Dream sequence, radiation ward. Day
EMMA, *dressed in a white coat, walks down the empty hospital ward until she comes to Craven's bed.*

6:5   Craven's room, radiation ward. Day
CRAVEN *wakes up. A nurse is staring at him. She is wearing regulation white overalls.* CRAVEN *stares back at her before speaking.*
CRAVEN: They all drowned . . .
    (*He drifts back to sleep. The nurse walks away down to the end of the ward.*)

6:6   Dream sequence, radiation ward. Day
EMMA *sits on bed.*
EMMA: Dad?
    (CRAVEN *opens his eyes.*)
CRAVEN: Emm . . .
    (EMMA *holds out a small black flower.*)
    What's that?
EMMA: A present.
CRAVEN: It's black.
    (*She stretches across and puts it into the glass of water* PENDLETON *had given him.*)

---

*This line was omitted in the final edit of Episode Five.
†Harcourt deliberately misunderstands the reference to Sherlock Holmes, preferring to play on the mock-horrific thought that the IRA might be involved.

EMMA: It's an Arctic flower.
CRAVEN: They all drowned.
EMMA: I know. I was there . . .
CRAVEN: Why didn't you tell me?
EMMA: Dad, you were on their side.
CRAVEN: No!
    (CRAVEN *wakes up*.)

6:7   A disused quarry. Day

Nallers's car sweeps on to the flat, puddle-strewn amphitheatre of the quarry and parks by a couple of cars. There is not much to see but three cars, two with their doors open, and three corpses sprawling out. A couple of CIA agents wander from one to the other.

NEILSON, a senior CIA official, stands watching NALLERS.

NALLERS gets out of his car and crosses towards him.

NEILSON: Morning. I'm Neilson.
NALLERS: Nallers.
    (*They both turn and survey the scene of carnage.*)
    What happened?
NEILSON: There's been a shoot-out. Jedburgh and three of my
    men.
NALLERS: Where's Jedburgh?
NEILSON: He got away.
NALLERS: What about the plutonium?
NEILSON: He took it with him.
    (*There is a shout from up the hill.*)
AMERICAN: (*Distant voice*) Sir!
    (*The two men look his way.*)
    (*Distant voice*) We found another one.
NEILSON: Four of my men . . .
    (*Pendleton's car trundles into the quarry.*)
NALLERS: What about the police?
NEILSON: No, I haven't called them yet.
    (PENDLETON *gets out of his car. As* NALLERS *returns to his car, their paths cross.* PENDLETON *recognizes* NALLERS *and, curious that he should be involved, turns to look at him. Then he walks over to* NEILSON. *He shakes his hand and looks around.*)
PENDLETON: What happened?

6:8 A golf course, Scotland.* Day
A woman golfer strikes the ball from the middle of the course. It sails down the fairway. The ball bounces on the green and a hearty male voice cries out.

HEARTY GOLFER: Well done, Jemima!

JEMIMA: This girl's no slouch.

(*The* HEARTY GOLFER *shapes up for the putt.*)

HEARTY GOLFER: Right, Morag. I'll go with the four – put the pressure on . . . OK?

(JEMIMA *walks on to the green to look at her shot.*)

JEMIMA: (*To* JEDBURGH) You're in with a chance, my dear.

(JEDBURGH *walks across to* PETE, *the caddy, selects his putter and surveys the ground between the pin and the ball.*)

JEDBURGH: What do you think, Pete?

PETE: Six inches to the right.

(JEDBURGH *returns to the ball and lifts his putter. He finds it difficult to focus.*)

JEDBURGH: Piece of cake.

(*He addresses the ball.* JEMIMA *removes the flag. It swims in front of* JEDBURGH's *eyes. He opens his legs wider, addresses the ball again, then strokes it towards the pin. But his concentration is now gone. He looks up at the sky, trying to stay on his feet. When he hears the ball spin into the bottom of the metal hole, he is almost too far gone to fake surprise.*)

JEMIMA: Bloody good shot.

HEARTY GOLFER: Well done, sir.

(JEDBURGH *waves his putter and accepts the congratulations.*)

6:9 Outside Mrs Girvan's guest house, Crieff. Day
Jemima's car stops outside the guest house. JEDBURGH *gets out of the car*

JEMIMA: Home again, home again, jiggedy jig. Are you all right, old sport?

JEDBURGH: Yes, fine.

(*But he does not look well.*)

JEMIMA: You're not looking too good.

JEDBURGH: I think that old lady in there is trying to poison me. I'll see you later.

(JEMIMA *drives off.* JEDBURGH *walks towards the front door, carrying his golf clubs.*)

*The Scottish locations were originally included as a homage to John Buchan.

6:10   The hall, Mrs Girvan's guest house. Day

JEDBURGH *enters. He makes for the stairs, but* MRS GIRVAN *has been waiting for him. She is carrying a small plastic airtight box.*

MRS GIRVAN: Mr Jedburgh. You forgot your sandwich again today, Mr Jedburgh.

JEDBURGH: Mrs Girvan, mince between two slices of white bread is not my idea of lunch. I'd rather eat the damned Bible.

MRS GIRVAN: Mr Jedborough!

   (JEDBURGH *corrects her.*)

JEDBURGH: *Jedburgh.*

   (*He continues up the stairs.*)

6:11   Jedburgh's room, guest house. Day

JEDBURGH *is on the phone. He finally gets through. He leans forward and speaks loudly.*

JEDBURGH: Hernandez? *Cómo estad?* Darius Jedburgh. You requited me. Look, I'm the *hombre* who put the bomb in your bus about a year or so ago – knocked out about half your . . . Yeah. That's right. Yes, the gringo from Texas. Listen to me, Hernandez, I'm taking a vacation in Scotland – it's in Great Britain. Yeah. Kilmichael. Kil, as in the word, you know, death, murder; Michael, as in St Michael – the patron saint of the CIA . . . I know he is your patron saint, Hernandez, but haven't you wised up yet? Every time you pray to him he sends a copy to the Agency . . .

6:12   A call box on an A road. Day

CLEMENTINE *stops the car a few metres past the call box. Behind it Forestry Commission land slopes down towards the trees and is covered with bracken, ferns and saplings. She gets out, leaving the engine running, and walks round to the back of the car. She unlocks the boot and opens it. Close by we hear the rushing water of a stream. She pulls out a bag stuffed with men's clothes and walks with it to the side of the road and looks down into the bracken.*

CRAVEN *emerges from the trees. He is wearing a doctor's operating theatre smock.* CLEMENTINE *tosses down the bundle of clothes.* CRAVEN *picks them up and vanishes again.* CLEMENTINE *walks back to the telephone box and goes inside.*

6:13 Inside the call box. Day

CLEMENTINE *dials Chilwell's number. We intercut with his office in Whitehall.* HARCOURT *takes the call.*

HARCOURT: Harcourt.

CLEMENTINE: It's Clementine. I'm with Craven.

HARCOURT: What made him skip?

CLEMENTINE: He saw a lead coffin. It had his name on it.

HARCOURT: Well, at least he knows his days are numbered.

CLEMENTINE: Yes, he does. That's why he wants to find Jedburgh. And he wants a guarantee that he won't be hassled.

HARCOURT: Will he get the plutonium back?

CLEMENTINE: Yes, he feels that's his responsibility.

HARCOURT: Well, tell him to try Scotland. Grogan's there. He's at a conference at the Gleneagles Hotel.

(CLEMENTINE *puts the telephone down.*)

6:14 Chilwell's office, Whitehall. Day

CHILWELL *comes into the office.*

CHILWELL: This business at Northmoor.

HARCOURT: Yes?

CHILWELL: The Minister wants to know whether you sanctioned the operation.

HARCOURT: Well, in a roundabout way, yes.

6:15 The drive, Gleneagles Hotel, Scotland. Day

A sports car turns off the road into the drive which leads to the hotel. The driver is JEMIMA.

6:16 Outside Gleneagles Hotel. Day

The flags of the Nato countries are streaming on the flagpoles. A number of guards are on duty. Jemima's car sweeps towards the front entrance of the hotel.

She stops and JEDBURGH *gets out. He turns to say thank you to* JEMIMA.

LAWSON *comes forward to meet him. He is accompanied by an Italian-looking American,* BARLOTTI.

LAWSON: Darius Jedburgh?

JEDBURGH: Hello, Tuffy. How they hanging?

LAWSON: Never better. This is Carlo Barlotti. Brookings Institute.

BARLOTTI: Hello, Colonel, how are you?

JEDBURGH: Pleased to meet you.

(JEDBURGH *shakes hands with* BARLOTTI, *then looks at* LAWSON.)
Is Jerry Grogan coming?
LAWSON: Yes. But I'm told he'll be late. Business in London.
(BARLOTTI *follows* JEDBURGH *and* LAWSON *inside*.)

6:17   The Minister's office, Whitehall. Day

The MINISTER *looks up from his desk.* HARCOURT *stands by the other desk. He has a report in his hand.*
MINISTER: How many bodies?
HARCOURT: Four, Minister.
MINISTER: And three at the plant?
HARCOURT: Makes seven.
MINISTER: How long can this sort of thing go on for?
HARCOURT: Until he's caught.
MINISTER: Do you think he's mad?
HARCOURT: Well, he wasn't before. But he certainly is now.
(*He hands the report to the* MINISTER. *The* MINISTER *looks at it.*)
MINISTER: Now, this is the report on IIF.
HARCOURT: It's a copy. We sent the original to the Director of Public Prosecutions.
MINISTER: Why?
HARCOURT: Because it proves that there is a hot cell at Northmoor – built in contravention of IAEA* safeguards.
MINISTER: It was never under IAEA safeguards.
HARCOURT: The contamination in the reservoir can now be traced directly to it. They are liable to prosecution under the Radioactive Substances Act of 1960.
MINISTER: Is this really within your brief, Harcourt?
HARCOURT: Northmoor was producing plutonium illegally, contrary to the Nuclear Installations Act of 1968, the NPT and every other international agreement. They are breaking every law in the nuclear rule book.
MINISTER: Northmoor was producing very small quantities of plutonium, by a secret laser process which was classified as experimental. I knew about it and so did a number of my colleagues.
HARCOURT: You knew about it?

*International Atomic Energy Agency.

MINISTER: From day one. As an experimental station, with a defence component, it is not subject to any of the restrictions you have just quoted.

HARCOURT: I don't understand. I mean, if you knew what caused the contamination, why was I brought in to investigate it?

MINISTER: Because the Americans became suspicious.

HARCOURT: So my involvement was purely part of a deception plan?

MINISTER: Yes, if you like.

HARCOURT: But you must have known that I would find out what was going on in the end?

MINISTER: Yes, of course I did. I just thought you might take a little longer to do it, that's all – and you might have used slightly less unorthodox methods of breaching the mine than the likes of Craven and Jedburgh.

HARCOURT: I will not withdraw that report.

MINISTER: Well, that's up to the Cabinet. But I'd like to suggest that it's your duty to get the plutonium back, since you were ultimately responsible for its removal.

6:18   Outside a small country railway station. Day

CLEMENTINE and CRAVEN are sitting in the car. CLEMENTINE is very aware that this might be the last time she will see CRAVEN.

CLEMENTINE: How long have you got?

CRAVEN: Three days like this, and then it's rapidly downhill . . . or so I'm told.

CLEMENTINE: What are you going to do about it?

CRAVEN: I haven't – I don't know. I'd like to find Jedburgh first if I can.

CLEMENTINE: He still has the plutonium.

CRAVEN: I know . . .
(Silence.)

CLEMENTINE: You know I'm very fond of you . . . If there's any way I can. . . .

CRAVEN: You've already been an enormous help.

CLEMENTINE: You can't die alone, Ronnie . . .

CRAVEN: Why not? We all do, you know . . .
(There is a silence.)
I left a report of my investigations so far with my bank manager. (He begins to write a note to the bank manager.) If yo

give him this, he'll give the report to you. It was going to the
Chief Constable. Now I'd rather Gaia have it.
(*He looks up at her. There are tears in her eyes.*)
Don't try and come after me.

6:19   The small exhibition room, Gleneagles Hotel. Day
LAWSON *ushers* BARLOTTI *and* JEDBURGH *into the room, where a
number of Nato officers and civil servants are gathered loosely round a
table which carries the usual array of drinks. Among them is*
BENNETT, *who reacts with astonishment at Jedburgh's arrival.*
JEDBURGH *doesn't see him.*
As LAWSON *and* JEDBURGH *approach the table they meet* LEWMAR
and COLONEL DALY. LAWSON *introduces them.* JEDBURGH *sees*
BENNETT.
JEDBURGH: Hello, Bobby.
BENNETT: Hello. What the hell are you doing here?
JEDBURGH: I'm fulfilling a long-standing engagement.

6:20   The large exhibition room, Gleneagles Hotel. Day
There is a burst of applause as BARLOTTI, LAWSON, JEDBURGH,
LEWMAR *and* DALY *walk on to the stage.* LAWSON *approaches the
microphone and comes quickly to the point.*
LAWSON: Ladies and gentlemen, welcome to the second Nato
    Conference on Directed Energy Weapons.

6:21   Harcourt's office, Whitehall. Day
PENDLETON *picks up the telephone.*
PENDLETON: Hello, Pendleton.

6:22   A hallway, Gleneagles Hotel. Day
BENNETT *is on the telephone.*
BENNETT: This is Bennett.
PENDLETON: (*Voice over*) Who?
BENNETT: Bennett. I'm speaking from the Gleneagles Hotel in
    Scotland. Jedburgh's here . . .
    (*He listens to* PENDLETON's *exclamation then continues.*)
    At the conference . . . on the platform . . . about to take part
    in a debate on the High Frontier.
    (*Cut to* PENDLETON.)
BENNETT: (*Voice over*) What are you going to do about it?

6:23   The large exhibition room, Gleneagles Hotel. Day

LAWSON *continues with his opening address.*

LAWSON: The question is, 'How high is high?' (*He looks around at the large audience of generals and civil servants.*) With the latest development in star wars technology are we on the edge of a new space race? And what does that presage for the future of that other race, the human race?

6:24   The Minister's office, Whitehall. Day

PENDLETON *opens the door.* HARCOURT *is arguing with the* MINISTER.

HARCOURT: I have my own sources in Washington. They have sent me a complete rundown of what's going on there.
(PENDLETON *enters.*)

MINISTER: If you believe what comes out of Washington, you're naïve.
(*He looks at* PENDLETON.)

PENDLETON: I've had a call from Bennett – Jedburgh's at Gleneagles and he's not playing golf.

6:25   Gleneagles Hotel. Day

A helicopter arrives in the grounds. BENNETT *waits for it to land.* GROGAN *gets out.* BENNETT *greets him and ushers him towards the hotel.*

GROGAN: Bobby – what's up?

BENNETT: There's no time to talk. You'll have to go straight on to the platform.

GROGAN: Where's Jedburgh?

BENNETT: Inside.

6:26   The large exhibition room, Gleneagles Hotel. Day

LAWSON *is introducing* JEDBURGH.

LAWSON: Darius Jedburgh is an old friend.
(*Applause.* GROGAN *and* BENNETT *enter the hall.* GROGAN *stops momentarily on seeing* JEDBURGH. JEDBURGH, *on the platform, sees him. They stare at each other. Then* GROGAN *makes his way forward. Meanwhile* LAWSON *is completing his introduction.*)

For several years before his posting to London as an energy attaché at the US Embassy Colonel Jedburgh reported directly to the Director of Scientific Intelligence at Langley. In his time he has also been a member of the Standing Committee on Nuclear Materials Safeguards and the International Anti-terrorism Committee.

(GROGAN *makes his way on to the stage.*)

Finally, I'm sure that my last guest needs no introduction. Our first nuclear 'entrepreneur', the President of the Fusion Corporation of Kansas, 'the Henry Ford of the sunrise industries', ladies and gentlemen, Jerry C. Grogan.

(*A loud and prolonged burst of applause follows as* GROGAN *takes his seat on the stage.*)

GROGAN: Hello, Darius.

(JEDBURGH *looks up.*)

Where's my plutonium?

(JEDBURGH *smiles at him and continues to clap.*)

LAWSON: And so, without more ado, to open our debate on the future of space, I call upon the President of the Fusion Corporation Kansas – Jerry Grogan.

(*Applause.* GROGAN *gets to his feet and goes up to the microphone.*)

GROGAN: Ladies and gentlemen, I must apologize for my late arrival. However, I did not want to leave London until I had confirmation that my company's bid for International Irradiated Fuels is to be allowed to stand. (*He looks up before delivering the punchline.*) It is.

(*There is prolonged cheering.* GROGAN *puts his hand out to* BENNETT.)

Bobby.

(BENNETT *stands up and together they share the applause.*)

6:27   The Great North Road. Day
Clementine's car at speed.

6:28   Inside Clementine's car. Day
CRAVEN *looks sick. He has a paroxysm of coughing. The radio is on.*

NEWSCASTER: (*Voice over*) The decision this morning to allow the bid from the Fusion Corporation of Kansas for International Irradiated Fuels – the private British nuclear waste plant – was greeted in the city with cautious optimism. Fusion, which is rumoured to be a strong contender for substantial contracts for President Reagan's 'star wars' programme, will bring to the British company fresh capital and a new sense of purpose.

There's still strong opposition to the sale in some quarters. At a Nato conference at Gleneagles Hotel this morning . . .

6:29   The large exhibition room, Gleneagles Hotel. Day

JEDBURGH *is listening to Grogan's speech.*

GROGAN: When we unlock a chain reaction, the energy which is contained in it was put there in the first ten seconds of the universe's existence. That is an awesome thing, ladies and gentlemen. We are tapping into the very source of God's creation. Today we have access to that power but we do not control it. And that is the sole purpose of my corporation – to find a way to control it. When we have done so, we can say for the first time in the history of the planet, man will be in charge.

(*Applause.*)

6:30   A single-track road beside a river, Scotland. Day

Clementine's car glides down a country lane and comes to a halt by the river. CRAVEN *leans out of the car and is violently sick. He gets out, walks towards the water, kneels down, cups his hands and begins to drink.*

EMMA: That's enough, Dad.

(CRAVEN *looks up. She has materialized again.*)

6:31   The large exhibition room, Gleneagles Hotel. Day

GROGAN: What we are trying to do in Kansas at the moment is to take the plutonium bomb and explode it, in a vessel not much larger than the circumference of my arms, and to contain the energy in there. By harnessing that energy we can direct it in the form of lasers half way across the world to shoot down enemy rockets before they leave their silos. That is the capability for which we are aiming. It will cost us billions of dollars to get there, but in the end it will be worth it.

(*Polite applause.*)

6:32   The river, Scotland. Day

CRAVEN *looks out across the river.* EMMA *stands beside him.*

EMMA: You're getting angry again.

CRAVEN: I'm dying.

EMMA: Do you regret it?

CRAVEN: I feel so much is left undone.

EMMA: Other people will continue the job. You'll be with me.

CRAVEN: I still don't understand.

EMMA: Dad, it's happened before, you know. Millions of years ago when the earth was cold, it looked as if life on the planet would cease to exist. But black flowers began to grow, multiplying across its face, till the entire landscape was covered with blooms. Slowly the blackness of the flowers sucked in the heat of the sun, and life began to evolve again. That is the power of Gaia.

CRAVEN: (*Grimly*) It will take more than a black flower to save us this time.

EMMA: This time when it comes it will melt the polar icecap. Millions will die. The planet will protect itself. It's important to realize that. If man is the enemy, it will destroy him.

CRAVEN: Is this some kind of warning?

EMMA: All I'm saying is, don't spend your last hours seeking revenge, Dad. The planet will do it for us . . . in time.
(*She disappears, and* CRAVEN *is left looking at the water and the trees . . .*)

6:33   Outside Gleneagles Hotel. Day
Nallers's Granada draws up and parks outside the hotel bar. NALLERS *gets out. Another* MAN *gets out, goes round to the back of the car and opens the boot.*

NALLERS *scans the front of the hotel and the environs with a soldier's expertise. He scribbles a note, folds it and places it behind the windscreen wipers. Then he walks towards the bar entrance.*

6:34   The large exhibition room, Gleneagles Hotel. Day
GROGAN *is still speaking.*

GROGAN: I believe that fusion motors will power the great spaceships of the twenty-first century which will leave the earth in their hundreds to colonize the solar system. That is ultimately what the phrase 'high frontier' means . . .

6:35   The small exhibition room, Gleneagles Hotel. Day
NALLERS *enters the room and looks around. He crosses to the drinks table.* GROGAN's *voice can be heard through a loudspeaker system.*

GROGAN: (*Voice over*) That is ultimately what the phrase 'high frontier' means . . . the historical expansion of man into space, with all the parallels it evokes of the rigours and heroism of America's nineteenth-century trek westward. Like our forefathers, we will be escaping poverty and tyranny and, as in the past, war will provide the anvil upon which our technologies will be forged.

(*During the speech* BENNETT *enters the room*)

BENNETT: The others?

NALLERS: On their way.

6:36   The large exhibition room, Gleneagles Hotel. Day

GROGAN *begins to sum up.*

GROGAN: I foresee within the next hundred years the beginning of man as an interplanetary being, a celestial warrior. And, furthermore, a solar empire for the United States of America, and her allies.

(*Applause.*)

Looking at our over-populated, over-exhausted planet, I don't see how we can turn our backs on such a future, no matter what it costs, or how long it takes.

(GROGAN *sits down beside* JEDBURGH. *There is prolonged applause and a standing ovation.* NALLERS *and* BENNETT *join* LAWSON *at the back of the hall.*)

6:37   Outside Gleneagles Hotel. Day

A Landrover pulls up behind Nallers's Granada. TWO MEN *get out. One of them picks up the folded note which has been left behind the windscreen wipers. He opens it and reads it.*

6:38   The large exhibition room, Gleneagles Hotel. Day

JEDBURGH *begins his speech casually.*

JEDBURGH: Ladies and gentlemen, thank you . . . 500,000 million dollars for a defence system for Washington DC seems a bit pricey to me. But then, I don't live there.

(*There is a wave of laughter from the audience. It encourages him. He begins his speech proper.*)

6:39   Outside the large exhibition room, Gleneagles Hotel. Day

BENNETT *and* LAWSON *exit from the Exhibition Room.*

BENNETT: He has to be stopped.

LAWSON: But he's an accredited speaker.

BENNETT: The man is sick.

(The two 'undercover' men come into shot. BENNETT *and* LAWSON *pause while they pass. They enter the Exhibition Room.* LAWSON *waits until they have gone.)*

LAWSON: This audience is 100 per cent secure. They can take anything he can throw at them.

(BENNETT looks at him and gives up.)

6:40 The large exhibition room, Gleneagles Hotel. Day

BENNETT *enters the room. The two undercover men are now at the back of the room standing beside* NALLERS.

JEDBURGH: Jerry Grogan suggests that in a hundred years from now the human race will leave the planet and move into space. Now, Jerry is a hell of a salesman. He has the gift of making such an unappetizing idea sound attractive. The way Jerry tells it, it sounds like an extension of the old Oregon Trail. It calls for the same 'American' virtues: self-reliance, independence, know-how. But it's not going to be that way. In this new international nuclear state that Jerry's a part of – they do not cherish such virtues – you got that straight from the horse's mouth, because I used to be a part of it. Read between the lines of a Jerry Grogan speech and you will find not the frontiersman but the Teutonic knight. Not democracy but despotism. This future nuclear state will be an absolute state whose authority will derive not from the people but from the possession of plutonium. And just to make sure we all know what we're talking about, here, I brought some of the stuff along with me today. *(He goes to his case and takes out two bars of plutonium.)* Two bars of weapons-grade plutonium. *(Immediately the whole platform, with the exception of* GROGAN *moves back from* JEDBURGH. *The audience begins to panic.)* I stole this stuff – on orders – straight out of Jerry's latest acquisition at Northmoor. Twenty-four people have died for this stuff, including me . . . All I have to do is bring these bars together and we will have a criticality.

GROGAN: Careful, Darius!

(The front rows of the audience are emptying, with shouts and cries of alarm. People stampede out of the hall.)

JEDBURGH: Four hundred 'rads', ladies and gentlemen – a lethal dose to anyone within a radius of ten yards. Get it while it's hot!

6:41   Outside the large exhibition room, Gleneagles Hotel. Day
The doors open and the audience pours out. LAWSON *and* BENNETT
*are caught in the flood. They try to force their way against the crowd
back into the room.*

6:42   The large exhibition room, Gleneagles Hotel. Day
As the audience retreats, JEDBURGH *turns to* GROGAN. *He brings the
two bars of plutonium together. There is a flash and* GROGAN *gasps.*
JEDBURGH *turns to the fleeing audience.*
JEDBURGH: Hey, what's the matter? Don't you all want to be part
of the new age of plutonium lunacy? Don't you want to see
mankind become enslaved to this new priesthood of
plutonium culture and see the earth become a desert – all its
natural resources plundered to build some New Jerusalem in
the Milky Way?
(*By now the seats are all empty.* JEDBURGH *laughs and lowers
himself on to the steps.*)

6:43   The small exhibition room, Gleneagles Hotel. Night
Whisky is being poured into a tumbler. Five of them are being filled up.
GROGAN *can hardly be seen, slumped in a deep-wing chair. The*
MINISTER *accepts a whisky.*
MINISTER: Why did you let him go?
(*A fire is burning in the grate.*)
BENNETT: We had no alternative.
MINISTER: None?
BENNETT: He still has twenty kilos.
GROGAN: In 'an explosive configuration' – his words.
(*The* MINISTER *crosses towards a box in the centre of the room
where* BENNETT *stands.* BENNETT *opens it. The* MINISTER
looks down at the two bars of plutonium.)
MINISTER: Are twenty kilos enough?
GROGAN: To dispose of the east coast of Scotland? . . . Yes.
(*The* MINISTER *looks at him.*)
MINISTER: If he was going to do that, he would have done it by now.
GROGAN: Nobody was prepared to take that chance.
MINISTER: Instead of which, a particularly sensitive relationship
between you and my government is public property.
(GROGAN *gives him a look, but no more. The* MINISTER *looks at*
LAWSON.)
LAWSON: We could have had a catastrophe in there.

MINISTER: Colonel.

(LAWSON *leaves the room. When he has gone the* MINISTER *turns to* BENNETT.)

What did he say about Northmoor?

BENNETT: Not much. The whole hall was in such a state of pandemonium, I doubt if anyone noticed. The man is quite insane. He completely misread Jerry's argument.

GROGAN: Did he? I thought he put his finger right on it. Either we stay or we go.

MINISTER: Go where?

(*Nobody answers. The poor chap seems completely at sea.*)

Well then, what are we going to do next? We shall have to find him.

(*He looks at* HARCOURT.)

HARCOURT: I think we should leave it to Craven.

MINISTER: Bennett?

BENNETT: There are alternatives.

(*The* MINISTER *looks at* BENNETT. LAWSON *re-enters the room.*)

LAWSON: There's a telephone call from Inspector Craven – for Mr Harcourt.

MINISTER: (*To* GROGAN) Would you have any objection if we left it to Craven?

(GROGAN *looks at the* MINISTER.)

GROGAN: As long as he finds the plutonium, it's OK by me.

MINISTER: Well, Harcourt, you'd better make sure that he's fully briefed, hadn't you?

6:44 The golf club, Gleneagles Hotel. Day

PORTER: He used to play here twice a week.

(*The* PORTER *leads* CRAVEN *towards the locker room.*)

He said he felt at home.

CRAVEN: When did you see him last?

PORTER: A couple of days ago now.

6:45 The locker room, Gleneagles golf club. Day

The PORTER *makes for Jedburgh's locker.*

PORTER: He was a good loser, which is just as well. We have a lot of strong players.

(*He unlocks it.*)

CRAVEN: OK, that's fine. Thanks.

(CRAVEN *looks inside. At the bottom of the locker is the empty Harrods bag and a plastic container with a congealed mince sandwich inside. On the bottom of the container is a sticker proclaiming that it belongs to Mrs Girvan, Girvan Guest House, Crieff.*)

6:46 Outside Gleneagles Hotel. Day

A Ford transit draws up outside the hotel. It parks behind Nallers's Granada and the Landrover. NALLERS *walks over to the driver.*

6:47 Harcourt's bedroom, Gleneagles Hotel. Day

HARCOURT *enters the room.* PENDLETON *is at the window watching the scene below.* HARCOURT *crosses over to him and looks down. He can see* NALLERS *in conversation with* BENNETT. *There are now three cars tucked beside the side of the road.*

HARCOURT: Who's that man?

PENDLETON: Nallers . . . He drinks at the Chelsea Barracks . . .
    He's rumoured to be the state executioner.

HARCOURT: Who would he be after – up here?

PENDLETON: It could be you, old boy. The Minister didn't take
    too kindly to that report of yours.
    (HARCOURT *looks affronted.*)
    But it's more likely to be Jedburgh.
    (*There is a knock at the door.* PENDLETON *opens it.*)
    Ah, good. Thank you.
    (HARCOURT *continues to stare down at the men outside with distaste, then he turns and looks at the tea tray* PENDLETON *is holding.*)

HARCOURT: I thought I ordered oatcakes.

6:48 The track to Kilmichael. Day

Clementine's car lurches up the track towards the half-hidden lodge. CRAVEN *is driving. He stops and gets out.*
He moves round to the back of the house. There is the sound of a rushing stream. He finds a door and rings the bell. JEDBURGH *opens the door.* CRAVEN *turns as* JEDBURGH *appears.*

JEDBURGH: What took you so long?

6:49 The living-room, The Lodge, Kilmichael. Day

A wood fire is burning in the grate. JEDBURGH *tosses another piece of wood onto it as* CRAVEN *enters.*

CRAVEN: How have you been feeling?

JEDBURGH: Sick. (*He looks at* CRAVEN.) Boy, have I ever been sick . . . You come alone?

CRAVEN: Yeah. What the hell are you doing up here?

JEDBURGH: Mostly dying. I've bought the farm boy. You talk to Harcourt?

CRAVEN: Last night.

JEDBURGH: He tell you I was at Gleneagles?

CRAVEN: Yeah. You caused quite a stir.

JEDBURGH: Yeah. Nothing on TV, though, I see.
(JEDBURGH *sits down*.)

CRAVEN: No. They've got that screwed down tight.
(CRAVEN *walks to the window and looks out*.)

JEDBURGH: Yeah. What about you?

CRAVEN: What about me?

JEDBURGH: How long have you got?

CRAVEN: Two weeks.

JEDBURGH: That's too bad . . . It was a helluva mission though, huh?

CRAVEN: You didn't complete it.
(JEDBURGH *looks up*.)

JEDBURGH: They were waiting for me with guns, weren't they? My own people, Craven. They started shooting at me. Honour went out the window the day they invented that stuff.

CRAVEN: Do you know what Harcourt told me last night? Grogan had reached the conclusion that the Inquiry would stop the takeover so he decided to get the plutonium another way. Then he thought of you. Who would walk into a cave full of radiation? You would – given the right scenario. All he had to do was make a call to Washington to make sure they fed you the right orders. They didn't just betray you. They made a fool of you.

JEDBURGH: No shit, Sherlock. You think I didn't figure that out?

CRAVEN: Where is the plutonium?

JEDBURGH: It's at the bottom of a loch.

CRAVEN: What shape is it in?

JEDBURGH: It's in pretty good shape. I packed it in chalk. At its core I put a pound of plastic explosive.

CRAVEN: You turned it into a bomb?

JEDBURGH: Yeah.

CRAVEN: Why?

171

JEDBURGH: 'Cause that's the problem with plutonium, Craven. It's limited in its application. It is not user-friendly. But as a vehicle for regaining one's self-respect, it's got a lot going for it. Damned right I turned it into a bomb.

CRAVEN: Is it armed?

(JEDBURGH *looks at him.*)

Fused?

JEDBURGH: There's a detonator, if that's what you mean. (*He pulls a bullet from his top pocket.*) It's a plutonium bullet.

(*He tosses it over to* CRAVEN, *who examines it.*)

CRAVEN: Would it work?

JEDBURGH: Well, fired from a high-velocity rifle, it just might.

CRAVEN: A nuclear explosion?

JEDBURGH: It'd be one hell of a way to go, huh?

CRAVEN: It seems rather hard on the rest of Scotland.

JEDBURGH: Yeah, that's what I thought, too. Especially the golf courses. So, I decided against it.

CRAVEN: What other ideas have you had . . . to end it all?

JEDBURGH: Well, I called up this especially humourless bastard called Hernandez. He runs this rinky-dinky terrorist outfit. I'm supposed to be on his death list. So I invited him up. He hasn't showed.

CRAVEN: Where's the plutonium?

JEDBURGH: Loch Lednock – ten miles west of here, by the dam.

CRAVEN: You mind if I use the phone?

JEDBURGH: You're going to call Harcourt?

CRAVEN: Yes.

JEDBURGH: He'll only turn it over to Grogan. They'll screw you the same way they screwed me.

CRAVEN: I'll have to take that chance.

(*He turns to exit.*)

JEDBURGH: Craven!

(CRAVEN *turns back.*)

They'll trace the call.

CRAVEN: They?

JEDBURGH: The opposition. They'll come looking for us.

CRAVEN: If we're lucky, they will.

(*He goes out of the room.*)

6:50   Harcourt's bedroom, Gleneagles Hotel. Day
The telephone rings in the bedroom. PENDLETON *picks up the phone.*
PENDLETON: Pendleton.

6:51   The hall, The Lodge, Kilmichael. Day
CRAVEN *speaks carefully into the telephone. Intercut with*
PENDLETON.
CRAVEN: I've found him.
PENDLETON: What about the stuff?
CRAVEN: Loch Lednock. By the dam. Be careful. It's packaged.
   (*Cut to* PENDLETON.)
   I'll meet you there tomorrow. Eight o'clock.
   (*He puts the phone down.*)

6:52   Harcourt's bedroom, Gleneagles Hotel. Day
PENDLETON *hears* CRAVEN *hang up. There is a silence. Then he*
hears another click, then the burring sound. He slowly replaces the
receiver.
HARCOURT: Well, has he got it?
PENDLETON: He knows where it is . . . We meet him eight
   o'clock tomorrow morning. Loch Lednoch.
HARCOURT: He'll be dead by then. I just hope he gave you the
   right instructions.

6:53   The kitchen, The Lodge, Kilmichael. Night
CRAVEN *and* JEDBURGH *are sitting at the kitchen table. The whisky is*
out. So is Jedburgh's automatic. Both are slightly drunk.
JEDBURGH: 'It was the year of the preacher . . .'
CRAVEN: 'It was the *time* of the preacher . . .'
JEDBURGH: 'It was the time of the preacher
         In the year of 01.
         When you think it's all over,
   (CRAVEN *joins in singing.*)
         It had only begun.
         And he cried like a baby.
         And he screamed like a panther
         In the middle of the night.'
JEDBURGH: You remember that, Craven?
         'He saddled his pony
         And he went for a ride.'
   (CRAVEN *looks at* JEDBURGH.)

173

CRAVEN: I am no longer seeking vengeance.

JEDBURGH: You know what you are, Craven? You're something special. You've been freeze-dried from some earlier epoch, just waiting for this to happen.

CRAVEN: Waiting for what to happen?

JEDBURGH: All this. The confrontation between good and evil.

CRAVEN: And what side are you on?

JEDBURGH: The side of the angels, boy. Always have been.

CRAVEN: Jedburgh, you are not, and never will be, on the side of the angels.

JEDBURGH: There are angels who will stand by me. St Michael, for instance.

CRAVEN: Then you do believe in Gaia?

JEDBURGH: As an idea, or what?

CRAVEN: As an idea.

JEDBURGH: You mean do I believe that the Earth Goddess will defend herself against all dangers?

CRAVEN: Including man . . .

JEDBURGH: Man will always win against nature.

6:54   Outside The Lodge, Kilmichael. Night

A number of cars with dim headlamps lurch slowly up the track towards the lodge. A Ford transit brings up the rear. In the lead car is NALLERS. *The cars come to a halt.* NALLERS *gets out.*

6:55   The kitchen, The Lodge, Kilmichael. Night

CRAVEN *and* JEDBURGH *hear the noise in the distance and are still.* JEDBURGH *looks into* CRAVEN'S *face.*

JEDBURGH: You were saying?

CRAVEN: I think you're wrong.

6:56   Outside The Lodge, Kilmichael. Night

The back doors of the transit open quietly, a lead coffin is pulled out and is left on the grass. It is marked 'Danger. Radiation'.

6:57   The kitchen, The Lodge, Kilmichael. Night

The sound of the approaching raiders can be sensed rather than heard by both men.

CRAVEN: On my way here I had a weird conversation with Emma. She warned me about a black flower which, she said, would

spread across the Northern hemisphere and melt the polar
icecap.

JEDBURGH: Grogan would zapp it.

CRAVEN: She said that the planet will turn against mankind and
destroy him.

(JEDBURGH *hears another noise.*)

JEDBURGH: Have you ever been in Afghanistan, Craven?

CRAVEN: Is this relevant?

JEDBURGH: I was out there last year, studying the drinking habits
of the Russian soldiers. Now, they'll drink anything as long as
it's alcohol-based: glycol, anti-freeze, brake fluid . . . But the
black flowers are out there, Craven. On the mountains. The
Afghans eat them.

CRAVEN: I think you're taking the piss, Jedburgh.

JEDBURGH: I am merely confirming the existence of the black
flower. And if Grogan don't zapp them, the Afghans will.

(*They hear a noise. Both stop and listen.*)

Shit.

(*He looks at his automatic.*)

CRAVEN: I think you're wrong. If there is a battle between the
planet and mankind, the planet will win.

JEDBURGH: Where's that going to leave you?

CRAVEN: On the side of the planet.

(*They listen to the sound of men approaching.*)

JEDBURGH: Do you want to wait for them inside, or do you want
to go outside and meet them head on?

CRAVEN: I don't see the point of moving from this spot.

JEDBURGH: The point is, Craven, to take as many of the bastards
with us as we can.

(*He stands.*)

CRAVEN: Why?

JEDBURGH: Because they are going to have our ass.

(JEDBURGH *switches off the light and exits.*)

6:58 The small exhibition room, Gleneagles Hotel. Night
Harcourt's glass is being refilled. A dinner is in progress. GROGAN,
BENNETT, HARCOURT, PENDLETON, LAWSON *and the* MINISTER
sit around a large table. The conversation turns to the next meeting.

HARCOURT: Well, what's the next one?

LAWSON: Geneva. 'Nuclear Non-Proliferation Treaty'.

HARCOURT: Same old circus?

LAWSON: Well, we get some new faces. And the old ones drop
    out . . .
HARCOURT: What's for pudding?

6:59 The stairwell, The Lodge, Kilmichael. Night
Close-up of JEDBURGH. *He turns off the light in the hallway and
searches the rooms for signs of intruders. He cocks his automatic.*

6:60 The small exhibition room, Gleneagles Hotel. Night
The reception continues. PENDLETON *and the* MINISTER *are talking
together.*
PENDLETON: You will come tomorrow?
MINISTER: Yes. But I have to swim off Sizewell in the afternoon.
There's all this talk about the nuclear state but every weekend sees
one of us swimming up and down outside some nuclear power
station while the world's press takes snaps from a safe distance on
shore. Makes me sick . . .
    (PENDLETON *looks at him with a certain morbid curiosity.*)
PENDLETON: How sick?

6:61 The kitchen, The Lodge, Kilmichael. Night
CRAVEN *sits at the table. He holds a pistol in his hand.*

6:62 The stairwell, The Lodge, Kilmichael. Night
JEDBURGH *steps into the hall and pivots. The sounds of the impending
assault are all around him. He aims and fires. He fires again.*

6:63 The kitchen, The Lodge, Kilmichael. Night
CRAVEN *sips his whisky. He can hear the gunfire outside in the
hallway.*

6:64 The stairwell, The Lodge, Kilmichael. Night
JEDBURGH *is on the stairs. He fires two more rounds.*

6:65 The kitchen, The Lodge, Kilmichael. Night
*The kitchen door is blown open and a dark shape comes through the
door. Simultaneously a window is splintered by another charge. Three
men storm in and rush at* CRAVEN. *All three hold guns to his head.*

6:66 The stairwell, The Lodge, Kilmichael. Night
JEDBURGH *shoots a man at the top of the stairs. He falls.* JEDBURGH

turns to reload but is suddenly overcome by a coughing fit. NALLERS
appears at the top of the stairs.
NALLERS: Colonel Jedburgh!
    (JEDBURGH *turns.*)
JEDBURGH: Yes, sir.
NALLERS: What's the problem?
JEDBURGH: No problem.
    (NALLERS *shoots him.*)

6:67   The small exhibition room, Gleneagles Hotel. Night
Champagne is poured into Grogan's glass. GROGAN *looks up and
smiles.*
GROGAN: Normally I don't drink champagne, but tonight is an
    exception, I think.

6:68   The kitchen, The Lodge, Kilmichael. Night
The three men are still pointing their guns straight at CRAVEN.
NALLERS *enters the room.*
NALLERS: Is this Craven?
CRAVEN: Just do it. Do it.
NALLERS: No, no, old son. You're on our side.
    (NALLERS *and the men exit.* CRAVEN *shouts out.*)
CRAVEN: I am not on your side.

6:69   Loch Lednock. Day
HARCOURT's *voice, reading his letter to* CLEMENTINE, *can be heard
over the action.*
HARCOURT: (*Voice over*) My dear Clemmy, within hours of
    Jedburgh's death and in conditions of great secrecy, the
    plutonium was recovered from Loch Lednock.
    (*A helicopter flies in over the loch. From the top of the hill*
    PENDLETON *and* HARCOURT *watch the operation below.*)
HARCOURT: (*Voice over*) It was an IIF show. No one else would
    take responsibility for the stuff – certainly not Her Majesty's
    Government . . .
    (BENNETT *is supervising the recovery of the plutonium, a difficult
    job. Several men, wearing protective clothing, gather around the
    package as it is brought up from the loch.*)
HARCOURT: (*Voice over*) Myself and Pendleton turned up just to
    'show the flag' – and to remind Grogan that this was only the
    first round. Yes, Grogan was there, watching the proceedings

like some twentieth-century vampire, although after his exposure to Jedburgh's plutonium at the conference I don't hold out much for his chances.

(*The helicopter hovers over the group of men as the plutonium is put into a net and attached to the helicopter's winch.* HARCOURT *is observing the scene from his vantage point through a pair of binoculars.* GROGAN *is watching the events from his car on the shore.*)

GROGAN: (*Speaking into his walkie-talkie*) What's the hitch?

BENNETT: We're just making sure it's secure.

(*The helicopter rises into the sky, the plutonium swinging below it.* PENDLETON *and* HARCOURT *watch the helicopter cross the dam and head down the valley.*

CRAVEN *can be seen standing on the top of a hill overlooking the loch, watching.* PENDLETON *and* HARCOURT *catch sight of him.*)

HARCOURT: (*Voice over*) You asked about Craven. The last we saw of him was up on the hill overlooking the loch, staring down at us like a wild animal. Neither myself nor Pendleton felt it appropriate to wave. Besides, by my reckoning, he was not long for this world. When we left he was still on the hill.

(*The whole group begin to make their way down the glen.* HARCOURT *and* PENDLETON *can be seen through the rear windscreen of one of the cars, looking back up the hill.*)

(*Voice over*) I only wished we could have shouted out some words of comfort . . . told him that in the end, the earth, Emma's beloved Gaia, would be saved from ultimate destruction – and that the good in all of us would prevail . . . but in the circumstances, I don't think he would have believed it.

(CRAVEN *stands on the top of the hill.*)

CRAVEN: (*Shouting*) Emma!

HARCOURT: (*Voice over*) As we drove down the valley, I thought I heard a cry, but it was lost in the noise of the helicopter. When I looked back he was gone.

(*Dissolve through to winter. A wide shot of the loch and surrounding hills, then a close-up of the spot where* CRAVEN *stood the ground is covered in snow, through which black flowers are beginning to grow.*)

(*Roll end titles over this.*)

Background to *Edge of Darkness*

The following outline of what went on before Emma's murder was drafted by me as a basis for discussion by the production team. The intention was to provide a detailed account of what actually happened, and to explain events which the scripts sometimes did little more than allude to. The point of this exercise was to see whether or not the scripts made sense from all angles, and if not, whether the scripts or 'back story' should be amended. One of the details which was subsequently changed was the existence of a second survivor of the Northmoor raid. This character was eventually cut out.

The Beginnings

In August 1983 radioactive isotopes, caught in the scanner at the Corrie Reservoir outside Craigmills, brought the pump station to a halt and caused a public outcry.

Minute traces of caesium and ruthenium, thought to have been windborne from Sellafield, eighty miles north-west of Craigmills, were found in the water and it was some weeks before the reservoir was officially cleared of contamination.

Friends of the Earth, concerned about the effect of emissions of low-decaying isotopes from the Windscale towers, were quick to point to the Corrie Reservoir as a first-class example of what they had been worried about since 1978.

Officials at the Sellafield plant were equally quick to deny any responsibility and came up with all sorts of graphs about prevailing winds, temperatures and cloud base at the time of the autumn equinox, all of which were ignored by the press, who knew a good story when they saw one.

Tony Marsh, a Sellafield engineer, was sent to take samples of the Craigmills water, and his report was the first (and only one) to point a finger at the Northmoor Nuclear Storage Plant as the possible culprit. Northmoor, a small waste facility to the west of

Craigmills, was run by a private company, International Irradiated Fuels (or IIF as it liked to be called), whose managing director was Robert Bennett.

Marsh confirmed that isotopes of caesium and ruthenium had been found at Craigmills consistent with those given off in the reprocessing of spent fuel at Sellafield. This appeared to condemn Sellafield out of hand, but Marsh pointed out that the Northmoor plant had recently been given permission to store spent fuel from the Magnox power station in deep caves under the moors. These Magnox rods were known to corrode rapidly in water, and it was possible that the toxic elements had seeped through the floor of the caves into the water-table beneath Craigmills. Such isotopes could have included caesium and ruthenium.

Friends of the Earth saw this as an attempt to divert attention from the deplorable conditions at Sellafield, and their attitude was reinforced by an appearance of Bennett on television, stoutly defending the safety record of his company, putting himself over as an altruistic servant of the public, taking on a dirty job no one else wanted to do, and implying that as a private enterprise company he was outside the lobby of self-interest which protected the big state firms, and so was a firm candidate for a scapegoat. The press took the same view as Friends of the Earth, although the scandal was now superseded by the issue of the Sellafield pipeline raised by Greenpeace.

What feeble resistance Sellafield was able to put up in its defence disintegrated when it was leaked that one of the isotopes not mentioned in the original discovery (but mentioned in Marsh's report) was krypton. This isotope is common only in the reprocessing of plutonium, not in the decay of Magnox rods. Since the only plutonium reprocessing plant in the country existed at Sellafield, the case now seemed to have been well and truly proven

In October, Marsh, who continued to proclaim Sellafield's innocence in this business, was killed in a road accident, and with his death the matter seemed to rest.

First Doubts

Two organizations, neither of which advertised itself, were not convinced by the media's coverage of the events. One was Gaia, a shadowy organization of scientists who were concerned with the ecological implications of their work. The other was a mini department attached to the Cabinet Office in Whitehall, run by

Pendleton and Harcourt, who had direct access to the secretary to the cabinet (and thus to the prime minister). Their brief was to look into anything which in their opinion warranted their interest. Northmoor evidently did.

Pendleton's lanky figure could have been seen poking around at the scene of Marsh's accident, and also at the pumping stations of the West Yorkshire Water Board, where he made sure that if there were any fresh incidents, he would be the first to be informed.

The Gaia interest was slightly more obscure. A mole at Windscale/Sellafield, convinced that Marsh's report was indeed accurate, sent a copy to an eminent engineer who had been a founder member of Gaia.

Who and what is Gaia? In 1977 a group of concerned scientists, engineers and civil servants met in London to discuss their opposition to Thorpe, the proposed nuclear reprocessing plant at Windscale. They were concerned with the social and scientific consequences of the plant, which would eventually turn Britain into a nuclear state; they were also worried about the ultimate environmental issues. They believed that plutonium could eventually destroy not only civilization but also life itself on the planet. Their fears were to a degree shared by President Carter of the United States, who was worried about the spread of plutonium on the world market, and the consequence which might follow if it were bought by a Khomeini or Gadaffi.

Carter encouraged the English scientists to form a respectable opposition to argue against the current establishment view that the nuclear state represented the best bet for post-imperial Britain. To this end he sent Darius Jedburgh, a top CIA agent, to London to orchestrate opposition to Thorpe and to lobby the 1977 Conference on Nuclear Proliferation which was due to be held in London shortly.

Although the group did not succeed in imposing their views on the conference or at the Windscale Inquiry, they were successful, along with Friends of the Earth and the Network for Nuclear Concern, in making a powerful case against the spread of plutonium.

Carter, a year later, alarmed by the progressive modernization of Russia's nuclear armoury, issued PD59, the now famous presidential directive which initiated a new nuclear arms race (the results of which are only now coming to light). PD59 changed the viability of Britain's plutonium programme. Instead of being an irritant in the special relationship between Britain and America, it became an asset.

Jedburgh, instructed to abandon the anti-Sellafield cause and to ditch its most lucid supporters, found it more difficult than anticipated. The organization went underground and, following the publication of Jim Lovelock's book, *The Gaia Hypothesis* (1979), it began to be known as Gaia, even though Lovelock's ideas were only marginally relevant to the now clandestine organization's aims.

Gaia grew rapidly in the years 1980 to 1984, particularly amongst scientific officers of the Civil Service. It got its biggest support following the Prime Minister's inept handling of the GCHQ union dispute in March 1984. That, plus the outcome of the New York/Washington Conference on the Nuclear Winter, did much to make scientists think of the serious dangers which now faced the planet.

It was at this stage in Gaia's development that Marsh's data became available to a senior member of its inner council. The logic of the Marsh report was as follows: if the quantities of krypton found in the reservoir water were not attributable to Sellafield, yet could only originate from a plutonium reprocessing plant, there had to be another plant somewhere, and that could only be Northmoor. The inference, unbelievable though it might seem, was that Northmoor was a clandestine reprocessing plant whose end product was plutonium. The political implications were mind-boggling. Such a plant could not have been built without official help, nor run without official approval. What's more, a great deal of effort must have gone into keeping it secret.

Northmoor, under Bennett's guidance, had benefited from the Conservatives' enthusiasm for privatization and from their deep distrust of Britain's nuclear establishment, which was currently reforming under new management at the Central Electricity Generating Board.

Bennett had persuaded the government to back a pilot scheme in the management of nuclear waste. As government-owned mines (purchased in the 1950s from the coal board for obsolete defence projects) lay dormant in Yorkshire, Bennett suggested that they should be leased to him to start a nuclear waste facility. He was determined to use them to develop his own methods of storage and to research new techniques for vitrification, etc.

In this he had the backing of much of the anti-nuclear establishment, who believed that the best way to handle waste was not to break it down as was being done at Sellafield (thus releasing its dangerous constituents) but to store it until new technology and engineering were developed which would make it safer to handle. This had the added advantage that, with the passing of time, many of the more powerful substances would have decayed and lost their toxicity.

In 1979 IIF were therefore given a limited go-ahead and in 1980 Bennett opened his gates to the waste of the world. 'Bring me your poor, your starving, and your . . .' had been changed by Bennett into 'Bring me your waste, your spent fuel and your sludge'. But his company articles limited him to low-grade storage only.

It was only in 1983, when a foul-up occurred in the processing of magnox rods at Windscale and a backlog of high-level waste began to build up throughout the system, ultimately threatening the functioning of the power stations themselves, that Bennett was allowed to begin to store high-level spent fuel, mostly plutonium-rich rock from the Magnox power stations.

The implications of what might be happening at Northmoor filtered down the Gaia organization to the younger echelons in the universities. These young, proto-eco-terrorists, not content to monitor the water of the Corrie Reservoir to see if there were any more leaks, decided to mount a raid on the Northmoor itself in the hope of finding the source of the plutonium.

The Northmoor Break-in

Emma Craven, a life scientist who had just joined the Craigmills Teacher Training College, having graduated from Cambridge, was given the job of organizing the break-in.

A year after the discovery of the first radioactivity in the Corrie Reservoir, six scientists, including Emma, broke into Northmoor, entering through disused mineshafts on a route devised by a local trade-union leader, James Godbolt, who had promised his expertise and aid.

The raid was an appalling tragedy. While returning through the drainage tunnels near the centre of the plant, the main party was engulfed by water and all four members drowned. Two escaped: Emma, who had been left at the sluice gates as part of the back-up (only four physicists were selected for the final reconnaissance) and Kenyon Peel, another biologist who had been left guarding equipment at the entrance to the Great Cave (the section which divided the deserted mineshafts from the walls of the plant).

Emma and Kenyon escaped but were unable to provide Gaia with any news about the reprocessing plant other than the death of their comrades.

Faced with a major crisis which might well rebound against them, Gaia made crude plans to disguise the disappearance of the four scientists in such a way that it would not cause comment. Since they came from different parts of the country, their disappearance could be temporarily explained by statements that they had gone abroad, etc.

Gaia was concerned that IIF would announce that their plant had been raided. But, significantly, nothing of the sort occurred. What did happen was that Kenyon Peel died in a motor accident a few weeks later and Emma Craven, whose father was a senior Yorkshire detective, was shot by a crazed ex-convict out on a vengeance trip. It was assumed he had wanted the father but in the heat of the moment succeeded in killing only the daughter.

While the hunt was on for the killer (a man called McCroon) and his sidekick (Lowe), Detective Superintendent Craven, Emma's father, began to make a few preliminary investigations of his own. He soon became aware that 'there was another dimension to the murder' and that it involved Northmoor. He began to doubt whether Emma's death was, as his fellow officers stated, simply a question of vengeance; he began to incline towards the view that she had been killed in an attempt to silence her.

While this was going on, another character was taking an interest in the events at Northmoor. Darius Jedburgh, the man who had set up Gaia, golfer extraordinaire, and the last of the old CIA field agents, living in London on what amounted to half pay, had become interested in the original press story about the Corrie Reservoir. Jedburgh, who was not as gullible as the science correspondents of the quality newspapers, read the Marsh report and at once concluded that the British were hiding illicit plutonium in the caves in an effort to fool their closest ally (the Yanks) about the true nature of their plutonium reserves.

Jedburgh commissioned a report on Northmoor, trying to use old contacts in Gaia to get to the bottom of the mystery. The report, which he forwarded to Harcourt and Pendleton, roughly confirmed the outline of the story so far.

Pendleton's and Harcourt's reaction on reading it was twofold. First, that the building of a hot cell at Northmoor for the reprocessing of plutonium could not have taken place without some official backing at the highest level; second, that they should proceed very carefully, for, although Jedburgh's report was very precise, its sources were non-attributable and the word 'alleged' occurred in the text on twenty-two occasions – not the kind of document to justify a full-scale search of the fifty miles of levels and corridors which made up the Northmoor plant.

They were, however, encouraged by two other developments: first, the death of Emma Craven had brought in the Yorkshire Police into the investigation and, in particular, Ronald Craven, an experienced police officer and a veteran of Northern Ireland, who was likely to leave no stone unturned in investigating Emma's past; second, a Parliamentary Inquiry was looming on the privatization of the nuclear industry. Northmoor, the pilot scheme, would come under close scrutiny, particularly as Jerry Grogan, the owner of the Fusion Corporation of Kansas, a rising star in the world of 'emerging technology', seemed to be keen to acquire IIF.

Characters

To help the actors, I drafted thumbnail sketches of the characters, which they could reject or accept as they saw fit. Some examples follow.

Ronald Woodhouse Craven

Ronald Woodhouse Craven was born in 1940 in the quiet desperation of the war. His father, who had never seen the sea till the time of his call-up, drowned in the Atlantic two years later. Ronald was brought up by his mother until her death in 1948 of breast cancer. The farm outside Manchester where they lived was then sold for a few pounds to pay her debts, and Ronnie went to live with his mother's sister Emily at nearby Craigmills.

All he recalls of the time when his mother died are silver aeroplanes in the blue sky and the trees near the farm where he used to walk. Of his father he remembers nothing but a faint smell of Blanco and Woodbine and his mother's cries in the night. Emily was a healer and it was through her that he learnt a great deal about animals; his great-grandmother had been famed in the country for her healing ways with animals. 'Woodhouse' had been her family name and Craven found out years later in a Sunday newspaper that Woodhouse, or *wudwusa*, means 'the wild man of the woods' – a European version of the Abominable Snowman, or Caliban in *The Tempest*. But the idea of a *wudwusa* was already familiar when he read this. A nature lover, Craven liked his own company and shunned others.

Craven, a child of Beveridge's reforms of the education system in 1942, went to the local grammar school. He received a grant for dinner money because of his straitened circumstances and also a grant towards his clothes.

From grammar school Craven went on to Loughborough College, where he wanted to study agriculture. However, he was involved in a pot-holing accident in Cheshire in which a number of students died, and this blew his mind. Dreams of his father walking out of the sea, which he had repressed as a youngster, now began reappearing nightly. Advised to take the rest of the year off, Craven shut himself up in a cottage on the moors, working as a shepherd. It was two years before he re-emerged, by which time his agricultural ambitions had gone.

It was 1961. He was twenty-one years old. It was a new Britain, the age of youth, the Beatles, freedom, optimism – 'you never had it so good'. Craven messed around with the art college types at Leeds, fell in love with and married Ann Wharmby, a Montessori teacher. Within the year she was pregnant. After marrying Ann, Craven joined the police force.

Craven's idea of the police force in those days was not a metropolitan one. He wanted to get back to the moors with his new wife and their child. His only experience of the police had been positive: in the Cheddar caves, where they had been so courageous, and later up on the moors, where sometimes his only contact with 'civilization' had been the little white van which ran across the hill twice a week. There had been emergencies when he had been called out to feed the sheep in the snow, to comb the ridge for lost hikers. He connected the police with accidents, emergencies and the extremes of hardship, not with law and order. By joining the police, he hoped his father would return to the sea. And he did, but it was a long time before Craven worked sheep again, or saw the wind comb the bog grass across the fells.

He was thrown directly into the policing of metropolitan Leeds. And, as the affluent society spread, Craven found himself attached to CID; as a CID officer proper, he worked first with the Drugs Squad – a completely new operation for Yorkshire – and then later out in the divisions. He did not get back to the country until he came to Craigmills in 1973.

Ann Wharmby was a big, soft-faced woman of calm demeanour

and stable disposition, whose parents never got over her marriage to Craven. A beautiful young woman with an air of mystery (evoked by the fact that she did not talk much), Ann had drifted among the Leeds art students, a prized companion of their most colourful personalities, until she met Craven. In Craven she found a strength and a disregard for rank and achievement which ran counter to her own rather fashionable views. After they began to live together she drifted out of the art scene and rarely visited her old haunts. Ann, who had trained as a Montessori teacher, loved children but had a stroke of bad luck with the birth of her own daughter – Emma was born in 1964 on the day preceding Wentworth, by Caesarian section. Craven always had the feeling that the operation had been forced upon his wife by a golf-mad gynaecologist who wanted his weekend free.

In the early years Ann experienced some difficulties with Emma (it was before the concept of 'bonding') and Craven found himself drawn into a much closer relationship with the child than would otherwise be considered normal. It was some time before Ann was able to come to terms with her feeling of inadequacy, but her relationship with Emma did stabilize and the couple moved to the house at Craigmills.

To pay for the house Craven volunteered for duty in Northern Ireland and, in 1973, when Emma was nine, he was sent to Portadown on the Irish border, attached to headquarters there as a member of the Special Branch. At Portadown he was responsible for the recruitment of informers in the Catholic section of the population. At that time intelligence information was in very short supply and was desperately needed.

Craven's strength lay in interrogation methods. He had established a reputation for 'getting information out of a corpse', his colleagues used to say. Like all good interrogators, this was not primarily achieved by violence. He was able to take over his prisoners, seeking out their emotional and psychological weaknesses and supplying a certainty which in time they came to rely on. They would supply information in return for these 'fixes'. (It is significant in this context that Craven frequently referred to his prisoners as 'patients'.)

It was therefore relatively easy for Craven to adapt his techniques to train informers. Like most police informers, they became psychologically wedded to their controller. One such person was McCroon, a passionate life-affirming Irish patriot on the fringes of the Belfast underworld.

During the time Craven was away, Ann developed a melanoma. The original operation proved successful but the condition recurred two years later and by 1974 she was dying. Ann's illness brought Craven back from Northern Ireland. His return to England left his informers high and dry. Some were coupled to new police officers but most were let go by his successor, cynically advertised as 'touts' (therefore spreading dissension in the provo ranks), or manipulated in plots where they were expendable. None was given the protection Craven had originally promised. McCroon fled to England and took to a life not dissimilar to the one he had left in Northern Ireland: he robbed sub-post offices and on one raid in Yorkshire killed a post mistress. It was the time of the Birmingham bombing. Craven was brought in to track him down, which he did punctiliously. McCroon admitted to the crime and got twelve years. This was in 1977.

The death of Ann in 1974 was a tremendous blow to Craven, even though it was cushioned by the nightmare progress of the illness. What little confidence he had in doctors waned even further when he saw their expertise crumble in the face of disease and death.

Refusing to mourn her passing, with no more than an angry visit to the grave where her pain-racked body had been buried, he gave himself over to his work, haunted by the fear that his trip to Ireland had in fact helped to bring on the illness. Emma became the sole reason for his existence, and his consolation.

He had a vivid memory of opening Ann's wardrobe to see three wool blazers for Emma, each one a size bigger than the other, and new shoes with an E fitting taking her up to fifteen years: things she had purchased before she died in the (justified) knowledge that in some ways Craven would not be able to cope. Ann, anxieties and all, lived on in Emma, sharing the house with the shadow of her mother, whose loss still ached like an amputated limb. With such a convergence of feeling Craven found no need to remarry or even have more than the occasional physical relationship. He had a number of female friends but their presence in the house was vigorously resisted by Emma, who felt from the earliest age that she was the mistress of the house and should come first in her Daddy's affections. Who was he to gainsay her?

Pendleton
Pendleton's background is ex-colonial (parents lived in Malaya and

later Kenya – coffee). Although English by birth, Pendleton was educated at Trinity College Dublin, after which he became a regular officer in the Parachute Regiment. He served in Aden, Indonesia, Vietnam (with the Australians) and Northern Ireland. Later he pursued an unsuccessful career in the City (stockbroking/insurance) while continuing to serve as a Territorial Army officer. Seconded to the SAS, he began to disappear off on various unofficial missions (the kidnapping of a British businessman; the guarding of British diplomats; the storming of hijacked planes).

He tends to resist offers to commercialize his experience (and train various counter-terrorist units throughout the world). He is not by nature an intelligence officer, but really a field man with extensive knowledge of anti-terrorist techniques. Divorced – twice – with no children, Pendleton's fatal flaw is women. An opera buff and theatre goer, Pendleton would have liked to have been an actor or an opera singer.

Harcourt
Solid middle-class background. Parents were international lawyers. Father an official with the United Nations, died with Dag Hamershold in a plane crash. Educated at Winchester and Cambridge. Studied law, took Silk in 1976. Married prospective Tory MP. Two children. Lives in the country.

Made his name with Games Board investigation of gambling casinos; Lloyd's investigation of supertanker sinkings – a massive conspiracy to defraud insurers; secret negotiations for the return of Hong Kong to the Chinese.

Freeman of the City of London; member of the Honourable Company of Silversmiths; on the board of a dozen companies; refused knighthood because he disapproved of the Falklands War (relatives in Argentina); nevertheless accepted job to work in the Cabinet Office, having been recommended by Lord Rothschild. Good raconteur; likes raffish company; millionaire.

Darius Jedburgh
Jedburgh is a large Falstaffian figure who dominates the latter half of *Edge of Darkness*. Twenty years as a field operative in almost permanent exile has given him a jaundiced view of the human race and in particular of the men who run the CIA head office at Langley.

An anglophile, with the near belief that God is a golfer,

Jedburgh is also a devotee of Black Zen and the TV programme *Come Dancing*. Yet, with all his heavy drinking and hillbilly airs, Jedburgh is a tough operative who knows exactly what he is doing. And his tragi-comic ironical view of history and all the setbacks that the CIA has had to suffer – in a never-ending series of political defeats, from Vietnam to Central America – have not fogged his vision, which is focused well beyond the limits of current American policy and party dogma.

What Craven knew

Much of the discussion during the development of the scripts concerned structure. This was complicated by the fact that we all held differing views about the nature of the detective story. Martin Campbell, the director, took the view that a detective should ideally discover most of the story for himself. Bob Peck, who played the part of Craven, agreed. I believed that because of the complexity of the plot, Craven's task (and mine) would be simplified if he had foreknowledge of much of what had happened.

I sent the following memo to Martin Campbell in an attempt to establish agreement about what Craven did or did not know. This continued to be a subject for debate right up to the end of the shooting.

1 He is aware of the contamination of the reservoir the previous year. His daughter was involved in the investigation.

2 He has met Tony Marsh and discussed the contamination with him; again, Emma had worked with Marsh on his report. Emma and Marsh had disagreed violently politically but had reached the same conclusion: that the source of the pollution was probably Northmoor.

3 He had wondered if Marsh's death was murder.

4 He had had arguments with Emma about the legality and danger of going into Northmoor. He had not seriously considered she would do it.

5 He did not know that she had contact with Godbolt or that she was interested for her own reasons in the outcome of the inquiry into the voting fraud.

6 Because of pressure of work he had been neglecting her. He knew nothing of the plan of the break-in with the aid of her inexpert partners, her informer boyfriend, and the devious Godbolt; nor of the break-in itself, nor the appalling experiences she underwent; nor the aftermath of the break-in and the loneliness

she must have experienced. Part of his remorse (now cut from Episode Two) is that he had allowed her to carry such a heavy burden alone.

7 Craven becomes aware of a possible link between Emma's death and Northmoor for two reasons: he is convinced that McCroon and Lowe did not have the motivation to kill him on their own (Pendleton and Harcourt express a similar doubt but for different reasons). He is aware of the danger of coincidence, but the fate of the other Gaia participants does have an effect on him. It makes him even more suspicious, although there is still no evidence.

8 Craven's first confirmation comes with the murder of Shields; if that is cut from the story, his suspicions will be confirmed for the first time in Episode Four, when he sees the MI5 file on the R2 computer.

9 Marsh's report would *not* have alerted him to the idea that Northmoor was in any way connected with his daughter's death, or that Northmoor security were acting illegally. (They may have been acting secretly, which is something else.) Had he believed they were acting illegally, as Emma did, he would have done something about it.

10 It is important to note that a television audience, on learning the gist of Marsh's report, would immediately conclude that something nasty was going on in Northmoor, and that Northmoor was responsible for Emma's death. But the characters in our story would not necessarily jump to the same conclusion. They would be more circumspect about it, because they are not getting it out of a television script. To explain the Tony Marsh story at the end of Episode Two automatically gives the whole game away as far as our audience is concerned (it confirms Northmoor management as the baddies with the hot cell who will stop as nothing to keep their secret.) In Episode Five, however, the same information serves a different purpose; it shows how Pendleton and Harcourt (and Jedburgh and the CIA) had reservations which went back a long way and which are based on hard evidence. It confirms the care they have taken in assembling their case and shows that people in Whitehall are not all simple-minded cowboys.

Expert Advice on *Edge of Darkness*

Nuclear Power

*Walter C. Patterson is the foremost critic of the nuclear power
programme in the UK. He supplied us with much-needed technical
assistance but also provided a robust critique of the plot and made many
suggestions, some of which we were more than happy to take up. For
instance, he told us about the corrosion of the magnox fuel rods at
Sellafield as they lay in water-storage, which greatly added to the
legitimacy of the Northmoor plant. Most important of all, he believed
in the project, in Lovelock's Gaia and in the idea that complex
scientific issues can be the subject of popular television drama.*

The following is his first reaction to the scripts.

Patterson's Comments

The premise of the series is that there exists an underground
nuclear facility, privately owned, in which plutonium is being
illicitly separated. A group of people from an organization called
Gaia succeed in entering the facility and obtaining some of the
separated plutonium. They are discovered and four of the six are
killed by the company. Two escape, without the plutonium that
would demonstrate the truth of their investigations; both are
killed within a short time. Hearings are held in London about the
incident at the facility. Craven and Jedburgh use the same route
as the Gaia group into the underground facility, intending to seize
the plutonium. Their intrusion is anticipated. In the ensuing
events they succeed in obtaining some (all?) of the stored
separated plutonium but both receive fatal doses of radiation.
They escape separately from the facility, and later events unfold
accordingly.

Let us take the various points one by one:

1 A plausible context for the existence and operation of the Northgate* facility might be as follows. The government wants to 'privatize' the nuclear industry. One of the fastest-growing areas of interest is management of spent fuel from nuclear power stations. The Northgate plant is set up as a 'demonstration' facility, to assess the available storage technologies for the various kinds of fuel, in particular magnox (metal) fuel, and oxide (ceramic) fuel. The traditional technology is storage of fuel under water, unprotected or enclosed in sealed canisters of various kinds. More modern techniques involve storing the fuel in gas-cooled magazines, either unprotected or, again, enclosed in sealed canisters. A 'demonstration' facility might plausibly have different types of fuel in various kinds of storage, including the pond storage that necessitates the water-supply that plays a significant part in the setting and the dramatic action. It would also justify the delivery of magnox fuel to the facility. Magnox fuel was originally designed specifically to produce weapons-plutonium, at Calder Hall and Chapelcross. A modern 'commercial' facility would be unlikely to receive magnox fuel, certainly not for storage under water; the fuel deteriorates rapidly in water. But if Northgate is a 'demonstration' facility to provide technical experience to private enterprise this problem can easily be circumvented. This would also make plausible the accumulation of radioactivity in the water system; in real life such contamination, as a result of decaying magnox fuel left too long in water, is a serious problem at British magnox power stations.

The detailed layout of the underground facility can be discussed later. But the hot cell, its nature and its operation, must be clearly understood by the production team if the action is to be plausible.

The scenario might be something like this: the main storage facilities include a surface entrance able to accommodate spent-fuel transport flasks into the underground cavern. (Its establishment underground can be explained by the difficulty of getting planning permission above ground.) The main storage pond is in the pond, with assorted shielded handling facilities for transferring fuel into and out of the pond, for sealing it in canisters and for storing it in shielded gas-cooled bunkers and the like. There will also be laboratories for examining samples of fuel, to study its behaviour in various storage regimes. These laboratory facilities can plausibly

*The name was later changed to Northmoor.

include most of the hardware that might in fact be required for a hot cell; its purchase has therefore a legitimate cover.

The hot cell itself is, of course, concealed in a side cavern, with entrance to it restricted to a handful of trusted (and crooked) personnel. Fuel can be diverted from the fuel-examination lab into the hot cell by means of remote-handling apparatus invisible from outside the shielding.

The hot cell consists of a single large room. In its centre is a heavily shielded bunker, with thick windows and the accessible ends of remote-handling gear. There will be heavily shielded pipes and conduits about, and perhaps a track across the floor along which a heavy-duty dolly can carry a shielded flask containing magnox fuel rods from outside the hot cell into the room and through an airlock into the interior of the central bunker or 'cave' (the conventional nuclear term for such a shielded remote working area).

There will be access ports on the wall of this 'cave', out of which can be taken the containers of separated plutonium. The plutonium can be in three physical forms. The separation process will produce plutonium nitrate solution, more about which below. The liquid solution can be converted into either plutonium metal or plutonium oxide powder. These conversion processes need not, however, take place behind heavy shielding, but might well be done inside a glass-fronted 'glove box' along one wall of the cell. (I'll suggest below a possible dramatic consequence of this.)

The intense radiation from the spent fuel comes in fact not from the plutonium but from the 'fission products' in the fuel, such as caesium. These fission products will be extracted inside the shielded cave, into an acid solution; it must then be kept shielded, or possibly removed inside a flask on the same dolly as was used to transport the fuel into the 'cave'. Alternatively, the highly radioactive fission product solution might emerge in a shielded pipe, to some unspecified storage or volume-reduction unit in an adjoining chamber. (I will suggest below a possible dramatic consequence of such an arrangement.)

2 I would recommend strongly the use of the name International Irradiated Fuels, and the acronym IIF, rather than British Irradiated Fuels, if only to reduce somewhat the possibility of aggro with the real-life British Nuclear Fuels. The international bid for the company and the involvement of Grogan need not be

explicitly identified with his desire for plutonium for use in space weapons. That application is not really plausible; just say he wants it for so-called 'emerging technology' weapons-research; the acronym ET has actually come into use already. The possibility of other, less reputable outlets, should also be underlined. Note that one elaborate theory attributes the death of Karen Silkwood to her discovery of a top-level plot to export plutonium to Israel.

The events in the cavern might go as follows: in the first event, the Gaia party find their way through the caves to the hot cell. They manage to gain entry. In the hot cell, in the glove-box for plutonium manipulation, the find samples of solid plutonium metal in small ingots, plutonium oxide powder in metal trays, and plutonium nitrate in solution in glass flasks. While attempting to remove the samples they inadvertently cause (in a way we need not specify) a criticality. This triggers criticality alarms and alerts the company security forces. It also gives the Gaia members a fatal dose of neutron and gamma radiation. The Gaia party eludes the guards and escapes into the connecting caves with some of the plutonium ingots. Once in the labyrinth of caves they may lose the guards. It is entirely plausible for the security chief therefore to call for sluice-gates to be closed or opened to divert water from the pond-supply into the escape-tunnel. He can use the twofold justification that these 'terrorists' must not under any circumstances be allowed to get away with plutonium, and that in any case they were all doomed to die of radiation exposure.

We can indicate that Emma was one of the lookouts, outside the hot cell when the criticality occurred. We need not go into detail about the water system except to indicate that it is extensive and complex, controlling large-volume flows below and above ground, some of it in the natural cave passages suitably valved and gated.

3 The existing scenario of events in the hot cell with Craven and Jedburgh needs to be changed; the descriptions of rods in tanks, and criticality induced and so on, are technically wrong. However, a possible sequence of events might be as follows. Craven and Jedburgh enter the hot cell; they may have to evade guards outside the entrance. Once inside they lock the door and proceed to gather up all the plutonium samples from the glove box, extracting them through a lockchamber on its end or side. Jedburgh will refer to the need to keep the samples separated, and to be relieved that it is all in metal ingots, since managing glass flasks or powder would be

more difficult and risky. Presumably it will have been cast into ingots ready for Grogan. The ingots should be small, no bigger than Mars Bars: 'Don't just pile them into that carrier bag – unless you want to start up the first Harrods reactor . . .' They recognize the material as plutonium, because it is in the glove box; otherwise it might be any dull grey metal, like lead.

They have barred the door, and are ready to come out firing; they might be carrying tear gas grenades for the guards, which would give them a reason to have gas-masks and a plausible hope of emerging successfully with the plutonium. However, they have reckoned without the flask-entry port in the wall of the hot cell. It opens, and the security chief and his henchmen, behind a flask on a dolly, charge into the room firing. A stream of nickel-jacketed high-velocity slugs pierce the fission product from the central cave, and lethally readioactive liquid pours from the puncture, spraying all over both Jedburgh and Craven. They use their tear-gas grenades and escape from the hot cell into the caverns . . . and later incidents follow.

Some notes on points of detail (there will doubtless be others). The hearings in London must of course be in camera. If the committee consists of MPs, it must be a special Select Committee with security clearance. We can discuss what need be explicitly specified and what may be left implicit and unexplained. If the existence of the hot cell and the plutonium-separation activities are illicit, as I understand they are supposed to be, we shall have to revise the testimony delivered by the IIF witness; he certainly cannot allude to 'theft of plutonium' without giving the game away to the committee. If desired, I can supply sample technical dialogue for the testimony, and also for the sequences within the Northgate facility. Indicentally, I notice in the *Financial Times* of 12 May a reference to a resource and energy company called Northgate. I presume that will not cause complications?

I have not here attempted to correct minor details of dialogue and incident; we can deal with them when scripts and design are closer to final form. Please copy new drafts to me as they are written; I'd also be happy to advise if necessary on detailed design of the visuals for the Northgate facility, including the hot cell itself, when they are available.

Walter C. Patterson
May 1984

The Police

Police input in a television drama can be double-edged. Most of their objections to scripts can be overcome, but if you find yourself in disagreement with them and they are offering facilities for shooting, then you are in a bind. Either you do as they suggest or you risk losing their co-operation.

London police get very blasé about scripts because there are so many film units shooting in the Metropolitan area. Provincial police forces tend to be much more enthusiastic, as was West Yorkshire. Their input into Edge of Darkness *added to its authenticity. It was their idea that Craven would be subjected to a fingerprint test within an hour of Emma's death.*

The following is an example of their comments on the scripts, summarized by a BBC researcher.

Craven's car: A or B reg. 1.6 Sierra/Datsun (mileage allowance). Car radio unlikely; portable radio and aerial or harness. Craven might have a bleep.

Murder: after 21.00 hrs; most personnel would have gone home. 999 call to duty officer in Force Control.

First vehicle: within four or five minutes: twenty-year-old constable in panda car, and ambulance (Metro, Escort, Chevette); unless Emma had a wound to the heart and was 'very dead' the ambulancemen would move her. Otherwise they would leave the scene almost immediately.

Under the circumstances a sergeant might well accompany the PC. Craven would meet them outside the house and try to establish a 'safe' route. He wouldn't forget his years of training.

Second vehicle: uniformed inspector and other PCs (including WPC) would arrive in a second panda car, the cleanest! They would be trying to get hold of the local detective.

Third vehicle: two detective constables (aged twenty-five to thirty) in an unmarked car; a five-year-old Hillman Hunter. The detectives would alert CID inspectors (either the DI or DCI). (The Chief Superintendents of uniform and CID would be alerted.)

Fourth vehicle: the uniformed chief superintendent (possibly in civvies but very smart) would arrive on his own. As it's his division, he'd be alert and officious. By now fluorescent orange tape would have been used to seal off both ends of the road; cones (yellow) might also be used. An inner and an outer circle would soon be established. The PC and WPC at the road blocks would use their personal radios to contact the duty officer; he would log all visitors on the computer as they arrive, providing a security check and an instant up-date facility.

The chief superintendent would ask for an *incident kit* to be set up. This would involve the distribution of *paper suits* (white). Obviously in our case they would need waterproof suits (disposable).

Fifth, sixth and perhaps seventh vehicles: scenes-of-crime officers would arrive to take photos, collect fingerprints and make plaster casts. Yorkshire now intend to video all murder scenes for their own reference. (Videos would not be acceptable as evidence in court.) One would be delegated exhibits officer.

Eighth vehicle: the police surgeon (an ordinary GP) would arrive in a Range Rover (before the senior investigating officer); he would certify death; the body would not be moved.

Ninth vehicle: the coroner's officer, a sergeant in plain clothes, would arrive in a three- to four-year-old car.

Tenth, eleventh and twelfth vehicles: two forensic scientists, experts on shooting and general science. They would be in suits and in good cars. Their arrival would coincide with that of the pathologist from the Home Office. (The local pathologist arrives on a motorbike, it seems!) They would all be handed paper suits and waterproofs (orange/yellow) with plastic overshoes. (West Yorkshire Police suggested use of armbands, though they don't use them for this purpose.)

A *safe path* would be taped out to the body and the house; because of the weather duckboards would be essential. Cables might be run from the house, but more likely is . . .

Thirteenth vehicle: a generator and/or a jeep with green-shaded lamps on stands. These would be very carefully positioned by one man (in order to minimize contamination of the scene). It is possible that the lights would be from a white (motorway-style) jeep.

Fourteenth vehicle: a van would deliver various bits of equipment – tents, more duckboards, cones, etc. A plastic tent on a frame 6ft x 6ft x 6ft.

Sixteenth vehicle: the police press officer (Barry!) would arrive in a white Sierra. (In such a murder the police might have a four-hour start on the press.) He would wait at the outer cordon with a white card: 'POLICE PRESS POINT', and would arrange interviews at regular intervals.

Seventeenth vehicle: a low loader would arrive to take Craven's car to the lab for fingerprinting.

Eighteenth vehicle: a dual-purpose hearse would arrive to remove the body. Body probably not bagged, but a body sheet would be provided; the body would be rolled on to this and then placed in a black plastic coffin 'shell'. The exhibits officer would go with the body.

As the body was removed *everybody* would go with it to the mortuary for formal identification, etc. (though Craven might go at a later stage): senior investigating officer, detective chief superintendent, superintendent, exhibits officer, two forensic scientists, pathologist, two scenes-of-crime officers, coroner's officer.

Other props: video camera; hasselblad or larger format cameras for black and white stills, duckboards; 2-inch fluorescent orange tape; lamps; scenes of crime kits for sample collection; polaroid cameras; yellow cones; plastic sheeting for protecting tyre marks etc. (they might improvise with dustbin lids); bushes, etc., would be covered with sheeting.

In the morning plans and measuring would take place, though some measuring for line of shot and range might take place the night of the shooting.

A PC would definitely stay outside Craven's house to protect the scene of the murder; this is a fundamental rule and would not be broken under *any* circumstances. Also, Craven, to have his own gun, would need a firearms licence. It would therefore be essential to take swabs of Craven's hands within a couple of hours of the shooting. Naturally, Craven would be horrified at this, but he'd do the same himself under different circumstances. It would be necessary to prove in court that he hadn't fired one of his own guns and perhaps murdered Emma. His guns would have to be removed for testing (and for safety, in case of revenge). Throughout the scene no smoking, no gum; and hands in pockets!

Resumé: Approximate arrival times for Emma's murder

21.15   Murder
21.17   999 call
21.22   Uniformed PC and sergeant
21.24   Uniformed inspector. PCs and WPC
21.40   Two detective constables

21.50	Either detective inspector or detective chief inspector
21.52	Chief superintendent
21.53	Coroner's officer/police surgeon
23.25	Coroner's officer/police surgeon
	Two forensic scientists/pathologist and police escort
	Lighting/tents
00.30	Coroner's officer arranges for disposal of body
	Press arrive

Jones would be a detective sergeant. He would always refer to Craven as 'Sir', or use his rank. He would not take over the inquiry as his rank is too low.

Policemen (especially from Yorkshire) drink *beer* (not vodka and orange); whisky possible and, at a pinch, gin and tonic. Beer and crisps unlikely at the murder scene, though whisky bottle *de rigeur*.

Ross and Craven would use Christian names (generally).

Answering machine: 'Mr Craven' or 'The Cravens are out . . .' If Ross had been drinking he would have a police driver.

Absolutely *no collusion* between Godbolt and Ross! This is the *sine qua non* of West Yorkshire Police Force co-operation. He would never have direct access to the appointing officer; nor would he be so pally with Craven.

Ross might say: 'Officially you're nothing to do with this inquiry . . .' (and use innuendo); he would never carry on and give Craven a verbal *carte blanche*. Again, the advice to take a gun should never be voiced. Craven would have to find some other (unofficial) way.

A shoulder holster, or waist belt, is possible.

'I Remember Lowe' sequence. Every detective remembers every detail of each murder conviction. To quote the Bradford boys: 'It's like the first time you make love; you remember everything each time you crack a case . . .'

Episode Three, Craven's 'soft technique' on Lowe said to be 'absolute rubbish'. They use a 'soft technique' – rough interrogation followed by sympathetic detective – but holding hands and kissing! Not in Yorkshire!

The press man would not know Lowe's name, though he may have heard of the accident; suggested line: 'How's the suspect?'

Re computer: West Yorkshire Metropolitan Police only knew of the PNC, thought there may well be a government one. PNC entries may have 'Confidential' and give a contact name.

Lowe's file would be on *microfiche* on the PNC. A printout would give his convictions and a reference for Criminal Records Office. Again, probably microfiche and photo.

John Darrah, *The Royal Camelot: Paganism and the Arthurian Romances*, Thames and Hudson, London, 1981.

James Lovelock, *Gaia: A New Look at Life on Earth*, Oxford University Press, Oxford, 1979.

Walter C. Patterson, *Nuclear Power*, Penguin Books, London, 1983.

— *The Plutonium Business*, Paladin Books, London, 1984.

Vladimir Propp, *Morphology of the Folk Tale*, University of Texas Press, 1969.